STRANGE MAGIC

A WITCHES OF CLEOPATRA HILL NOVEL

CHRISTINE POPE

Dark Valentine Press

This is a work of fiction. Names, characters, places, and incidents are either the product of the author's imagination or are used fictitiously. Any resemblance to actual events, places, organizations, or persons, whether living or dead, is entirely coincidental.

STRANGE MAGIC

ISBN: 978-0-9883348-9-2
Copyright © 2016 by Christine Pope
Published by Dark Valentine Press

Cover design by Lou Harper
Book layout by Indie Author Services

To learn more about this author, go to
www.christinepope.com.

STRANGE MAGIC

CHAPTER ONE

ZOE SANDOVAL ENTERED HER AUNT'S HOUSE, THEN CLOSED
the front door behind her as she called out, "Aunt Luz?
It's Zoe."

Only silence met her ears, which was exactly what
she'd hoped for. Yes, her aunt—and the de la Paz clan's
current *prima*—had said she was going down to Mesa to
have lunch with Zoe's cousin Alexis, who was expecting her first child, but those plans could have changed.
Fortunately, though, the big pueblo-style house that
had come to Luz after the former *prima's*—and Zoe's
grandmother's—death was absolutely still. Luz's husband David would be at work, of course, and their
daughter, the only one of their three children who still
technically lived at home, was attending school down
in Tucson, at the University of Arizona.

Which meant Zoe had the run of the place, at least for the next few hours.

On the surface, this didn't seem so very odd. Almost as soon as Zoe's aunt had become *prima* after Maya passed away, she had given her niece a set of keys to the house, saying that of course the *prima*-in-waiting should have access to the library there, to all the books and writings accumulated by more than ten generations of de la Paz *primas*. However, Zoe sort of doubted Aunt Luz would be very happy to discover the actual reason why her niece had slipped into the house while everyone was away. Well, once the clan had been presented with a done deed, they'd just have to accept what had happened and learn to deal with it.

Six years earlier, when she'd first been informed by her grandmother Maya that she would be the next *prima* after Luz, Zoe hadn't been exactly overjoyed to hear the news. She liked being a witch just fine, had loved exploring her talents with plants and potions and healing. It was a useful gift, one always needed in a clan as big as hers. But a *prima* couldn't call her life her own, always had to be there for the family, couldn't even choose her own husband, had to let the universe decide who would be her consort—the title given to a *prima*'s spouse.

That part was the worst. All right, sometimes the whole consort thing worked out just fine, like the way it had with Angela McAllister and Connor Wilcox. Connor was smoking hot, and if Zoe could be assured of one day having a consort like him, she'd be a lot more resigned to the loss of her personal life that being *prima* entailed. But that kind of perfect match wasn't always guaranteed. Whatever force or power dictated which man should be the consort of the *prima* seemed to be mainly concerned with choosing someone who could provide the necessary DNA to father powerful children. There was supposed to be some sort of soul bond involved, but unfortunately, it didn't always work out that way, no matter what the witch clans' traditions might claim otherwise.

Although Zoe's grandfather had died when she was only four, and therefore she couldn't remember him very well, she did know that her grandparents' marriage had been mostly a disaster. Her grandfather drank too much, and, from what Zoe had been able to gather, had cheated on Maya with a number of civilian—non-witch—lovers.

But they'd had two daughters, with Luz turning out to be much stronger than her younger sister, and so she became Maya's heir. Andrea, Zoe's mother, hadn't seemed very upset about being passed over, and who could blame her? She got to have a nice life with her warlock/lawyer husband, and a fancy house in Fountain Hills, while Luz had to do everything with the shadow of one day being *prima* hanging over her. It turned out that Luz's children were decently talented, but her daughter Alicia certainly wasn't strong enough to be the *prima*-in-waiting. So, as sometimes happened, the mantle went not to the *prima*'s daughter, but to Luz's niece Zoe...whether she liked it or not.

Even though Zoe knew the house was empty, she couldn't help almost tiptoeing as she made her way from the grand two-story foyer and down the hallway that led to the library. Although it was early March, Phoenix had already begun to heat up, and so she could hear the faintest hum of the central air conditioning working away in the background. That was the only sound she detected, however—no worries about the housekeeper cleaning in another part of the home, or a gardener working with a blower outside. Zoe obviously had the place to herself.

The library was a large room with built-in bookcases on every wall and a wrought-iron chandelier hanging over the round table in the center of the space. Off to one side was a leather chair with a matching ottoman, the perfect spot to put your feet up while you perused a book of spells or took notes from one of the old diaries on plant lore.

Zoe didn't intend to relax while she was here, though. She had something far different in mind.

The book she wanted was on one of the higher shelves, but she didn't have to waste time looking for a step stool. No, she merely extended her hand, and the book came floating down to her. Just one of the little powers that had appeared after she'd become the *prima*-in-waiting. She wouldn't come completely into all her inborn gifts until she'd met her consort and bonded with him, but during the past year, ever since she'd turned twenty-one, she'd seen how these little parts of her talent had begun to awaken, how one day she would be able to command much more than merely an ability to work with plants and mix up cures for colds and hangovers…once she'd completed the necessary soul-bond with her consort.

Her consort. There was the real problem. Almost as soon as she'd celebrated her twenty-first birthday, Zoe had been subjected to the consort search, which had to be the most demeaning ritual ever devised by witch-kind. The only way to know whether a guy was the "one" was to kiss him—and that had meant a whole lot of kisses with a whole lot of men she felt absolutely no attraction to.

And the problem was, she didn't have any basis for comparison. Both her mother and her Aunt Luz had assured Zoe that she'd just "know" as soon as she kissed the right candidate, but since she'd been prevented from having any kind of romantic contact with a guy, she didn't know the first thing about kissing, unless she counted what she'd seen in the movies or on TV...and she had a feeling those on-screen embraces didn't exactly reflect reality.

Not that some of the possible consorts hadn't been handsome. It wasn't as if Aunt Luz had gone out of her way to find unappealing candidates. She'd even reached out to the Wilcoxes and the McAllisters for help finding possible matches, which Zoe definitely appreciated. Those Wilcox warlocks tended to be pretty damn hot. The McAllisters less so, on average, but anything was better than getting hooked up with a distant cousin whom you'd been seeing at family gatherings ever since you were old enough to remember them.

Unfortunately, no one had worked out so far. Not a Wilcox, not a McAllister, not some fourth or fifth cousin from the de la Paz clan. Although she'd never voiced the worry aloud, Zoe had begun to wonder if Matías Escobar's attempt to kidnap her so he could take control of her powers had screwed up something inside, had made her unable to form the proper consort bond. True, Matías hadn't kissed her—he'd probably been waiting to get her alone before he did such a thing—but still. The whole situation was so messed up that she didn't know what to think.

And that was why, about a month ago, as her twenty-second birthday loomed and she still hadn't met any viable candidates, she had an unexpected and completely insane idea pass through her mind.

What if I make my own consort?

No, not in a Frankenstein sort of way. Zoe wasn't so desperate that she thought digging up pieces of dead men and stitching them together to make her dream consort was a viable solution. But she'd seen the spells when she was going through the library, familiarizing herself with aspects of her family's witchcraft that she'd never seen utilized so far, but might encounter on that far-off day when she herself became *prima*.

Spells of summoning, of word and thought made form. Such things hadn't been attempted in years and years, mostly because there was always a risk of the summoning turning out badly, but that didn't mean those spells couldn't work. Zoe knew she was strong, had felt her awakening powers thrumming within her over the past year. And as candidate after candidate came and went, and she still didn't have a consort, she began to formulate her own desperate plan.

She'd written down a list of all the ideal qualities she wanted from her consort—handsome, of course, and smart, and with a sense of humor. Chivalrous, but not condescending. After all, she would be the *prima* one day, the person in charge. That didn't mean she didn't want someone who would open doors for her, and pull out her chair at a restaurant. Maybe that wasn't a modern way of thinking, but the de la Paz clan did tend to be kind of old-fashioned.

So, someone really gorgeous, like *telenovela* stars Jencarlos Canela or William Levy. In fact, Zoe had printed out a bunch of images of William, since, after a good deal of hemming and hawing, she decided she liked him best. She'd brought those pictures with her today, a visual aid to use in her summoning. She set them down now on the round table in the middle of the room, and opened the book of spells. The spells were written in Latin, not Spanish, but she figured she could manage. Anyway, her Spanish wasn't all that great, to be perfectly honest; the odd word might slip in here and there, but her parents always spoke English at home, and that meant Zoe and her brother Zander did as well. Some members of the clan were just the opposite, and only used English when they had to, like going out shopping and so on, but somehow they all managed to understand one another.

Mostly.

Fingers shaking with nervousness, Zoe flipped to the page that contained the spell she wanted to use. She'd heard the McAllister witches in particular were a little more freeform, and didn't necessarily rely on books of spells to cast their magic, but in the de la Paz clan, if you were going to cast a big

enchantment, you went back to the words that earlier witches and warlocks had set down. Those spells
had worked in the past, so there was no reason to
think they wouldn't work now.

All right. Her eyes scanned the page as she refa-
miliarized herself with the Latin words. For something so big, it was really a short spell, only four
lines. Then she arranged the images of her ideal man
on either side of the book, so the spell might draw
its power from those pictures, take her thoughts and
wishes and desires, and give them form.

For a long moment, she hesitated. This was crazy.
Deep down, she knew it was crazy. But her birthday
was less than two weeks away. How in the world
were they going to find a consort for her in that span
of time, when the search had been going on now
for more than eleven months? Sure, stranger things
had happened, but did she really want to count on
that? If she turned twenty-two and still didn't have
a consort, she'd never have the full use of her powers. She'd be crippled as *prima* when it was her turn
to run the clan, and that would leave the de la Paz
family far too vulnerable. Yes, the McAllisters were
stalwart allies, and it seemed the Wilcoxes could be
trusted as well, now that Damon Wilcox was no longer at the head of that clan, but one couldn't say the
same about the Santiago family in California, the

clan that had spawned the warlock who'd tried to kidnap her.

Almost unconsciously, she ran her hands over the skirt she wore, smoothing the cotton fabric. Back when Matías had tried to seize her from the Paradise Valley Mall, she'd been going through a rebellious phase, with silly T-shirts from Hot Topic and Doc Martens and that streak of bright pink in her hair, the one that had made her parents so angry when they'd first seen it. Afterward, she'd reassessed her appearance in terms of her future role in the clan and had realized that really wasn't how a *prima*-in-waiting should dress. She got rid of the pink streak, the combat boots. Now she wore a lot of dresses and skirts, and sandals and flats. Her parents were relieved by the change in her style, and Zoe had to admit to herself that it actually had made her more comfortable. Jeans and lace-up leather boots could be damn hot in the depths of a Phoenix summer.

She looked down at herself, at the full knee-length retro-style skirt with its pattern of a city skyline, accented with sequins, and the flat leather sandals she wore. Definitely girly, but wasn't that something the dream man she was about to conjure would appreciate?

There was only one way to find out.

A deep breath. Another. In the back of her mind, a little voice was telling her to stop now, to put the book away and fold up the pictures of William Levy and stuff them back in her purse. She could clean up all evidence of ever being here, go out to her car, and call her friend Amber and see if she wanted to meet at the mall for a movie or something. You know, ordinary things, fun things that a girl of twenty-one would do.

Not standing here in her aunt's library and trying to conjure her perfect man out of thin air.

"Coward," she said aloud. The syllables seemed to ring in her ears. No way was she a coward. When Matías had tried to kidnap her, sure, at first she'd gone along because of that horrible mind-control talent he had, but as soon as she'd woken up enough to figure out what was going on, she'd tried to fight back. Would a coward have done that?

No.

So she breathed in again, and imagined exactly what would happen. She'd say the words of the spell, and her dream man would appear in front of her, smiling and handsome, admiration clear in his eyes. She would hold out her hands to him, and he'd take them. And then he would lean down and press his lips against hers, and all the wonder and fire and heat of a true consort's kiss would run through her, and they'd be sealed forever. It would be perfect.

Reassured by that rapturous image, she turned her attention back to the book and ran her index finger down the lines of the spell, once again mentally repeating the words. She'd translated them into English with the help of one of those online translators, and it was in English that those words echoed in her mind, even though the syllables that emerged from her mouth were the original Latin. Or at least she hoped the Latin was close enough, since she really wasn't what you'd call an expert.

From shadow to light
From night to day
From dream to reality
Become what I say

The air in the library shimmered, as if thousands of the world's smallest fireflies had suddenly decided to appear there and perform an intricate dance. Zoe looked on, eyes wide with wonder. It was working. The spell was working. She could feel it, feel the heat and the hum in her veins as the magic she'd been born with moved outward and acted upon the real world.

Golden light danced and waved, and then began to coalesce, slowly taking on the form of a tall man. No true details yet, only a glowing shape with broad shoulders, two arms, long legs.

Was the head shifting toward her slightly, as if the glowing shape had just realized someone stood there and was watching as it grew more and more solid? Zoe's mouth went dry, but she forced herself to stand her ground. True, she had thought her dream man would appear immediately, but it was fine if the process took a little longer than expected. Aunt Luz still wouldn't be home for some time. By then, Zoe and her conjured consort would be gone. There would be a ton of explaining to do, but once everyone saw how happy they were together, how clearly made for each other—no pun intended—she knew that all would be forgiven.

Since it—*he*—seemed to be looking at her, she decided she'd better say something. Maybe if he heard her voice, he would latch on to it like a lifeline, could use its encouragement to hasten his transformation.

"I'm here," she said softly, the words a little hoarse because her throat was still so dry for some reason. "I've been waiting for you. Please...come to me."

A blink. At least, she thought it was a blink, although since the shape didn't have eyes yet, what she'd seen was more like a strange shadow passing over the two places where his eyes should be. And then it began to move toward her.

Despite her best efforts to remain where she was, she couldn't help taking a step backward. No, that was absolutely the wrong thing to do. She needed to

welcome this apparition, not act as if she was afraid
of it.

Although, in that moment, she realized she was
afraid. No, she couldn't be afraid. She'd brought it—
him—into being. She was just nervous, faced with
something entirely outside her normal experience.
Anyway, he seemed to be growing more solid as he
stared at her, features gradually taking shape even
while she watched.

No. *No.*

Because the face that had begun to emerge wasn't
anything close to the *telenovela* star she thought so
handsome. It was twisted, misshapen, a face put
together by someone who didn't really know what a
human being was supposed to look like.

She took another step backward, frantically
thinking of what she could do to reverse the spell.
Something had gone terribly wrong, that much was
clear. She had to send this thing back to wherever it
had come from.

Its arms reached for her, and she let out a frightened little squeal. Her mind raced, trying to come up
with a counter-spell. But she couldn't think of anything. She'd been so certain this would work....

"Zhoooooo..." it said, and all her veins seemed
to turn to ice. Was it trying to say her name?

Madre de dios....

Maybe a banishing spell? She had to try. "Unwanted spirit, leave now. Leave this space. Go back whence you came. Only light and healing energy are allowed in this place!"

It paused, staring at her. Now it did seem to have some sort of eyes, but they were only black pits in that lumpy caricature of a face. For the longest moment, it did not move, but at least it had stopped heading toward her. Then its slash of a mouth parted in a snarl, and it reached out with one hand, fingers curved into claws.

No time for spells. No time for anything except a burst of her own raw energy, dragged up from deep inside and flung at the creature. A flash of pure white light soared outward and hit it in the chest. It let out a cry of pain, but it did not fall back.

Shit, Zoe thought. *Shit, shit, shit.*

But she'd hurt it. She didn't even know exactly how she'd managed to hurl that ball of light at the thing, but the action had seemed almost instinctive, as if the *prima* power buried within her had known exactly what to do, targeting the creature without damaging any of their surroundings.

Well, she'd have to do it again.

Another flare of light, this one bigger and so bright that Zoe was half-blinded by the flash when it exploded against the monster's chest. This time it did stagger backward as it released a roar of pain. And then it turned and ran, melting into nothingness, slipping through the wall of the library as if the thick adobe didn't even exist.

For a long moment, Zoe only stood there, her breaths ragged, adrenaline sharp and spiky along every nerve ending. Yes, she'd managed to banish the thing...but where had it gone?

She knew she should go after it. Unfortunately, her legs refused to obey her as she tried to move toward the place where it had melted through the wall. She realized her body was probably just trying to protect her. Who knew if she'd be successful at driving it off a second time?

All right. Only one thing she could do. With trembling fingers, she reached for her purse where she'd left it sitting under the table and pulled out her cell phone. Went to her contacts list and pushed the entry for Luz Trujillo. As the call connected, she thought,

I am in so much trouble....

CHAPTER TWO

Evan McAllister dropped the hood on his '70 Barracuda and wiped his hands on the rag hanging from the back pocket of his jeans. Changing out the spark plugs on the beast was a real pain in the ass, but he'd refused to alter a thing about the car's original equipment—hadn't switched the carburetors over to EFI, hadn't swapped out the ignition system. About the only concession he'd made to comfort was installing an aftermarket A/C unit, but that was because Verde Valley summers could be brutal, and he didn't much enjoy sweating to death every time he had to stop at a light, thus eliminating even the slight relief the open windows provided when he was actually in motion.

Working on the car helped to keep his mind off a whole host of things, up to and including his ex-wife.

No doubt egged on by her new lawyer husband, she'd been making noises about how she thought the hush money she'd received from the McAllister clan just wasn't enough, and that they'd better cough up some more if they didn't want her telling the whole world about the witches in their midst.

Scowling, Evan threw the dirty rag into the metal container he reserved for anything that might combust. He knew the elders would work it out somehow, but in the meantime, her latest salvo just meant more judgmental looks from members of the clan who hadn't approved of his marrying Kelly in the first place. Yes, the divorce had been final for almost two years now, but some people just didn't want to let it go.

After letting his eyes run over the sleek, dark lines of the Barracuda, and reassuring himself that he hadn't left any oil smudges behind, Evan went into the house and washed up at the kitchen sink. The silence around him seemed too hollow, even though he'd been living there alone ever since Kelly took off. Maybe he should have sold the place after all. He knew Bryce McAllister, one of the elders, wasn't too thrilled about the way he'd stayed down here in Cottonwood instead of moving back up to Jerome after the marriage fell apart.

But at first Evan had hoped Kelly would change her mind and come back, and after that—well, his flat in Jerome felt too small after living in the house, and anyway, the flat didn't have a garage. In Jerome, he would have had to beg garage space so he could work on his car. Besides, the flat was more than earning its keep as an Airbnb destination, and since Evan paid his cousin Kirby a stipend to keep an eye on things so he wouldn't have to keep coming up to Jerome to check on the flat, he really didn't see any reason to change the setup.

Just as he was about to throw the paper towel he'd used to dry his hands into the trash, Evan's cell phone began to buzz. A frown creased his brow, and for a second or two, he contemplated not answering it at all. Right then he just wanted to get a beer from the fridge and sit down and relax. His back ached a little from spending so much time bent over the engine compartment of the car, and he could use the downtime.

But he didn't get that many calls, and when he did, it was usually either one of his parents, checking in on him, or maybe one of his cousins calling to see he wanted to go over to Main Stage and play pool or something. Evan had to smile at the calls from his parents; you'd think he was some kid out living on his own for the first time, instead of a grown man of almost thirty.

The third type of calls were the ones he didn't get very often, but when he did, he never knew what to expect. His talent was an unusual one, a gift that witch-kind didn't see in every generation, the way you usually had a healer and a seer and a weather-worker. Most people called him "the fixer," which was close enough, since he had the ability to track down spells that had gone awry and exert his powers on them so they'd be rendered harmless.

Luckily, he wasn't called on to use his gift all that often, because the members of the McAllister clan were pretty circumspect with their magic and didn't tend to make the kind of mistakes that would require his services. Even so, he knew he could expect to hear from the elders on "official" business at least a couple times a year.

If his phone was ringing because of the third kind of call, then it didn't really matter whether he ignored it or not. They'd just keep trying until he eventually picked up.

So he went over to the table in the breakfast nook, where he'd set down his phone before heading out to the garage. A quick glance at the phone's display told him that the caller was Tricia McAllister, one of the clan's elders.

He didn't quite sigh, but he could feel himself let out a breath as he picked up the phone and swiped the button to take the call. "Hi, Tricia. What's up?"

No greeting. Just a tense, "The elders need to talk to you. How soon can you be at my place?"

"Twenty minutes," he replied. It didn't actually take that long to get from his house up to Jerome, but he'd need to change out of his sweaty T-shirt and greasy jeans before he went to meet with the elders. He might have known them all his life, but he still needed to show them the proper respect.

"See you then," Tricia said, then hung up.

That was kind of strange. Usually when these sorts of things came up, whoever was calling him would at least provide a general idea as to why he might be needed. But Tricia hadn't let slip a single detail. What, was she worried that the NSA was snooping on their phone calls or something?

Come to think of it, maybe that wasn't such a crazy idea after all. But if the government did actually know anything about the secrets the witch clans had been hiding all these years, its sure didn't give any sign of possessing that knowledge. Anyway, he had enough to worry about without dragging those kinds of conspiracy theories into the situation.

He headed down the hall to the bedroom and paused at the foot of the bed so he could strip off his T-shirt and jeans, then toss them into the hamper. Someone else might have thrown them on the floor, but Evan hated messes and kept his house neat—neater, actually, than when Kelly had lived here, since she tended to leave a trail of empty glasses and discarded shoes behind her.

The day was fairly chilly, despite the sweat he'd worked up while laboring on the Barracuda. He got a long-sleeved henley-style T-shirt from one of the drawers and pulled that on, along with one of his less faded pairs of jeans. The elders would just have to live with his work boots, since the only other shoes he owned were a pair of dress lace-ups that hadn't seen the light of day since his parents' anniversary dinner last fall, and some flip-flops for those truly brutal Arizona heat waves.

He headed back out to the garage and started up the car. It roared to life with a satisfying, throaty growl, and he nodded in satisfaction. Maybe the Barracuda did take a lot more work than a more modern vehicle, but a new Honda or Toyota wouldn't have the same soul.

Besides, it wasn't as if he had much else to do with his spare time.

The day had clouded up while he was working in the garage, and he hoped it wouldn't rain. That would mean another session in the driveway once the storm had passed, doing another three-step wash to get rid of the spots.

Yeah, 'cause that's not obsessive or anything, he thought as he backed out of the driveway and headed down toward Main Street. *It's just a car.*

Blasphemy.

Maybe. His parents had given him the car on his eighteenth birthday, and Evan and his father had spent countless hours restoring it, looking up matching-numbers parts to rebuild the engine, doing the prep work to smooth the body before it was sent in for its new coat of shiny black paint. Stephen McAllister, Evan's father, was a sculptor who specialized in big welded pieces, so he knew a thing or two about working with metal.

Anyway, all that effort was probably a sign that Evan obsessed over the car more than he should. But it just seemed to him that if you put that much love and attention into something, then you should care what happened to it.

It was getting toward four o'clock, which meant some people were already on their way home from work, and others were headed into old town Cottonwood for a drink at one of the wine tasting rooms, or to a restaurant to catch the first part of happy hour. He drove carefully and slowly, ignoring the admiring stares from some of the people out on the sidewalks. The Barracuda did tend to attract a lot of attention, but he was used to that sort of thing by now.

The growl of the Hemi engine as he headed up the winding highway into Jerome helped ease the tension in his neck. He didn't know what was going on, but he'd helped his clan with dozens of these problems before, and he had no reason to believe this time would be any different. Someone got a little over-zealous with a weather spell, or maybe tried forbidden love magic and attracted the wrong person. It didn't really matter what it was, since his talent seemed capable of unraveling even the worst magical knots.

Luckily, Tricia's big Victorian had a nice drive-way, so he was able to park there rather than on the street. Almost as soon as he knocked on the pale blue front door, she was there, opening it. Unlike a lot of the McAllister witches, she was neatly and stylishly dressed, in slim jeans and a short light green cardigan. With her carefully bobbed hair, Tricia had always looked to Evan as though she should be the head of the PTA or maybe the social committee at a country club, rather than the elder of a witch clan.

"Come on in, Evan," she said, gesturing him inside.

The interior of the house was as neat as Tricia herself, although it had been decorated with Victorian antiques that seemed a little fussy to him. Maybe she'd tried to match the decor to the house.

She led him into the living room, where Bryce and the third McAllister elder, Allegra Moss, already waited on the couch. Unlike Tricia, Allegra looked every inch the distracted witch, from the mousy, graying hair piled untidily on top of her head to the flowing dark skirt she wore with her baggy sweater.

"Hi, Bryce, Allegra," Evan said as he headed over to the wing chair where he usually sat during these meetings. They'd done this often enough that it had become something of a ritual by now.

However, he realized as he looked at the elders that they appeared uncharacteristically grim. That is, Allegra and Tricia, who had also just sat down on the couch, appeared far grimmer than usual. Bryce pretty much looked that way all the time.

"Evan," Bryce said, his tone brisk, "Angela asked us to handle this, since she's up in Flagstaff right now, and she didn't want us to have to wait while she drove down here."

It had to be fairly important if Angela was involved. Usually the McAllister *prima* was fairly hands off, unless something particularly big had happened. "Okay," Evan said, tone cautious. "So exactly what is going on?"

The elders exchanged glances. Allegra nodded at Tricia, as if encouraging her to speak.

Tricia smoothed her bright red bob with one hand. "About a half hour ago, I got a call from Luz Trujillo."

Evan felt his eyebrows go up. "The de la Paz's *prima?*"

"Exactly. It seems they've run into a bit of a problem, and they need our help. Or, more specifically, your kind of help."

As far as he knew, the de la Paz clan didn't have anyone with his kind of gift, so the request didn't seem that strange. What did feel sort of odd was that they'd waited this long to ask for his particular help. Surely they must have had spells go awry over the years.

But then, witch clans tended to be fiercely independent. The lines had started to get a little more blurred lately, true. Even so, Evan wondered what in the world had gone wrong that they'd be reaching out for help now.

Bryce snorted. "'A bit of a problem'? Sounds like their little *prima*-in-waiting might have placed the entire clan in jeopardy."

"Bryce, we don't know that for sure," Allegra put in, her voice so mild that the interjection was just barely a rebuke. She turned her watery blue gaze on Evan and continued, "But it does sound as if she's gotten in over her head by using a spell that was forbidden for a very good reason. Now they need our help. I'm actually very encouraged that they reached out to us. It says a lot about inter-clan cooperation and all that."

"Well, that and knowing I'd find out eventually, since Caitlin is married to Luz's son," Tricia remarked dryly.

Right. Evan had almost forgotten that Tricia's daughter had married Alex Trujillo, the son of the de la Paz prima. It wasn't as if he'd gone to their wedding. Back then, about six months ago, he'd still been too angry about Kelly's abandonment and their subsequent divorce to have any desire to attend a wedding, especially one all the way down in Tucson. No, he'd stayed home and worked on his car. "What kind of spell?" he asked.

Again the three elders glanced at one another. This time, it was Bryce who replied. "They want to talk to you in person about that. Considering that their future *prima* is involved, we have to respect their wishes. So we need you to drive down to Scottsdale and meet with Luz Trujillo."

"Just Luz?" Evan knew he'd have to meet with the prima herself, but he also would need to speak with the *prima*-in-waiting, too, if she was the one who'd cast the spell.

"She didn't say," Bryce replied. "I suppose that's for them to decide. But we said you'd be happy to help."

Of course you did, Evan thought sourly. *That's how it works—you snap your fingers, and I come running.*

That wasn't precisely fair. It wasn't as if the elders had ever made an unreasonable request of him. But sometimes it was kind of rough to be the only person with your particular kind of gift, because you didn't have the option of calling someone in to be your relief pitcher, so to speak. You had to do it all on your own.

"Okay," he said, after a short pause. "I'll need to go by the house and get a few things, but you can let Luz Trujillo know that I'll be down there in a couple of hours."

The elders probably noticed his hesitation but decided not to comment on it. What could they say? He'd agreed to take on the task.

As for all the mystery surrounding this "forbidden" spell the de la Pazes' future *prima* had cast—well, he'd find out the truth soon enough. For now, he just needed to get going.

Zoe sat on the worn leather couch in her aunt's living room, hands clasped together. Both her parents stood by the fireplace, looking angry and worried and nervous all at once. Aunt Luz ended the call and set her phone down on the side table next to the arm chair that faced the sofa.

"He's on his way," she said.

Both Andrea and Luis Sandoval visibly sagged with relief. "And he'll be able to help?" Luis asked.

"The McAllister elders seemed to think so."

Maybe she should also be feeling relieved, but Zoe wasn't quite ready to go there yet. She didn't know anything about this Evan McAllister. He hadn't been among the candidates sent to meet her, so he must be older. In her mind's eye, she imagined some scowling middle-aged man who would read her the riot act about her recklessness before he bothered to say whether or not he could truly do anything to rid the world of the monster she'd unleashed upon it.

Anyway, she'd already had her talking-to. She wouldn't bother to say she didn't deserve it, because she did, but there had to come a time to set the scoldings aside and get down to business.

But it seemed as if Luz wasn't quite done with her yet, because her normally full mouth pulled into a flat line as she looked at her niece, and she said, dark eyes flashing, "Don't think just because one of the McAllisters is coming here to bail you out that this is the end of the matter."

"Did I say I thought that?"

"Zoe," her father said in a warning tone. The stern expression he currently wore was one she didn't often see, since in general he tended to be fairly easygoing. Zoe didn't much care to be on the receiving end of it.

Right then, she'd had enough. Even though she knew the enormity of her mistake dictated that she should just sit there meekly on the couch and take anything her family handed out, something in Zoe rebelled at the notion of being so passive. Why should they get to be so judge-y? Her mother hadn't had to deal with the humiliation of kissing random guy after random guy in a stupid quest to find her ideal mate. No, she'd been able to meet up with her husband the old-fashioned way. You'd think Luz would be more sympathetic, since she'd been right where Zoe was standing now. But apparently Uncle David had been Aunt Luz's first candidate, and they'd kissed and known they'd found the perfect person, so Luz wasn't forced to look any further than that.

None of them understood what Zoe had been going through.

She got up from the couch and planted her hands on her hips. "Don't you think I know I screwed up? But what none of you want to talk about is how I shouldn't have been forced to cast that spell in the first place!"

"No one *forced* you to do anything, Zoe," her father said. His tone was even enough, but his dark eyes flashed fire. Did he look like that when he was arguing a case in front of the judge? She didn't know, because she'd never actually seen him at work in the courtroom. "You cast that spell because you were frustrated...and selfish."

All right, true enough. Even though she knew how petulant the words sounded, she burst out, "And none of you understand what it was like, to have to kiss all those guys, whether or not I thought they were cute, just because of some stupid tradition!"

"Zoe!" Andrea Sandoval exclaimed, looking truly scandalized. In that moment, the resemblance between her and her older sister seemed particularly strong. "It is *not* a stupid tradition. It is because our *primas* have been with exactly the right man that we have stayed strong all these years."

"Oh, like Grandpa was exactly the right man for my *abuela?*" Zoe shot back.

"Enough," Luz said, and raised a hand. "We will not have that discussion about my mother—*or* my father, may they both rest in peace. What you did, Zoe, was perform an extremely dangerous piece of magic, one that has rightly been forbidden for hundreds of years. Believe it or not, I do understand something of your frustration. Do you think it gives your parents any joy to see you suffer disappointment after disappointment? Do you think it pleases me? We have all been on edge ever since Matías Escobar tried to kidnap you, because his actions pointed out how truly vulnerable you are. We would all be much happier if you had found your consort early on."

For a long moment, Zoe said nothing. Her thoughts churned this way and that, because she knew that Aunt Luz was right, that they had come so very close to completely losing control of the situation. Sure, she'd been watched over since the day Maya had identified her as the *prima* who would succeed Luz, but she'd still managed to have something of a normal life. Boys were off limits, of course. Otherwise, though, she wasn't that much different from the other girls she'd gone to high school with, participating in classes and extracurricular activities, and going to the movies and shopping and just hanging out. The only thing that had been strictly forbidden was going to parties alone, because Zoe's parents knew kids drank at those things, and where there was drinking there were loosened inhibitions and all manner of risks. She'd always had a cousin tag along with her, just to make sure nothing went sideways.

Ever since Matías had tried to steal her away, though, she'd been watched even more closely. There were de la Paz cousins in her classes at Scottsdale Community College, and less obtrusive observers when she went out with Amber or some of her other friends to shop or eat or whatever. Zoe had even seen her Uncle Jack show up occasionally, which just made her want to shake her head. Not that she had a problem with Jack—he was her favorite uncle, the youngest of her father's four brothers—but you'd think a detective with the Scottsdale police department would have better things to do with his time.

In fact, she was pretty sure someone in the clan had followed her when she'd driven here to Aunt Luz's house to cast the fateful spell, but once they'd seen where she was going, they hadn't bothered to stick around. Too bad, because maybe then there might have been a witness to see where the monster had gone.

Hoping she could steer the conversation elsewhere, Zoe said, "Maybe we don't need Evan McAllister's help at all. Maybe the thing just... disappeared."

Luz shook her head. "No. I fear we are not that lucky." She paused then, one hand lifted before her, the gesture she made when attempting to sense magical currents on the air. "I can tell it is still out there. Where exactly, I'm not sure, except that it's somewhere in the area, possibly to the south of here. My senses aren't strong enough to pinpoint it more than that. But there is definitely a wrongness, like running your hand over a piece of smooth silk and feeling a snag beneath your fingertips. We will require Evan McAllister's talents to help us track it down."

Deep down, Zoe had known it wouldn't be that easy. She also knew she'd have to participate in neutralizing the spell, since the McAllister warlock apparently required some input from the original spell caster for his own gift to work properly. So she'd have to suffer the company of this Evan person, whoever he was, and hope that he wouldn't turn out to be too much of a judgmental jerk.

Otherwise, attempting to locate the monster might prove to be even more problematic than conjuring it in the first place.

CHAPTER THREE

THE DRIVE DOWN TO SCOTTSDALE WAS UNEVENTFUL. EVAN hit a little traffic once he turned onto the 101 Loop and headed east, but the majority of the cars were going in the opposite direction, traveling back to their homes in the western suburbs at the end of a long week.

He had to wonder what all these ordinary residents of Phoenix would think if they ever discovered that a large witch clan lived right in their midst, that some of their lawyers and teachers and cops had more about them than met the eye.

That would never happen, though. The de la Paz clan was just as careful as the McAllisters and the Wilcoxes when it came to hiding their true nature. However, it had to be a strain. He was used to the setup in Jerome, where more than half the town was part of the extended clan, and the civilians who did live there full-time were in on the secret. The arrangement allowed for a much more relaxed attitude when it came to using their powers, although the McAllisters still did their best to keep things on the down-low.

Even so, he knew he'd have to be careful while down here in the big city. His power wasn't a showy one. On the other hand, just like every other witch or warlock out there, he also had the ability to unlock doors and summon fire and cause others to focus their attention elsewhere when he really didn't want to be noticed, which meant he could perform magic spells that might raise a few eyebrows if any civilians happened to be looking in the wrong place at the wrong time.

Of course, he thought, as he pulled off the highway onto Cactus Road and headed east toward the hills, if he really wanted to be unobtrusive, he probably should have rented a car, some boring subcompact thing. Even in this upscale area, he had noticed a few heads swiveling as he drove past.

Luz Trujillo's house was on a quiet street of large, expensive homes on more generously sized lots than you might expect to find in this part of the world, where everything felt much closer together than most of the residential parcels in the Verde Valley. The *prima*'s home had been built in the traditional hacienda style, of stucco with a red tile roof. A dark gray Audi SUV was parked in the driveway, a small pale blue Fiat next to it. He had to pass through a gate into a courtyard where a fountain played and baskets of flowers brightened up the overhangs. The air here was warm, but not hot, a contrast to the chilly day he'd just spent up in Jerome.

Although he hadn't seen anyone, Evan couldn't shake the feeling that he was being watched as he paused in front of the large door of dark wood and knocked. Well, that wasn't terribly surprising. The clan's *prima* lived here, and so someone always had to be on their guard.

The door opened, and a tall, good-looking Hispanic man in his late forties looked out. When he saw Evan, his somewhat tense features relaxed into a smile. "Evan McAllister? I'm Luis Sandoval, Luz's brother-in-law."

"Hi, Luis," Evan responded, and extended a hand. He'd known as soon as the door opened that a warlock stood before him, since he'd experienced the usual tingle on the back of his neck that he felt whenever he encountered another person with witch-blood for the first time.

"Come in," Luis said, stepping aside so Evan could enter. "They're waiting in the living room."

They. So that meant it wasn't just Luz who'd be present at this meeting. Good—he wanted to hear what had happened from the *prima*-in-waiting herself.

Evan followed Luis from the impressive two-story foyer down a hallway, and then into a large room with a big fireplace—unlit now, on this mild spring day—and a series of windows that looked out onto the courtyard. In that room were three women, two of them attractive and slender, also probably in their forties, with sleek dark hair and simple sleeveless dresses. They resembled one another enough that Evan guessed they must be sisters.

The third one, though....

She was much younger than the other two, early twenties, and so he thought she had to be the *prima*-in-waiting. However, to say she wasn't what he'd been expecting would be a massive understatement. For some reason, he'd been picturing someone like his cousin Angela, who was pretty but not that concerned with her appearance, and who always seemed to go around in jeans and cowboy boots and the barest traces of makeup, if any at all.

This girl—well, for one thing, she was wearing a knee-length skirt that showed off her slim brown legs, and with the skirt a fitted scoop-neck T-shirt that didn't do much to hide the curves of her body. Her eyes were big and brown, with lashes so long that at first he thought they must be fake. But no, they seemed to be all hers, just like the fullness of the breasts under the thin shirt. Silver gleamed around one slender ankle, and more silver shimmered from the charm bracelet on her right wrist.

And her mouth....

He had to tear his eyes away, because he knew he was staring, and the last thing he should be doing was gawking at the de la Paz clan's *prima*-in-waiting the way a starving man might stare at a particularly juicy steak.

"Hi," he said quickly. Too quickly, he thought, but he had to do something to distract himself. "I'm Evan McAllister."

"Hello, Evan," said one of the two older women. She'd been sitting in an armchair, but rose then and came to him, one hand extended. "I'm Luz Trujillo. This is my sister Andrea. And this"—she hesitated so briefly that Evan could have almost imagined that she hadn't paused at all—"this is my niece Zoe, and our future *prima*."

He nodded in her direction but didn't trust himself to do much else. She was watching him, her eyes slightly narrowed, but otherwise her expression seemed almost blank, as if she wanted to make sure he couldn't discern much of what she was thinking just by looking at her.

"Would you like to sit?" Luz asked. She gestured toward the chair she'd just vacated. "And there's water, or lemonade."

For the first time, Evan noticed a silver tray sitting on the large coffee table of dark wood. On that tray were a set of thick glasses with cobalt-blue rims, and two matching pitchers. His mouth did feel dry. Some water would probably be a good idea. "Water would be great."

Andrea moved from her position by the fireplace to pour him a glass of water, then handed it to him. "We thank you for coming," she said. Her voice wasn't quite as low as her sister's, but it still had the same slightly husky edge. Sexy, really.

Evan wondered if Zoe's voice had that same quality. So far she hadn't spoken a word.

"Not a problem," he said easily as he made his way over to the chair Luz had indicated and sat down. "I'm here to help."

"That means a good deal to us," Luz said. "There was a time when our clans did very little to aid one another."

No point in disputing her comment, because Evan knew it was only the truth. Yes, the de la Pazes and the McAllisters had been friendlier than most, but even their cooperation was a fairly recent development, brought about mainly because of the friendship between Maya de la Paz and the McAllister's former *prima*, Ruby Lynch. In the past, it had been safer for clans to isolate themselves, since too much cooperation could open the door to activities that might be more easily detected by the civilian population.

So he just nodded, and ventured, "If you could tell me exactly what happened? Right now I'm not really sensing anything that needs to be fixed."

Which in itself was odd. Usually when he was called to set a spell on the right course, or banish its effects completely, he could feel the wrongness as soon as he set foot in the place where the spell had been cast. Here, though, there wasn't anything, except the faint whisper of magic he felt coming from both Luz and Zoe. That didn't surprise him, because he could feel the same sort of gentle hum whenever he was around Angela or her husband Connor. Evan had always assumed it was simply because a *prima*— or a *primus*, or a *prima*-in-waiting—had more magic about them than the average witch or warlock. At any rate, it wasn't bothersome, and tended to fade into the background after he'd been around them for a little while.

However, he guessed that the thrum he felt when he looked over at Zoe didn't have much to do with his magic-sensing abilities....

After he asked the question about what had happened, she appeared uncomfortable for the first time. She shifted on the couch and studiously avoided looking at anyone in particular. The charm bracelet she wore jingled faintly as she pushed a lock of long dark hair over one shoulder.

Luz was the one who spoke then. "I'm afraid Zoe was feeling impatient. The search for a consort can be frustrating, and she became anxious. We were all anxious," the *prima* added quickly. "But we had no reason to believe that the search wouldn't have a satisfactory result."

"I screwed up," Zoe said. Her voice did, as he'd hoped, have that slight husky edge to it, a warmth that sounded more mature than the twenty-one he knew she must be. "I just didn't want to wait anymore. My birthday is less than two weeks off. So I used this."

Lying on the couch next to her, halfway hidden by the full skirt she wore, was an old book. She lifted it, and opened the volume to a place somewhere near the end, then held it out to Evan.

"See for yourself."

He took the book from her, handling it gently because he could tell it was old and fragile. In fact, he experienced a little thrill at realizing that he held an actual book of spells, or grimoire. McAllister magic didn't really work that way—each member of the clan used their magic based on their own inborn gifts and abilities. Yes, they had some spells they used at common rituals, like the ones recited at the Samhain observance, or the Yule celebrations. Most of their enchantments, though, they made up as they went along, depending on the current need.

But clearly the de la Paz clan did things differently. It wasn't that one method was good and one bad, more that they had descended from different traditions.

When he looked down at the page, though, Evan couldn't help frowning. He didn't know why he'd expected the words to be in English, but he couldn't read what was there. Latin, he could tell that much. His foreign language experience was two years of German in high school, which wasn't going to help much here.

Zoe seemed to note his consternation, because she said, "On the surface, it's simple. 'From shadow to light, from night to day, from dream to reality, become what I say.'" She spoke the words quickly and without inflection. That was the only safe way to utter the words of a spell aloud when you didn't actually mean to cast it. The intention was everything. And it helped that she had said the words in English, not Latin.

"Sounds harmless enough," he remarked.

Luz and Andrea exchanged a glance, and Luis spoke up. "Well, that's the problem. Sometimes it's the simplest-sounding spells that have the most potential to go wrong."

"It went *very* wrong, I assure you," Luz said. "Zoe was trying to conjure her perfect consort, but what appeared…wasn't."

The *prima*-in-waiting winced. Evan supposed it must have sounded even worse when put so baldly. But no wonder the spell had gone sideways. He couldn't imagine anyone in his clan—not even Angela and Connor working together—attempting such a high-powered enchantment. To conjure a human being from thin air? Zoe had to be strong, or she wouldn't be her clan's next *prima,* but he had to wonder why she'd thought she could ever be successful at such a thing.

To his surprise, she was the one who spoke next. He'd assumed she would prefer to let her aunt do the talking for her. "It was a monster," she said. "Shaped like a man, and around the same size, but its face—" Her words faltered, and she pulled in a breath, as if to give herself strength to go on with the story. "Anyway, it looked completely solid, real, but it was able to go through the wall of the library as if it wasn't there."

"Did you try to talk to it?" Evan asked. To be honest, he wasn't sure if he would be capable of rational discourse if he were ever confronted by such an apparition. Zoe, however, seemed fairly calm about the whole thing, if embarrassed that she'd been driven to such lengths.

"I did, at first. But then it made this horrible snarling noise and reached for me, and it just felt so wrong that I did what I could to drive it off."

"How?"

"My—my powers. I mean, the *prima* powers I have inside me. I'm not as strong as I will be once I'm matched with my consort and my gifts are fully awakened, but it was enough to make the thing go away. I had to hit it twice before it ran, though."

Evan paused for a moment and resisted the urge to run a hand through his hair. So apparently there was now some monster running around the greater Phoenix area, a monster with the ability to walk through walls. Which meant it probably could come and go as it pleased, wherever it pleased.

Great.

Still...he had to respect what Zoe had done to get rid of the thing. Yes, it was her mistake that had summoned it here in the first place, but to stand her ground and try to fight back, rather than run away and get help? Those actions seemed to indicate some pretty serious *cojones,* so to speak.

But then, she would be the de la Paz clan's next *prima.* Evan had never met Maya de la Paz, but he'd heard the stories about her. She made his late Great-Aunt Ruby sound like a pushover. It seemed Maya's daughter was just as tough, and her granddaughter as well. At least he could count on some good backup while he was here, although in that moment, he had to admit to himself that he was somewhat at a loss. Zoe had no reason to be lying about what had happened, but he still couldn't catch one whiff of the creature, whatever it was. And if he couldn't do that, then they stood a slim chance of catching it and sending it back to whatever plane of hell it had come from.

In the meantime, he figured he might as well start at the beginning and work out from there. "Did you do any preparations for the spell back at your house?"

Zoe looked confused for a second, then nodded. "Yes. I found the spell here, but I did all my research at home."

"Research?"

She didn't exactly sigh, but her chest rose and fell as she let out a breath. Evan made sure to keep his eyes fixed on her face, but it wasn't easy. He hadn't counted on her being so distracting, and he didn't quite know what to do about it. "Which hot *telenovela* guy I wanted my 'perfect' consort to look like."

That had to have been excruciating for her to admit. He said, "Thanks, Zoe. Then I guess that's where we should go next."

"Our house?" Luis asked.

"If it's okay."

"Of course," Andrea said hastily. "You can follow us there. It's about fifteen minutes from here."

"Sounds good." Evan set the water he held down on the little painted table next to him, careful to use the coaster, then stood up.

Zoe got up from her seat as well, reaching down to retrieve the purse that had been sitting on the floor next to her.

"What do you think you will find?" Luz asked, her tone frankly curious.

"I don't know," he admitted. "But I've got to start somewhere."

Could this have been any more embarrassing? Zoe didn't know. All she did know was that she thought she would rather have admitted the truth behind the creation of her consort to the judge-y older man she'd first imagined, rather than the actual Evan McAllister.

Damn, he was smoking hot. She hadn't even contemplated that possibility, mostly because she'd just assumed that someone who wielded his powers and had his kind of responsibility had to be someone a lot older than she was. All right, he still had to have a few years on her, looked to be somewhere in his late twenties, maybe as much as thirty, but that wasn't such a big age difference, was it?

She told herself that even entertaining such a thought was crazy. Evan had to be way too old to be considered consort material, or surely the McAllisters would have sent him down to see if he was the "one." In general, candidates weren't more than three years older than the *prima*-in-waiting they were trying to match. Trying to guess someone's age could be tricky, but she thought he had to be at least twenty-eight or twenty-nine, maybe even more than that.

And when they left the house to go to their cars—her parents in their Audi SUV, Zoe in the Fiat her parents had bought her for her twenty-first birthday—she watched as Evan headed toward a shiny black piece of muscle car parked just behind her parents' SUV. She didn't know much about cars, but whatever he was driving, it was pure sex on wheels, just like he was sex on legs.

Stop that, she commanded herself. *He's here to help. He's not your future consort.*

Too bad, though. She'd never seen a guy with hair his color, a deep, deep red that you almost thought was brown until the sunlight touched it. He didn't have a redhead's complexion, though; he was sort of fair-skinned, but she hadn't seen any freckles, and she guessed he'd be more tanned in the summertime when he had a chance to get outside more.

From what she'd heard, Jerome was a lot colder than Phoenix.

Then again, wasn't just about any place colder than Phoenix?

She pulled away from the curb, and the shiny black monster Evan was driving fell in behind her. A glance in her rearview mirror told her he'd put on some sunglasses for the drive. It was hard to tell for sure, but she thought they were black Ray-Bans, to match the car.

Sigh.

With some difficulty, she forced her concentration forward, on making sure that she didn't inch too close to her parents' Audi, and she frowned at herself. Being all distracted and girly around the man who'd been sent to help her was exactly the wrong thing to do. She needed to focus. He'd said he hadn't been able to detect the creature, but what did that mean? Maybe it really was gone, and what Luz had sensed was just a weird echo of a false positive. Or maybe she'd sensed something else entirely, and not the creature Zoe had summoned.

Which in a way was worse. She didn't want to think that her hometown harbored an even worse threat than the monster. No, it was probably that Evan had never encountered anything like this before in his life, and so the usual rules just didn't apply.

That thought didn't reassure her very much, but she told herself that the McAllister elders wouldn't have sent him here if he didn't have something to contribute. This was a different kind of magic from what he was used to. He was bound to need some kind of an adjustment period.

So her thoughts hummed along as she followed her parents down to Shea Boulevard, and then up into the hills east of Scottsdale. Just beyond was the Fountain Hills suburb where her house was located, although they had to climb some more hills to reach her street. The whole time she was acutely conscious of the gleaming black car a few yards behind her. She wondered about it. From what she'd heard, the McAllisters weren't really into material stuff and tended to live like a bunch of hippie leftovers in their ramshackle mountain town. But there was definitely nothing ramshackle about that car.

Her parents turned onto their cul-de-sac, and then up into the driveway and the far left garage bay where they always parked the Audi. Right next to that was her mother's BMW, while the far right bay was reserved for Zoe's Fiat. In another year and a half, her younger brother Zander would be driving, but by then she should be long out of the house, married to a consort she hadn't even met yet.

If she ever met him.

She decided she could heave an exaggerated sigh, since there wasn't anyone around to hear it. So that's exactly what she did, right before she grabbed her purse from where it had been resting on the passenger seat and got out.

Her parents were already standing in the driveway, waiting for Evan, who had parked at the little bit of curved curb in front of their house. As he came up the drive, he pushed up the sleeves of his shirt, clearly bothered a little by the heat. It might have only been early March, but temperatures had inched into the eighties the last few days.

Not that she minded, because now she could see his forearms, strong and with a dusting of dark hair. She wondered if it was just plain brown, or whether it was also dark red. On his left wrist he wore a bulky dark watch, one of those sporty chronograph things.

Oh, yeah, definitely hot.

She swallowed, and was saved from having to act like a rational human being by her mother saying, "Come on in, Evan."

They all went inside. Zoe could tell from the startled flicker of his gaze upward that he was surprised by the opulence of the house, its gleaming columns and shining travertine floor. Well, they probably didn't have houses like this in Jerome. Everything there was old, and often not all that well-maintained. Or at least that was what the cousins who'd been brave enough to venture there claimed. Zoe had never been, because the *prima*-in-waiting was supposed to stay in her own territory. Previously, that particular rule hadn't felt too limiting, because the southern part of Arizona was a pretty big place to roam around in, but now she found herself wishing she had been to Jerome, just so she'd have a better idea of how foreign her own surroundings must feel to Evan McAllister.

"My room is upstairs," she offered. Both her parents lifted their eyebrows, and she went on, "Well, that's where I was doing my research. On my *computer*," she added for emphasis in case they still didn't get it. "And then my lab is out in the casita."

"Lab?"

"My talent is potions, and some healing. That is, making healing potions. I can't just lay on hands and heal someone like Valentina and Alba, our two healers, can. So I do a lot of work out in the casita."

"Why don't we look at the casita first?" Evan asked. Apparently he'd also picked up on the vibe that her parents didn't particularly want him in her room.

Which was stupid, because he had acted completely professional this whole time, not a flicker in his eyes to indicate that he'd even noticed she was female. Zoe could tell, because she'd done her best to watch him sideways and from under her eyelashes, so he wouldn't notice. It was definitely safer that way, but....

Since she'd already allowed herself her one sigh of exasperation for the hour, she said, "Sure. It's this way."

He offered a faint smile for her parents, who also smiled in return, although Zoe had the feeling that they'd started to pick up on some vibes and weren't happy. Or maybe it was only that they didn't like the idea of having an attractive unattached warlock around their daughter. Evan didn't wear any rings; she knew, because she'd looked at his left hand almost as soon as she laid eyes on him.

Also, the secret was out now when it came to *primas* and their consorts. Yes, it was always better to be with the one who completed her soul bond, because then a *prima*'s powers would be able to reach their fullest potential. However, a *prima* didn't have to be with her soul mate to be pretty powerful on her own. And that made Evan's presence here problematic, to say the least. Because she could already feel how attracted she was to him. So attracted that she couldn't prevent the thought from crossing her mind that if she could be with him, then this stupid consort search would have to stop, and her family would finally leave her alone.

She knew better than to betray anything of what she was thinking, however. Instead, she took Evan through the kitchen and out the door that opened onto the cover patio. A little beyond was the infinity pool, and off to one side was the casita—pool house, lab…whatever you wanted to call it.

The door was always kept locked, and she'd left her purse in the house, but that didn't matter. Zoe laid her hand on the doorknob and it turned easily. Inside was the space she'd taken over once her talent with herbs and potions had really begun to manifest itself. Long tables to either side, and an apartment-sized gas stove for the times she needed to use heat to get the effect she desired. Sprays and sprigs of all sort of herbs hung from the walls, lending their riot of scents to the air. The ductless A/C unit on the far wall hummed into the quiet.

"Wow," Evan said as he looked around. He appeared genuinely impressed, too, although Zoe didn't know him well to decide whether she was reading his expression accurately.

"So this is where I work," she said. Now that they were alone together, in this space where she usually kept the blinds drawn to avoid damaging any sensitive potion components, she couldn't help feeling a little awkward. He seemed so much taller when he was standing close to her like this. Of course, it didn't help that she was barely five foot three in her bare feet. She had always hated that she hadn't inherited her mother's height, had turned out to be vertically challenged just like her grandmother Maya.

"It's quite the work area." He moved away from her, taking a few steps farther into the room so he could inspect the equipment and all the herbs hanging from the walls. "Where do you get all these?"

"We have a garden in the side yard," she explained. "I grow what I can there. But I also have to buy a lot of imported stuff, because the climate here isn't that great when it comes to cultivating things. We looked into building a greenhouse, but the association wouldn't allow it. Said it wasn't allowed under the CC&R's, or something stupid like that."

During this speech, Evan's eyebrows had knotted together, as if she'd suddenly started to babble in Spanish and he was having a difficult time following what she'd just said. "Association?"

Right. Homeowner's associations probably weren't a thing in Jerome. "Homeowner's association. There are all these rules we have to follow if we live in this neighborhood. You can't paint your house pink or purple. You can't add a second story if the house wasn't built that way originally. You can't leave cars on the street overnight. That kind of thing. It's so everything stays looking nice."

"Sounds kind of extreme."

Zoe shrugged. She'd spent her whole life here, so she was used to the way things worked. "Better than having pink and purple houses everywhere, I guess. Although purple is my favorite color."

He smiled at that, just a little. What a great smile, too, with the way his hazel eyes seemed to light up, and how the crinkles showed at the corners of those eyes.

But she shouldn't stare. Had she been staring? Crap, she'd better say something fast. "Anyway, I work in here when I'm not doing stuff for school."

"You're in college?"

"Just the local community college. There didn't seem to be much point in trying for ASU—the logistics would have been a total pain, since it's way across town instead of only a few minutes from the house. Anyway, I would have had to drop out once—well, once I found my consort. So I just didn't bother with the whole thing."

A nod. He even looked vaguely sympathetic, as if he'd figured out that being the future *prima* of a clan wasn't exactly a bed of roses. So many restrictions, so many things you couldn't do….

"Did you do any of your research in here?" he asked then, his tone turning brisk.

"Some. I mean, I brought my laptop in here a few times when I had a long-simmering potion that I had to babysit."

"Hmm."

What he meant by that, she had no idea. She leaned against one of the lab tables and watched as he moved to the far end of the room, where a blind-covered window took up most of the wall. He paused there for a long moment, then raised one hand to touch the wooden blinds. A faint frown pulled at his dark brows.

"What is it?" she asked. "Do you sense something?"

Why he'd be able to do something like that here, when he'd come up empty back at Aunt Luz's house, Zoe didn't know. But magic wasn't always logical. It had its own whimsical nature, and sometimes did as it pleased.

Evan didn't answer right away. When he spoke, he sounded abstracted, as if he was concentrating on something far away. "Maybe," he said at last. "I don't know for sure. I did feel something, like a finger trailing through still water. Something upsetting the pattern."

Which sounded suspiciously like what Aunt Luz had said about sensing a snag in an otherwise smooth piece of silk. Same concept, only a different metaphor.

"Which means it's still out there," Zoe said. Deep down, she'd really been hoping that once the creature got bored with wandering around Phoenix, it would pop back into whatever dimension it had come from. But she should have known the universe wouldn't be that kind.

"Yes," Evan replied, still in that same somewhat faraway tone. His fingers—long and strong-looking— moved down the edge of the blinds. "Somewhere to the south, I think, but the sensation is so faint that it's really hard to tell."

"Maybe we should drive that way, see if we can find anything," she suggested. As the words left her mouth, though, she thought of how desperate she must have sounded.

And how much of that was really wanting to go find the creature, and how much just wanting to have Evan drive you around in that car of his? she thought then.

Zoe really didn't want to know the answer to that question.

To her surprise, he appeared to take her suggestion seriously. "That could work. If we get closer to where it's gone, then it might be easier for me to get a clear read. Right now I might as well be asking a Magic 8 ball to tell me where the thing is."

"Okay," she said at once. If he really was going to go along with her crazy idea, then they should go now before he had a chance to change his mind. But...she should probably propose that she should drive, just in case he couldn't focus on driving and tracking at the same time.

But when she ventured to ask the question, he shook his head. "No, it's actually better if I'm driving. Sometimes I feel as if the car is helping me just as much as my talent is."

Relief, and a certain measure of excitement, went through her. "It's a pretty amazing car. What is it?"

"A '70 Plymouth Barracuda," he replied, clearly proud of his ride. "My father and I restored it together. It looked like it was headed for the scrap heap before we started working on it."

Zoe didn't know much about cars, except the new fast ones that a lot of her cousins liked to drive, but she had to admit that it was pretty cool that he had done a lot of work on the car. It meant he wasn't afraid to roll up his sleeves and get dirty.

And then she had to stop her brain from continuing that particular line of thought, because her mind immediately went to an image of how he might look bent over the engine, grease streaking his bare arms, maybe his shirt hiking up to reveal the hard, flat stomach underneath.

No, she told herself. Just that one word, but for the moment, it was enough. If she didn't stay focused, she feared the worst might happen…or the best, depending on how you looked at it.

"Okay," she said briskly. "Let's go catch a monster."

CHAPTER FOUR

ANDREA AND LUIS SANDOVAL DIDN'T LOOK THRILLED about their daughter taking off with him in the Barracuda, but neither did they try to stop her. And that, Evan thought, was probably about as good as it was going to get.

Not that they had anything to worry about. He'd already vowed to himself that he would be a perfect gentleman, no matter how drop-dead gorgeous their daughter had turned out to be.

It was hard not to stare, though, as she went around to the passenger side of the car, her long jet-dark hair shimmering in the breeze. And that little silver chain around her ankle was distracting as hell.

Didn't you use to like blondes?

If asked that question a few years ago, then yes, he probably would have said he preferred blonde women.

Kelly was blonde, bright-haired and blue-eyed, the perfect girl-next-door cheerleader type. Zoe couldn't have been more her opposite, and yet....

And yet he knew he shouldn't be paying any attention to the *prima*-in-waiting, except to help her with this seemingly impossible quest and then get the hell out of Phoenix before things got any weirder.

She climbed into the passenger seat and looked around with some interest. The inside of the car felt blazingly hot, so Evan turned on the air conditioning to full blast.

"It came with A/C?" she asked, as if surprised that something as antediluvian as a vehicle built in 1970 would have such creature comforts.

"No," he said as he pulled away from the curb and pointed the car in the direction they'd come from. That weird tingle or twitch or whatever you wanted to call it felt a little stronger now that he knew where to look for it. He definitely needed to head south. "It's an aftermarket system. I installed it a couple of years ago."

"Oh." For a few seconds she didn't say anything. Then she shifted in her seat so she was half turned toward him, and he caught a faint drift of something sweet-smelling. Perfume, or maybe just what she used in her hair?

He swallowed and kept his eyes on the road. "What's south of here?"

Zoe looked vaguely startled by the question. "Well...a lot of things. I mean, technically we're north of Scottsdale here in Fountain Hills, so there's Scottsdale, and then Tempe and Mesa and Chandler and Gilbert. Phoenix is big, you know."

Yeah, he'd known that intellectually, but he hadn't really processed the idea of its vastness until he'd started driving around on its streets. It would be so easy to get lost here. Of course the car didn't have a nav system, and he'd never bothered with GPS because he knew the Verde Valley and its environs like the back of his hand. True, there was the map function on his phone, but again, he'd never had much need for it.

"So...they're as crowded as the parts we've already driven through?"

Zoe gusted out a little breath between her full, glossy lips, as if she had been about to laugh and then decided it wouldn't be appropriate. "Yes. There are little open areas here and there, but you know, it's a city. All those places are cities. We've got millions of people living here. "

Of course they did. A huge haystack, with one ant that wasn't supposed to be there crawling around somewhere in the middle.

"Okay," he replied, even though he knew the situation was far from okay. The car had begun to cool down now that they were driving, but he could still feel sweat trickling down his back. Why the hell hadn't he changed into a T-shirt before he drove down here?

Because it was still in the sixties when you left Jerome, he told himself. *The temperature in Phoenix wasn't exactly high on your list of priorities when you were getting your stuff together.*

Zoe was staring out the car window at the high-end houses passing by. Not that they should be anything new to her, since she'd lived her whole life in this area. Evan wondered what that would be like, to be surrounded by everything new and shiny, to not always be patching roofs and replacing siding and shoring up hillsides that had a tendency to slip an inch or three each year.

But then he felt it again—that strange tingle at the back of his neck, almost as if a small insect was crawling across his skin. He had to resist the urge to slap at the place, like he'd expected to find a gnat or a mosquito there.

South…but south and east, toward those strange spiky mountains he could just barely glimpse out the driver-side windows.

"What are those?" he asked, jerking his chin toward the unfamiliar peaks.

"What?" she responded, and then seemed to notice where he was looking. "Oh. Those are the Superstitions."

Reassuring name. "Are there people living out there?"

"Not really. I mean, I guess people go to hike there and stuff, but it's not what you'd call populated." She shifted in her seat once again so she was nearly facing him full on, at the same time pulling at the seatbelt so she wouldn't get tangled up in it. "Do you think it's in the mountains?"

He didn't bother to ask her what she'd meant by "it." "I'm not sure. Maybe. I'm feeling something in that direction, but I can't tell how far out it's coming from."

For a moment, she didn't say anything. Her hands smoothed the fabric of the vintage-looking skirt she wore. "I'm not really dressed to go hiking."

No, she wasn't. In a perfect world, he'd be taking her out for a drink or something. If she drank. There was so much he didn't know about Zoe Sandoval.

"Well," he told her, "let's just drive in that direction. If it looks like we're going to be heading into some rough terrain, we'll stop and turn around."

"And let it get away?" She shook her head, full mouth set with determination. "I can manage."

Evan had a sudden flash of her climbing up a rocky mountain path in those flat sandals. Better than high heels, he supposed, but her footwear still wasn't what he would call practical. But he could tell she was determined to make this right. "We'll see what happens. How do I get out in that direction?"

By that point, he'd pulled onto the 101 Loop southbound, just because it felt like the right direction to go. But he really didn't know where the freeway went after that.

"Um...give me a sec," Zoe said. "I don't go out that way very often. I think the 60 east, but let me check." She fumbled in her purse and pulled out a big iPhone, one of those pink metallic ones. It had a sparkly protective case, also pink. She seemed to notice Evan giving it the side-eye, and added, somewhat waspishly, "You have a problem with pink?"

"Um...no."

"Good." She entered her passcode and then brought up a map, dragging it around on the screen with one finger. "Yes, the 60. We still have about five miles to go."

Thank the Goddess for technology...and that Zoe seemed to know what she was doing with it. Evan wasn't sure why he should be surprised by that, even if he himself was the type who tended to ignore the more advanced features on his own phone. He had to admit that it did help to have her there in the passenger seat, playing navigator. Kelly had been useless at that sort of thing, mostly because she'd grown up in the Phoenix area and seemed to have a mental block when it came to learning where everything was in Cottonwood or even Sedona. Prescott she could handle, probably because that was where you needed to go if you wanted to do any serious shopping.

But he really didn't want his thoughts to head down that particular pathway, not when he had much more serious matters to occupy his mind right now.

"What will you do if we catch up with it?" Zoe asked then. The half-irritated expression she had worn a moment earlier was gone; now she just looked worried.

"Guess I'll figure it out when that happens," Evan said.

A finely arched eyebrow lifted. "That's your plan?"

"Mostly, I don't plan." She cocked her head at him, as if urging him to explain further, so he went on, "That's not how my talent works. Every magical spell that goes wrong is a little different in *how* it's gone wrong. So I have to be near it, feel it, and then I can begin to work through *un*working it, if you know what I mean."

She nodded, dark eyes solemn. "I think so. But… have you ever fixed anything like this before?"

"No. That doesn't mean I can't, though. I just won't know until it's right in front of me."

"That's kind of scary."

Just kind of? Evan thought. But he didn't say that out loud. He knew she was nervous and worried, and beating herself up for getting them in this situation to begin with. Admitting that he was anxious and tense—and yeah, a little scared—wouldn't help at all.

"Not really," he said, hoping he sounded strong and confident. "I'm used to it by now. I've never run into anything I couldn't handle."

The eyebrow went up again. "Really?"

"Really."

He wouldn't bother to tell her that dispelling wonky weather spells or toning down the effects of a love potion gone sideways wasn't exactly the same thing as driving off the sort of inhuman being she'd summoned. But at least he hadn't been lying when he'd said that he really had been able to manage everything he'd come across.

So far.

They drove in silence for a few minutes after that. Evan saw the turnoff for the 60 east and took it. Out here, the freeways weren't quite as busy, although he still saw plenty of cars occupying the road. After they'd gone a few more miles, he felt that buzzing, prickling sensation on the back of his neck again, only much, much stronger. Without thinking, he changed lanes, then pointed the Barracuda toward the Power Road off-ramp.

"What is it?" Zoe asked. "Is it here?"

"I think so," he replied, slowing down as he approached the bottom of the ramp. That tingly sensation seemed to tell him he should head south, so he turned right. Coming up on the left was a large apartment complex. The pull in that direction was so strong he winced.

"You feel it?"

"Yes," he said shortly. "Don't you?"

She shook her head, fingers tight around the pink iPhone she still held. "Nothing. That's kind of sad, isn't it? I mean, I summoned the thing, and I can't even sense where it is."

"At least one of us can. That's what's important." He aimed the Barracuda at one of the driveways leading into the apartment complex, then drove along slowly, passing carports and open-air parking areas for guests and resident overflow. The place was clean and well-kept, almost mercilessly bright under the hard Phoenix skies, even though the sun was now edging toward the horizon.

Why the hell would an unearthly creature take refuge in this kind of place? Evan could understand if the monster had decided to go roaming around the Superstition Mountains—that sounded like its kind of place—but this particular corner of suburbia? He didn't get it.

But his current incomprehension certainly wouldn't stop him from pursuing his goal. Evan kept driving along slowly, waiting for that uncomfortable sensation at the back of his neck to intensify further, to tell him just where the heck he could find his quarry.

Then he heard it, even over the rumble of the Barracuda's engine. A woman screaming from somewhere off to the left.

Zoe shot him a look of consternation. "Is it—?"

"Probably. Let's go."

He pulled the car into one of the guest parking spaces—luckily, there were several available, probably because it was late afternoon on a weekday—and stopped the engine. Zoe slipped her phone back into her purse, but then tucked the bag under the seat, as if she'd realized that she would need both hands free for whatever might come next.

They hurried over to one of the sidewalks, then ran in the direction of the screaming. Evan wondered why he didn't see anyone else responding, but realized that most of the people who lived in the upscale-looking complex were probably still at work, or maybe on their way home. Actually, that could only help him out. The fewer witnesses to what was happening, the better.

The walkway curved around the building, heading toward a large man-made pond bordered by more sidewalks. Trees grew along the greenbelt, already lush with leaves in this much warmer climate, while the trees up in Jerome were still mostly bare.

The screams abruptly stopped, but Evan knew where he and Zoe had to go. To that one clump of trees to the left, which provided shade and shelter.

Shelter for what, he wasn't sure he wanted to know.

He and Zoe came around the final curve, and her hand went to her mouth, as if she'd had to stifle a scream of her own. Not that he could blame her.

The creature—well, she'd said it was a monster but hadn't gone into much detail. It was tall, several inches taller than his own six foot two, and oddly proportioned, with overly wide shoulders and arms that seemed much too long for its torso. That was the least of it, though. As if it had sensed them approaching, it turned at once, so Evan was able to get a good look at its face.

It was like staring at a waxwork that had begun to melt. None of its features were in the right place, the nose off to one side, the mouth skewed, one side much higher than the other. Its rage-reddened eyes locked on Zoe, and it let out a hideous roar, right before it let go of the young woman it had been holding—clearly, the source of the screams—and came straight for them.

How the hell was he supposed to think in this kind of situation? Evan might have faced down a

human adversary once or twice before, but dealing
with a couple of drunks in a dive bar was a far cry
from confronting a rampaging monster that looked
as if it had climbed right out of hell. Anyway, this
was when his power was supposed to take over and
tell him exactly what to do. Now, though, he could
only stand there, instinctively placing himself in
front of Zoe even though he didn't know what he
could possibly do to stop the juggernaut that was
bearing down on them.

But then he felt a sharp pain in his side, and
realized Zoe had just elbowed him in the ribs so he
would step out of the way.

"I've done this before, remember?" she said
grimly as she raised her hands.

Bright light flared outward, hitting the creature
in the chest. It let out another of those roars, but
she didn't flinch, only sent another of those blinding
flashes toward the creature. This time it staggered,
and she didn't waste any time, but kept throwing
improbable fireball after fireball at it, until at last it
let out a screech and disappeared.

Zoe stopped then and bent over slightly, palms
flat against her skirt as she tried to catch her breath.
Then she glanced over at Evan and shot him a sar-
donic glance, right before she said, "Exactly who's
supposed to be protecting who here?"

CHAPTER FIVE

As far as knights in shining armor went, Evan was definitely falling down on the job. Zoe pulled in another breath, then reminded herself that she was going to be *prima* one day and that she could take care of herself, thank you very much.

"Sorry—" Evan began, but she just shook her head.

"It's okay. I've fought it off before. You haven't."

He still didn't look convinced. However, she really didn't feel like getting into an argument right then, because now with the creature gone, even if just temporarily, she needed to focus on its victim. A young woman—girl, really, probably younger than Zoe herself—was slumped at the base of one of the eucalyptus trees.

Shit. If the monster had been responsible for hurting someone...or worse...she knew she would never forgive herself.

She ran over to the girl, Evan just a pace behind her. Without thinking about what she might be doing to her skirt, Zoe knelt in the grass next to the unknown young woman. She had long dark hair and wore a knee-length skirt similar to the one Zoe had on. In fact, at first glance, she looked a lot like Zoe herself.

No....

Evan caught it, too; his face was grim as he looked from her to the girl and then back again. But he didn't bother to comment, only reached out and took her wrist, apparently so he could feel for a pulse.

"She's alive," he said, and Zoe went limp with relief. "I think she just fainted from shock."

Well, that wasn't too surprising. Zoe figured she probably would have done the same thing if she'd been a civilian confronted by such an unearthly apparition.

She stood up and brushed at her skirt, which seemed none the worse for wear. "What should we do?"

Evan didn't appear all that certain, either. "I'm not sure. I hate to just leave her here. Maybe we should call 9-1-1?"

That sounded like a good idea. They could call for help, but make sure to be gone before anyone in authority showed up. The last thing they wanted was to attract any attention to themselves. Yes, the de la Paz clan had witches and warlocks in most of the police departments in the greater metro Phoenix area, but Zoe didn't know if any of them worked in this particular neighborhood.

"Okay," she said. "Do you have a phone?"

An expression of consternation passed over his face. "It's in the car."

As was hers. "Why don't you give me the keys?" she suggested. "Then I can go get both our phones."

He didn't look too thrilled by that proposal, but he didn't protest, instead began digging around in his jeans pocket for the keys. As he did so, however, the girl began to stir, her eyes fluttering open. For a second it looked as if she was about to scream again, but then her gaze grew more focused as she took in Evan, kneeling in the grass next to her. Incongruously, she even began to smile.

Well, Zoe supposed she might smile, too, if she opened her eyes and expected to see a monster, and instead saw Evan McAllister staring down at her. At the same time, though, an odd little spark of jealousy flared in her. That girl had no right to be looking at him like that....

"Are you okay?" Evan asked. His air was calm, but slightly worried, just as any normal person might be if they found someone passed out under a tree. "We were walking by and saw you lying there...."

"I—" The girl blinked and shook her head. Zoe realized the resemblance between her and the stranger was superficial enough, since the nameless young woman wasn't Hispanic and had blue eyes. It was just the long dark hair and what she'd been wearing, really. "I thought I saw something, but now I don't know. Everything just went black."

"Probably the sun," Evan said easily. "It's pretty bright today. Do you live near here? We can walk you back to your apartment...."

The girl's gaze flicked from Evan to Zoe, and her eyes narrowed slightly. She probably had just noticed that the hot guy who'd come to her rescue wasn't alone. "No, I'm fine. I mean, yeah, I live here, but I think I'm okay." She pushed herself to a standing position while Evan watched. Zoe didn't know him very well, but she could tell from the way he kept watch that he was ready to dive in and help if the girl turned out to be not as steady on her feet as she'd thought.

"Are you sure?"

"I'm sure. Thanks." And then she hurried past Zoe, not even giving her a second glance. Zoe didn't know whether the rudeness was because she was embarrassed by the way she'd fainted, or because of disappointment that her rescuer wasn't alone.

Either way, she was gone, walking swiftly down the path toward one of the banks of apartments.

So, too, was the monster, but Zoe couldn't even be all that relieved about its disappearance. She somehow knew, deep in her gut, that once again it had only been sent away from their immediate vicinity, not back to whatever plane of hell it had come from. They'd have to track it down once more and try all over again.

In the meantime, though, she knew she needed a drink. There had to be someplace around here where they could find something to take the edge off.

Maybe once she'd gotten a beer or two into him, Evan would open up enough to explain exactly why his talent hadn't saved them this time.

He must have still been off balance from their encounter with the monster. That was the only reason Evan could think of as to why he was now sitting in a place called BJ's Brewhouse, having a brown ale while Zoe sipped at a margarita. The restaurant was packed, too, and he hadn't been sure they'd even be able to get a table, but one miraculously opened up just as the hostess took Zoe's name. More *prima* magic? He couldn't hazard a guess. Right then he was feeling a little shell-shocked, but he had picked up one vital piece of information.

At least now he knew that she drank.

"I'm really sorry about that—" he began after the waiter had dropped off their drinks and disappeared.

Zoe waved her hand. "Whatever. At least I was able to get rid of the thing. But you need to be honest with me, Evan. Do you think that's going to happen again?"

In other words, *Are you going to blow it again?* "I don't know," he replied. He hated not being able to give her a more definitive answer than that, but he had no idea what else he could say. It was on his lips to tell her that this sort of thing had never happened to him before, but that kind of excuse would just make him sound like some poor bastard in an erectile dysfunction commercial. Lifting his shoulders, he added, "This really isn't like the times I've had to fix spells gone wrong up in Jerome."

"I guess not." She sipped some more of her margarita, and Evan had to force himself not to stare at the way her full lips puckered around the straw. "And I know all I did was make it go someplace else. It's not banished."

Of course not. He'd already figured as much, because if Zoe really had managed to get rid of the creature altogether, she would have looked a lot happier as they left the scene of the crime, as it were.

Thank the Goddess that the girl who'd fainted was apparently the only witness.

And that girl…Zoe's sharp eyes couldn't have missed the superficial resemblance between the two of them. Evan doubted it was a coincidence.

Almost as if she'd been reading his thoughts, she said, "I don't like that she looked like me. I mean, not exactly, but…."

"It makes sense," Evan said. "You summoned it here. Even though you keep driving it away, it's going to keep trying to come back to you, or at least to people who look sort of like you."

She winced slightly. "I know. And that just makes the whole situation suck that much harder. I have no idea what we can do to warn people. I mean, there are probably a ton of girls my age in the Phoenix area with long dark hair. Maybe not quite as many who wear skirts, but still."

He couldn't argue with that. It wasn't exactly the sort of information you could feed to the local police departments, or the local news, telling girls in that enormous group that they might be targets. The creature's patterns wouldn't even help him to track down who the next victim might be. Why it had come here, some twenty miles away, when there had to have been suitable targets much closer to Zoe's home in Fountain Hills, Evan couldn't begin to guess.

A long pull at his beer didn't help much to settle his state of mind, either. This had all been a huge mistake. What was the point of coming at all if he couldn't even use his talent to help the de la Paz clan? He wouldn't allow himself to be too concerned about what his failure might do to clan relations, because everyone knew that sometimes there were instances where a witch or warlock's talent failed them, for whatever reason. However, he really didn't want that to happen to him in this instance.

For some reason, what he hated most was the idea of letting Zoe down.

"Can you feel it?" she asked then, her voice carefully neutral.

On the drive here from the apartment complex, he'd attempted to reach out with his gift and see if he could get any sense of where their quarry had gone. Right then, he hadn't been able to feel anything. He tried again now, hoping that maybe the beer would have loosened him up enough that he could get past his disappointment and worry, and accomplish something useful.

All he got was a complete blank, not even the faintest sensation that something was off in the greater Phoenix area. "No," he replied, his tone flat. "Not a damn thing."

"Maybe it's lying low," she said. "Maybe I hurt it a lot this time." She paused then, one pink-polished fingernail tapping against the straw in her margarita glass. "This may sound strange, but I really don't like the idea of hurting it. I mean, I brought it here. This is all my fault. It probably doesn't even know what it's doing."

Possibly. Evan just didn't have enough context to begin to guess what might be going on in the creature's mind—if anything. It could be acting on pure instinct, in which case Zoe's feelings of guilt might be somewhat misplaced. If he'd known her better—and if he hadn't worried that she might misconstrue the gesture—he would have reached over and patted her free hand where it rested on the tabletop, just to give her some of the reassurance she so obviously needed.

But since he wasn't quite that brave, he had to settle for saying, "I know it's hard, Zoe. I guess maybe you have to look at it this way—however it ended up here, it's someplace where it doesn't belong. It'll be a mercy to send it back where it came from."

Those words elicited a nod, although she didn't look all that convinced. She drank some more of her margarita, big dark eyes studiously looking away from him. Once again he was astonished by the length of her lashes, the way they could shutter her expression and make her very hard to read.

At last she said, "I suppose you're right. So... what are we going to tell my parents, or Aunt Luz?"

"The truth." He might have been blowing it mightily so far, but Evan wasn't stupid enough to try to conceal anything from the de la Paz *prima*. She needed to know what was going on.

"They're not going to like it."

"Probably not. But I have a feeling they'd rather hear an unpleasant truth than a lie."

Zoe tensed somewhat at the word "lie," but she didn't try to argue with him. "You're right, of course." She turned away from him so she could dig through her purse, producing her cell phone a moment later. "I'll go ahead and call, and let them know what happened."

"Wait," he said.

Her eyes widened. "So you *don't* want me to tell them the truth?"

"No, it's not that." Evan hesitated, trying to stop and analyze why exactly he'd told her that she shouldn't call her parents, or the *prima*. After all, they needed to be kept apprised of what was going on.

But then he realized he'd told her not to call because he had experienced another of his twinges, one so faint that it almost hadn't registered at all. If they had another lead, they should go ahead and follow up on it. Maybe that way they'd have something more promising to report.

"You felt it," Zoe said. Her tone was flat, so Evan knew it wasn't a question.

"Yes," he said. "Not much. But something. So I guess we'd better get moving."

She nodded, then bent her head slightly so she could take a long pull at her margarita, draining the rest of what was left in the glass. That sounded like a good idea to Evan; he finished off the inch of beer he had remaining, then lifted a hand so he could flag down the waiter and pay the tab.

Or rather, attempt to pay it. As soon as their waiter left the little leatherette case with the bill on the tabletop, Zoe swooped in and grabbed it.

"Oh, no, you don't," she told him. "You're down here helping out my clan. That means drinks are on me."

"Okay," he said, not bothering to protest. After all, she did have a point. Besides, you only had to look at her house to know that her family had a hell of a lot more disposable cash than he did.

She appeared pleased that he hadn't argued, and slipped a twenty into the sleeve that held the check. Then she slung her purse over her shoulder. "Well, let's go. Any idea where we're headed?"

"Not yet," he admitted. "Maybe north."

"'Maybe north'?" she repeated, looking skeptical.

"It was a tiny twinge. Let's just get in the car and see what happens."

Her mouth quirked slightly at his reply, but she didn't say anything else, only slipped out of the booth and headed toward the front door. As Evan followed, he thought of the possible implications of his last remark and wanted to groan. No wonder Zoe had appeared as if she was fighting back a grin.

Because it was only too true that the back seat of the Barracuda had seen more than its fair share of action....

Evan didn't say anything as they pulled out of the parking lot at BJ's Brewhouse and headed back to the freeway. Just as well, because Zoe couldn't help wanting to grin every time she glanced over at him. It had been an innocent slip-up, but since she'd already been harboring a few impure thoughts about him, she had to force herself not to look over her shoulder at the back seat so she could gauge whether it was big enough for certain extracurricular activities.

Instead, she sat quietly in the passenger seat and watched as they headed west on the 60. However, when they came to the interchange with the 101 Loop, Evan passed it by. So were they not heading north after all? Or had the twinge he'd felt been farther west, and then north?

That seemed to be the case, because he jogged onto the 10 Freeway, and then the 51 so they were pointed north once again. Zoe knew this part of town a little better, just because her mother liked to shop at the Biltmore shopping center, and they were only about five minutes away from the exit now. Had the creature decided to prey on young women shopping at the MAC cosmetics store there, or was it thinking that maybe lurking in the dressing rooms at Saks Fifth Avenue was a better idea?

She shuddered at the mental image that thought conjured, and Evan glanced over at her. "You okay?"

"Sure," she replied. "So...do you know where we're going yet?"

"Not really. I can feel it sort of pulling me in this direction, but that's about all."

To her relief—or maybe her disappointment, since she'd found herself thinking if they ended up at the Biltmore center, maybe she could pop into the MAC store and replace the lip gloss she'd lost the week before—Evan passed the exit at Camelback Road and kept going, although she noticed that he stayed in the far right lane, just in case he had to get off the freeway quickly. A few more miles flashed past, and she wondered if he really was going to go all the way up to the top of the 101 Loop. Once there, he'd have to decide whether to head east or west, since the 51 dead-ended where it T-boned into the 101.

However, almost as soon as the thought crossed her mind, Evan turned on his blinker and got off at Cactus Road.

"So it's here somewhere?" she asked.

"I think so," he replied, his voice tense. "Someplace east of here."

Zoe nodded but didn't say anything. From the way his hands were clenched on the steering wheel, she could tell that he didn't like having to maneuver in this kind of traffic. Things had been clotty enough on the 51, since it was now past six o'clock, but the surface streets here were a lot worse.

Then she sucked in her breath and grasped the strap of her purse, as if clinging to that strip of leather might help to give her the reassurance she needed. Because coming up on the left was the Paradise Valley Mall, a place she'd avoided ever since Matías Escobar had tried to kidnap her there.

"What is it?" Evan asked. His eyes were fixed on the road ahead, but obviously he'd noticed something.

"Nothing," she replied. "I mean, that's the mall."

Behind the dark Ray-Bans, his eyes flicked over to the left and then returned to the motorists around him. Good idea, because he had to tap his brakes as some jerk in a Subaru cut right in front of them, headed for one of the mall entrances. "The mall?"

"Where I was almost kidnapped."

"Oh." He paused for a few seconds, clearly searching for something to say. "I'm sorry. I don't think I ever heard the actual name of the place where it happened."

"It's all right. I wouldn't really expect you to know. It's just...I haven't been back here since."

Another hesitation. "I can understand that," Evan said, the words coming out slowly and evenly, as if he was weighing each one with care to make sure he wouldn't upset her. "But if it makes you feel better, I don't think that's where we're going."

"We're not?" She couldn't think of what else might be around here that would be of interest to the creature. Off to the right were some condos, and then past that a golf course—

Evan abruptly stomped on the gas, sending the Barracuda shooting forward in a neck-cracking show of velocity. As Zoe clutched the "Jesus handle" above her head, she realized Evan was taking advantage of a small opening in traffic so he could cut over into the driveway that led to the Stonecreek golf course.

"We're going golfing?" she quipped, knowing how flat the joke must have sounded.

"We're not," he replied, slowing the car to a more reasonable speed so they wouldn't bottom out on one of the speed bumps in the driveway. "But maybe your monster is."

She couldn't really think of what to say in reply to that remark, so she just held on to the handle as Evan maneuvered the car into an open parking space. There were a few left, probably because people wanting to stop by the clubhouse on their way home from work wouldn't have made it this far yet.

Neither she nor Evan were wearing what you could call golf clothes, although Zoe thought she'd probably blend in just a bit better, since at least she did look like someone who could be going to the clubhouse. But Evan, with his faded jeans and henley shirt with the sleeves rolled up, wasn't exactly what you could call country club material.

This wasn't a country club, though. She knew that much, because there were members of the clan who liked to play golf, and they tended to talk about it at family gatherings, even though that sort of thing bored her out of her skull. Anyway, this wasn't the kind of place where you had to pay six figures to be a member, and so she guessed she and Evan would have a little more burn time before some staff member decided they looked out of place and came over to investigate.

"Where to?" she asked, after slinging her purse over one shoulder. Maybe dragging it along was a bad idea—fighting off monsters while having a Coach bag getting in the way could be a problem— but she didn't much like the idea of leaving it in Evan's car, either. She'd done that at the last place they'd encountered the creature, and had regretted not having her cell phone close by.

"That way," he said, then pointed toward a stand of pine trees a few hundred yards off.

It did seem like the kind of place where a monster might hide itself. What the creature thought it would find on a golf course, she had no idea, but they weren't really here to investigate the inner workings of its mind. They just needed to send it back where it had come from before it could cause any more trouble.

She followed Evan as he set out with a determined stride. Thank God she'd decided to wear these flat sandals when she got dressed this morning, rather than the wedges she'd first tried on. She could manage the wedges pretty well under normal circumstances, despite their near four-inch lift, but they definitely were not designed for traipsing around on a golf course.

As they walked, she had to fight to keep her gaze from locking on Evan's butt in those nicely faded Levi's. True, there wasn't anyone around to see her staring, and his focus appeared to be fixed forward, but what if he turned around unexpectedly? Then he'd catch her staring at his ass, and she couldn't imagine that would go over particularly well.

Also, the setting sun kept catching in his deep red hair, and she found herself wanting to run her hands through it, to feel it soft and heavy against her fingertips. A certain warmth moved through her, one that had absolutely nothing to do with the heat of a Phoenix afternoon beating down on them, and she made herself push those thoughts away. She couldn't be thinking about Evan McAllister like that. A distracted witch was a witch who made mistakes, and she'd screwed up enough for one day.

Then he lifted a hand, as if telling her to stop, although he didn't speak. One finger held to his lips, just in case she hadn't gotten the memo, he pointed toward the stand of pine trees. Zoe narrowed her eyes as she looked in the direction Evan had indicated, which was west, into the setting sun. Her sunglasses were still in her purse, and if she paused now to dig them out, she might lose her focus.

But in the next moment she forgot all about her sunglasses, because she caught a glimpse of a dark form moving among the trees, one she was pretty sure wasn't a caddy searching for a lost golf ball. A chill moved down her spine, despite the lingering warmth of the day.

What in the world was the creature doing here? Was there something about trees that had attracted it? After all, they'd found its last "victim" under a tree. Maybe that girl had just been in the wrong place at the wrong time.

Zoe didn't know, and she didn't dare ask Evan his thoughts, because it seemed clear enough to her that they needed to remain quiet so they might have the best chance of sneaking up on the thing. Whether you could sneak up on an otherworldly creature at all was something she didn't know for sure, but they had to try.

She came up to stand next to Evan, and together they moved gingerly toward the clump of tall pine trees. The shadow they cast was dark and cool, and she could feel it the second they were within the shelter of its shade. At the same time, she again felt that tingle travel down her spine, and wondered if it was the same sort of thing her companion experienced when he drew closer to the creature.

Because this time she could tell it was there. It had stopped, possibly because it had detected their presence in the same way they could sense it. Beside her, Evan might have been a statue, he stood so still. Was he communing in some way with his gift, trying to think of how he could use his own particular talent to get rid of the monster?

Zoe hoped so. At the same time, though, she couldn't forget how he had completely choked only an hour earlier. So she pulled in a breath and gathered her own strength, remembering how she had called the fire to her and used it to drive the creature away. The *prima* energy, not yet fully developed but still so powerful, burned within her, waiting.

Evan took a step forward. From within the trees, Zoe saw a glint of baleful golden eyes. Had its eyes always been that color? She couldn't even remember.

Or was the creature changing somehow, morphing into something else, like in those old *Aliens* movies, the ones that Zander loved but which always gave her nightmares?

Ice flooded through her at that notion, but she wouldn't let herself react. She had to be calm, no matter what happened.

Another step. Zoe forced herself to move forward as well. The charms on her bracelet jingled faintly, and she winced. Could the creature hear the metallic *clink* over the not-so-distant sounds of traffic out on Cactus Road? Once again, she didn't have a clue.

Evan stopped then, his head lifted into the wind, as if he was listening to something only he could hear. She hardly dared breathe, in case the sound of her breaths might be too loud.

And then from inside her purse came the infamous coyote-howl theme from *The Good, The Bad, and the Ugly*, the ringtone Zander had programmed into her phone as a joke and which she'd left there because she thought it was kind of funny, too, and at least different from the Taylor Swift or Katy Perry tunes her friends tended to favor.

At the moment, though, Zoe didn't think it was funny at all. She grabbed her purse, frantically digging through its contents so she could find her phone and silence it, but the damage was done. A horrible howl came from the stand of pine trees, and in the next instant, the creature burst out from the shadows.

God, it had changed. It seemed bigger somehow, and she hadn't been seeing things when she'd noted those glaring yellow eyes. At the same time, however, its features had shifted slightly, had become more human-looking, although still distorted.

She stared into that oddly altered face for a second, frozen in place as its gaze met hers. And then it seemed to fly upward, its body shattering into a million pieces which then coalesced into a whirling, smoky shadow, right before it disappeared.

Evan turned toward her, face so still she couldn't begin to guess what he was thinking. But the chill in his voice when he spoke was enough to tell her exactly how he felt.

Just one sentence, but it was enough to make her feel about two feet tall.

"Next time we go monster hunting, maybe you should shut your phone off first."

One screw-up after another. Could this day get any worse?

CHAPTER SIX

THEY WERE BOTH SILENT ON THE WAY BACK TO THE CAR. Evan knew he'd been kind of harsh, and he wished he'd kept his mouth shut, but there wasn't much he could do about that now. Zoe's jaw was set as she climbed into the passenger seat; once she'd buckled herself in, she pulled the phone out of her purse, looked at the display on the home screen, and said, "That was my Aunt Luz. I should probably call her back."

He didn't bother to argue, just nodded, because he knew you didn't ignore a call from your *prima,* even if she happened to be your aunt. Or maybe especially because she was your aunt and would just keep calling until she'd reassured herself that you were okay.

Just what the hell *had* that been back there? The creature, obviously, but it had changed, shifted into something different from the thing he'd first seen outside the apartment building out in Superstition Springs. It was bigger, looked more formed somehow, although Evan couldn't exactly put his finger on what had caused that change.

Yanking his thoughts back to the present, he paused at the exit from the golf course onto Cactus Road, not sure where to go.

Zoe murmured, "Turn right. We can take this street back into Scottsdale and then cut down to pick up Shea Boulevard and head back to Fountain Hills."

Back to her house. But where else could they go? It wasn't like he could pick up any sense of the monster. When it had shattered apart like that and then transformed into that strange swirling smoke, it was as if the tenuous connection he'd shared with it had been broken as well. He couldn't feel it at all. So he might as well take Zoe home.

As to what he planned to do next, well, he didn't have a frigging clue. Maybe he should just pack it in and go back to Jerome after he dropped Zoe off. It was clear enough that he'd gotten in way over his head here.

They inched along in the thick traffic, surrounded by people intent on getting home after a long work week. Evan thought it might be nice to only be concerned with the mundane minutiae of civilian life, of paying the bills and not pissing off the boss, rather than stuck trying to hunt down a monster that defied description. But no, that wasn't really true. Being a member of a witch clan came with its own particular set of unique problems, but he'd still rather be out here with Zoe, running around after the creature she'd summoned, instead of stuck in a cube farm somewhere shuffling paperwork around.

She had that damn pink phone out and was pressing a button on her contacts list. Her aunt, obviously, because in the next moment she said, "Aunt Luz? Yes, I'm fine—we're fine." A pause. "Yes. I mean, we saw it. But it—" Another pause as she bit her lip in frustration, clearly wishing she could get a word in. "No. It disappeared again. And it was up at the golf course across from the Paradise Valley Mall. No, because my phone went off and it scared it away. Or something like that." She stopped again, her free hand twisting a long lock of shining dark hair into a spiral.

Evan made himself stop looking and returned his attention to the traffic in front of them. The girl was distracting as hell, even when she was obviously irritated. Just another reason for him to get back to Jerome. For all he knew, it was Zoe's mere presence that had somehow been interfering with his powers. He'd never had anything like that occur before, but as his cousin Rachel was fond of saying, just because something had never happened in the past didn't mean it couldn't happen eventually.

Zoe ended the call by saying, "We're on the way back to the house. So I guess we'll see you in a few." Then she shoved the phone back in her purse, her lower lip looking mutinous.

He had to ask, even though he thought he knew the answer. "Everything okay?"

"No, not really. My aunt is annoyed that we didn't catch the thing and put it in a box and send it back where it came from."

"She really said that?"

"Of course not." Zoe shook her head and let out a breath. "With Aunt Luz, it's all in the *way* she says it, you know? And she's really not happy that we saw it twice and still couldn't get rid of it."

Well, Evan wasn't too happy about that, either. Once more, his feelings of complete inadequacy when it came to dispelling the creature threatened to overwhelm him. He needed to keep it together, though. During that last encounter, even though he'd been shaken by the change in the creature's appearance, he'd started to get more of a sense of the thing, of the way he might be able to shift the spell Zoe had used to bring it here to instead send it back wherever it had come from. If he'd had only a minute more to analyze the situation—

But he hadn't, because Zoe's damn phone had gone off at exactly the wrong moment. While he'd snapped at her about that, it really wasn't her fault.

He had his own cell phone shoved in his jeans pocket, and it could also have rung at a horribly inopportune time. No, it hadn't, mostly because he didn't get that many calls, but it *could* have.

"Well, she's welcome to try for herself," he said grimly, and Zoe chuckled. It wasn't much of a laugh, almost more a small throat-clearing, but at least it was something.

"You go ahead and tell her that," she said. "I'd love to see her reaction."

"No, thanks," he replied. "Your *prima* probably has a low enough opinion of me already."

That remark made Zoe's eyebrows go up. "Why would you say that?"

"I haven't done that great a job today, have I?'

She hesitated, then shrugged. "I guess neither of us have. But I don't know if Aunt Luz could have managed much more, even if she is *prima*. Maybe at tracking it down…she got a lot of that from my *abuela*, from Maya. They're both really good at sensing when magic has been used, and when people are in de la Paz territory who shouldn't be. But maybe that wouldn't apply in this situation, because we're not talking about a witch or a warlock here. We're dealing with something entirely different."

That was for sure. Evan thought again of the alterations in the creature's face. It had begun to look more human, even though it still had a long way to go. Was that the real problem, that in some way the spell hadn't been adequate to bring Zoe's "dream man" fully formed to this world, but if it had time enough…?

He shut down that line of thought real fast. Because otherwise he'd have to entertain the notion that, given sufficient time to change and develop, the monster could become a man, the one Zoe had called to her. Would she accept him, if he finally looked at her with the face she'd dreamed of?

Something in his expression must have bothered Zoe, because she said then, "Don't worry, Evan. We'll figure it out."

Better that she thought he was beating himself up over his failures that day. He made a noncommittal sound and kept driving.

Because no way in hell would he tell her he was worried that the monster might become a man, and that might leave Evan…where?

Exactly where you are right now, he told himself. *Absolutely nowhere.*

They pulled up in front of her house, and Zoe frowned. Parked in the driveway was her aunt's silver Lexus, but next to it was a black Ford Taurus, a car she didn't immediately recognize. As Evan turned off the engine, he followed her gaze to the unfamiliar vehicle.

"Someone you know?" he asked.

"I'm not sure," she replied, mentally ticking over possible members of the clan that Aunt Luz might have recruited for the search. Zoe wasn't too thrilled at any of the prospects. Bringing in Evan hadn't seemed too bad, because he wasn't a member of the family, and so less likely to start spreading stories.

Also, if she had to have help in this venture, better a handsome McAllister warlock than one of her numerous cousins.

"But I guess there's only one way to find out," she added, then pushed on the handle so she could climb out of the car.

Evan did the same, and together they went up the walk toward the front door. It did feel sort of strange to approach the house this way, since she was used to pulling into the garage and entering from the door that led into the laundry room. Once again she noticed the way he glanced around at his surroundings, taking them in. He did seem to notice a lot. Quiet, but you got the feeling that he was absorbing a lot of details even though he didn't talk about them.

They went inside. Almost at once Zoe heard voices coming from the living room, and so she headed in that direction, Evan still at her side. As those voices became more distinct, she realized whose car that had to be sitting in the driveway.

Her Uncle Jack, who worked for the Scottsdale police department. He'd probably driven one of the Scottsdale P.D.'s unmarked cars instead of his own Jeep Wrangler, for whatever reason.

She wasn't sure how she should feel about him being here. Yes, he was her favorite uncle, but in a way that made the situation even worse. She really didn't want him to know how badly she'd messed things up.

But…he was also the person in the clan who was best at defensive magic. Not like her cousin Alex, who could create a protective dome that shielded him and anyone else within a ten-foot radius from just about anything you could throw at it, but Jack knew the sorts of spells to help ward off dark magic, to create a zone around yourself so that the ill will of others couldn't affect you. No one had thought twice about a cop utilizing those sorts of spells, since his work did tend to bring him in contact with some not very nice people. However, Zoe had wondered from time to time why anyone else would really need those spells. All was well within their clan, and now that the Arizona witch families were all cooperating with one another, there didn't seem to be much to protect yourself from, magically speaking.

All right, she *had* thought that way…until Matías Escobar had nearly succeeded in kidnapping her. Then the reason for the existence of those spells had become pretty damn clear. And she could see why her aunt would have thought to summon Jack Sandoval now.

Zoe arranged a smile on her face as she entered the living room, even though she wasn't feeling all that cheerful. More like anxious and worried and a lot more inadequate than she wanted to be. But she didn't need to broadcast those emotions to everyone in the room.

Because there was Uncle Jack, and both her parents, and of course Aunt Luz. A casual observer might have thought they were just having a simple family get-together, because they were talking quietly, and a pitcher of iced tea and some glasses sat on the coffee table. But Zoe knew from the tension in their postures that this was no social visit.

"Hi, Uncle Jack," she said, since it seemed the best way to ease into the conversation, and because she'd noticed the way his gaze had shifted toward her the second she and Evan had emerged from the entryway. "This is Evan McAllister."

Her uncle rose from where he'd been sitting on the sofa and extended a hand. "Hi, Evan. Jack Sandoval, Scottsdale P.D."

"I'm not under arrest, am I?" Evan said with a slight smile, and a chuckle went around the room.

"Not at all," Luz said. She, too, got up from the sofa and then stopped a pace or two away from Zoe's uncle, while Zoe's parents remained where they were on the love seat, although they were clearly paying attention to every word being said. "But it sounded as if you could use a little backup."

"We did have a couple of setbacks," Evan began, sounding apologetic—so apologetic, in fact, that Zoe felt compelled to step in.

"Because we're dealing with something we've never seen before," she said quickly. "But I know we'll get better at tracking it. And at knowing what to do when we catch up with it."

"I don't doubt that," Jack said. "But at the same time, because we're dealing with a new threat, it makes sense that you should be better equipped to protect yourselves." Although he'd been smiling, his expression sobered abruptly. "We almost lost you once, Zoe. Do you really think we're going to let that happen again?"

She wanted to protest that of course it couldn't happen again, that this situation was completely different, and Matías was safely locked up where he couldn't hurt anyone ever again...but she held her tongue. It was impossible to say for sure what might happen, and in the meantime, better that she and Evan be as well-armed as possible.

"No," she said. "I get it."

"Good." Her uncle's gaze slipped over toward Evan, quietly assessing. Zoe could tell that the

McAllister warlock wasn't too thrilled by being inspected in such a way, but he didn't say anything, only stood there and looked back at Jack as if he was used to being subjected to that kind of scrutiny. The two of them were almost the same height, and in a weird way the scene reminded Zoe of a sequence from an old western, where two gunfighters would stare each other down to take their measure before pulling out their guns and trying to blow each other's heads off.

Although she sincerely hoped that wasn't what either Evan or Uncle Jack had in mind.

At last, her uncle nodded. Just barely, but she'd been watching for it, and she thought she saw the approval in his expression. Good. She wouldn't have to worry about them having the witchy equivalent of pistols at sunrise.

"Do you know any defensive spells, Evan?"

"Not really," Evan admitted. His shoulders lifted slightly. "That's not my talent. That is, I've had to protect myself a few times when the spell I was attempting to unravel got a little out of hand, but I don't think you're talking about quite the same thing."

"No, I'm not," Jack said. "I'm talking about having to defend yourself from an intelligent foe."

"But is it?" Zoe's father put in, getting up from the couch so he could involve himself in the conversation. "That is, I thought this was just another spell that went wrong."

"It might have started out that way," Luz said. "But we're dealing with some kind of entity here, even if we still don't know exactly what it is. So while we need Evan to assist with reversing the spell if possible"—for the briefest second, her eyes narrowed, as if she was becoming increasingly uncertain whether that would actually happen—"we also want to make sure that he and Zoe are equipped to take care of themselves in the case of a magical attack."

Her father didn't look too thrilled by that prospect. Zoe wasn't exactly happy about it, either, although at the moment she found herself more irritated by the way the *prima* had looked at Evan. After all, how many people could jump into a situation like this and fix everything right off the bat? Magic could be an amazing thing, but it still had its limits… as did the witches and warlocks who wielded it.

"So what are you going to teach us?" Zoe asked. They might as well get down to it, even though six o'clock had come and gone, and they'd have to start thinking about dinner in the not-too-distant future.

Or…would they? She realized then that she had no idea how long Evan had planned to stay down here in Phoenix. Maybe he'd thought this would be a simple project, and he'd just turn around and go home as soon as he was done.

Jack seemed to pick up on some of her hesitation, because he looked over at Evan again. "This is something that's going to take more than an hour or so. Where are you staying, Evan?"

"I—" He stopped there, his manner diffident. "I hadn't really thought about it. I did bring stuff for a couple of days, just in case."

"You can stay here with us," Luis Sandoval offered, and Zoe shot him a grateful look. Yes, maybe it would be weird to have Evan at the house all the time, but she also felt a little quiver of anticipation at the prospect. Maybe if she could catch a glimpse of him emerging from the bathroom, a towel wrapped around his waist after his morning's shower....

Evan, on the other hand, appeared more dismayed by the idea than anything else. "Um—I wouldn't want to impose. I can stay at a hotel." He paused, then asked, "If there are any around here, that is."

"Several," Luz said. This time her gaze went to Zoe and remained there for a few seconds, and her mouth tightened slightly. "I think it might be better if you did that, Evan. The de la Paz clan will take care of it for you."

"That's really not necessary—" he began, but she cut him off.

"No, I insist. We called you down here. It's the least we can do. I'll make the arrangements now.

The CopperWynd is closest to the house—I'll see if they have anything available."

She stepped away so she could retrieve her phone from her purse, then went into the dining room to make the call. Evan glanced over at Jack, clearly trying to ignore the look of disappointment Zoe knew she must be wearing right then.

"Well, I guess we'd better get started," he said.

The house was so big that it had its own exercise room, complete with a treadmill and stair-stepper and one of those Bowflex machines. No wonder Zoe's father looked like he could put someone through a wall. His height and the bulk in his shoulders probably helped a lot when he was arguing a case in the courtroom.

Did Zoe use any of this stuff? She certainly was slender, but that could have just been her natural build. Evan really didn't know for sure, and he sure as hell wasn't going to start ogling her then and there, not with her uncle standing in front of them. Talk about putting someone through a wall. All right, Jack Sandoval probably wasn't quite as broad as his older brother, but he was certainly tall and fit, and when he took off his sport coat and hung it from one of the treadmill's handles, you could see the way his biceps strained against the white dress shirt he wore underneath.

He also wore a shoulder holster, which he did not remove. Catching the way Evan's gaze traveled to the gun in that holster, Jack said, "Luz called me as I was coming off shift. Didn't have time to go home and change."

"Um, that's fine," Evan responded, then realized he probably sounded like a complete and utter idiot. He wasn't used to that. He'd always thought he could handle himself just fine. Dropping the ball when it came time to confront the creature had rattled him more than he wanted to admit. Also, there was something in the older man's self-assurance that made him feel as if he was just a dumb kid, even though Evan guessed that Jack Sandoval was probably only six or seven years older than he was. Definitely Luis's younger brother by a good bit.

But then Evan reminded himself that Jack's age wasn't really the issue here. Learning how to defend himself definitely was. That thing he'd seen back at the golf course had loomed over him, something Evan wasn't really used to. If it had come down to a physical confrontation, he wouldn't have been able to prevail against the creature. And Zoe? It looked as if it could have crushed her in one hand.

Of course, she'd already proved that she knew how to take care of herself.

"First off," Jack said, "I want you both to carry these." He fished in the pocket of his pants and pulled out a couple of black stones, each of them cut into rough facets, not smooth like jet.

"What are they?" Evan asked, even as he took the stone from Jack and held it in his hand, feeling the cool, slightly rough surfaces against his skin.

"Black tourmaline," Zoe responded. She took the second stone and slipped it into the pocket of her skirt. "It's used for protection. It helps to guard against evil spirits."

Privately, Evan had never bought into a lot of that sort of mumbo-jumbo, even though he knew many of the people in his own clan used combinations of crystals to aid them in their own magic and spell casting. His own gift had never required any sort of outside assistance, nothing but the raw power he'd been born with. Then again, that gift hadn't done so well today.

Jack gave an approving nod. "That's its most common use, but it also can help guide you toward a disruptive spirit. So if you're having trouble tracking down this entity—for lack of a better word—the stones can help you in locating it."

That would be useful. Yes, Evan's power had guided them to the creature several times now, but what would have happened if he hadn't wasted any time and had made a beeline toward it? Maybe then it wouldn't have had the opportunity to change so much.

And he really didn't want to think about how it might be changing again, might be morphing into something he couldn't even imagine. What if it kept growing in power and strength? Zoe's skill at sending it running was useful—and sort of amazing—but sooner or later they'd have to prevent it from escaping so they could drive it back to whatever plane of existence it had come from.

"Okay," Evan said, then put the stone in his jeans pocket. "Anything else?"

The look Jack gave him then was another of those measuring ones, the kind of flat stare that seemed to take in every detail of his appearance, his voice and inflection, cataloguing it for later use. The older man had been wearing a jacket, and had on a dress shirt and pants, and so Evan guessed he wasn't a beat cop, but some kind of a detective, the sort of man who spent his days ferreting out every detail of a case in order to bring a criminal to justice. Right then Evan could only hope Jack Sandoval wasn't so perceptive that he could see the impure thoughts he'd been having about his niece only a few minutes earlier.

"There's lots 'else,'" Jack responded, his tone casual. "But a lot of it depends on what you're up against. Now, when I caught up with that little creep who tried to kidnap Zoe, that wasn't too hard, because I knew what his talent was and made sure to cast spells so his magic wouldn't have any effect on me. This thing, though—it's not like any spirit or demon I've ever heard of, which makes it harder. The tourmalines are a start, something that works against just about any kind of negative energy. There are basic banishment spells, too. This is probably the simplest one."

He straightened then, dark eyes suddenly more piercing, as if he was staring past Evan and Zoe into some sort of void populated by hellish creatures no sane person would want to imagine. Voice strong and carrying, he said,

"To any spirits who threaten me in this place,
Fight water with water and fire with fire
Banish their souls into nothingness
Remove their powers to the last trace
Let these evil beings flee
Through time and space."

Although they stood in an ordinary enough room, surrounded by the trappings of ordinary sub-urban consumerism, Evan couldn't prevent a shiver from moving through him. Jack Sandoval's voice had deepened as he spoke the words of the spell, and for a second Evan got a flash of the man wearing dark robes, arms raised to fight off some unseen foe, even though Jack stood there in his regular street clothes, and in fact hadn't moved at all.

Evan had never experienced anything like it. Sure, he'd been present at the McAllister clan's rituals for Samhain, their invocations on occasions like Yule and Imbolc, and yet he'd never had the hair stand up on the back of his neck like this. In that moment, he realized the de la Paz witches must have faced terrible foes in their past, enemies that would make the dark magic–wielding members of the Wilcox clan, such as Damon Wilcox, look like Sunday school teachers.

No wonder they'd been so spooked by the prospect of Matías Escobar and everything he represented. They knew what they were up against.

Zoe felt it, too—Evan risked a quick glance over at her, and saw how her warm-toned skin suddenly looked paler, how her mouth had tightened, her jaw going tense. When she spoke, however, she sounded almost normal, except for the faintest tremor at the beginning of her question, gone so fast Evan wasn't sure he hadn't imagined it.

"Can we go over it again, Uncle Jack? I want to make sure I get it exactly right."

So he had her and Evan repeat the words, over and over again, until Evan was pretty sure he'd be able to say the damn spell in his sleep. He'd thought for sure he'd feel foolish intoning those same words over and over, but he hadn't. The sound of his own voice had been sturdy and sure, as if he, too, was hearkening back to a past his clan didn't really talk much about, when they'd been beset by enemies on every side, and had retreated to Arizona Territory to make a safer life for themselves.

"Good," Jack Sandoval said at last. "You've both got it. I think that's a good start. But now"—he glanced down at the slim, expensive-looking watch strapped to his wrist—"I think that's where we call it quits for the evening. It's almost eight o'clock, and you haven't eaten anything yet, have you?"

Evan shook his head. Zoe said, "No. I'll see if my parents can order something in for all of us."

"That's all right," Jack replied. "I need to get home. But if anything strange comes up—and I mean *anything*—you call me. I don't care what time it is."

"Yes, Uncle Jack," she said, although Evan didn't quite buy the demure note in her voice. It really wasn't her style, or at least didn't seem to be, based on their short acquaintance.

Jack didn't appear all that convinced, either, but he only gave her a grim smile and said, "I mean it, Zoe. You know what happens to heroes, right?"

This time it was her turn to shake her head.

"They end up dead." Jack retrieved his jacket from where it had been hanging from the treadmill's handle, shrugged it over his shoulder, and left the exercise room.

Evan and Zoe stared at each other for a long moment. Neither of them said a word.

CHAPTER SEVEN

MUCH TO ZOE'S DISMAY, EVAN LEFT SOON AFTER THAT, once Luz had given him the information about the CopperWynd resort where he'd be staying, along with directions. Now that the *prima* had accomplished her goal of making certain that her vulnerable niece and the McAllister warlock wouldn't be sleeping under the same roof, she departed as well, saying that she needed to get home. Zoe had given her a hug goodbye, because she knew if she didn't, Aunt Luz would know something was up, but Zoe wasn't feeling very affectionate right then.

Her parents ordered takeout from her favorite Chinese restaurant, clearly hoping that would cheer her up, but she was in no mood to be cheered. She ate her egg drop soup but picked at the lemon chicken, then announced she was tired and wanted to go to bed. Neither her mother or her father tried to stop her from heading upstairs to her room, although she could tell they wanted to talk to her some more, wanted to discuss what had happened to her that day.

Too bad. She was tired of talking. Or rather, she was tired of being talked *at,* and she had a feeling that was exactly what would happen if she stayed down in the dining room with them.

So she went up to the second floor, relieved beyond belief that her brother Zander was staying the night at a friend's house so a bunch of his geek buddies could be up until all hours playing *World of Warcraft.* Or maybe it was *Call of Duty.* She couldn't remember for sure, since she'd always thought video games were a big waste of time. But she was grateful now, since it meant Zander would be out of her hair until probably noon tomorrow, if not later. This whole situation was complicated enough without having to deal with his annoying questions. He never seemed to take much of anything seriously, and would probably laugh his ass off at her current predicament, amused beyond belief by the idea that some kind of supernatural monster was roaming around the city because his sister hadn't met a guy who could kiss her the right way.

Okay, it did sound terrible when you put it like that.

She'd snagged a fortune cookie as she left the table, more because no Chinese meal felt complete without one than because she was really hungry. Now she tore apart the plastic wrapper and shook the cookie into her palm, then cracked it open. A little white piece of paper fell out.

You will meet a tall stranger.

She wanted to laugh at that one. Well, she supposed it was true enough. She'd actually met two tall strangers today—one a horrible being from a strange dimension, the other a handsome McAllister warlock.

It would have been much better if she could have just met Evan McAllister.

Scowling, she threw the pieces of the cookie into the trash, along with the "fortune." Then she kicked off her sandals and fell on her bed, all the worry and fear and uncertainty of the day seeming to catch up with her then, to make every muscle in her body ache.

But that wasn't the only ache she was currently experiencing. She wished with all her being that Evan could have stayed here at the house. True, he was only a few miles away and could be here quickly enough if something happened, but that small bit of reassurance felt like cold comfort at the moment. Strange how she could miss him so much when she'd only known him for basically half a day. She did miss him, though—the flash of his smile, the warm light that entered his greenish eyes when she did or said something he found admirable.

Then, too, there was something quiet and contained and almost brooding about him, as if he was hiding a hurt he wanted to keep secret from the world. What that could be, Zoe had no idea. As far as she knew, no great tragedies had struck the McAllister clan any time in the recent past, except for the horrible loss of Roslyn McAllister at Matías Escobar's hands. But while it must have been terrible to lose a cousin like that, Zoe didn't think Evan had any close ties to Roslyn. Her brother was named Adam; Zoe knew that because Adam was now her cousin Alex's cousin-in-law. Or something like that. Alex's wife Caitlin and Adam McAllister were cousins—*real* first cousins, like Zoe was with Alex Trujillo.

Damn, she thought then as she stared up at the ceiling, *and I thought it was complicated enough keeping track of all the de la Paz cousins. It's going to start to get really crazy if we start having a lot more of these cross-clan marriages.*

Then again, she knew she could stand a good deal of craziness if it meant having Evan in her life.

And that, unfortunately, was the craziest thing of all. Although she'd been annoyed that she couldn't go out with guys the way her friends from high school did, had to act like she was second thing to a nun, for a long time it really hadn't seemed like the end of the world. She'd never met anyone she found all that attractive—at least not enough to go against her family's wishes—and so the lack of relationships hadn't bothered her much. In her mind, she'd told herself she would meet her perfect consort, just like Angela McAllister had, and then she'd get her own happily ever after.

Zoe hadn't counted on the consort search stretching out forever. She hadn't thought her happy ending might elude her, might turn out to be a terrible nightmare instead.

And she really could never have guessed that she'd meet a McAllister warlock who was far too old for her, and fall for him like a ton of bricks. She couldn't get him out of her mind—his warm, friendly voice, deep, but not *too* deep; the lush dark red of his hair; the way his eyes crinkled at the corners when he smiled. Even the tiny bits of grease she'd seen around his cuticles, as if he'd been working on his car when summoned and had cleaned up...but quickly, so he'd left evidence of the day's labors still showing on his hands.

For some reason, he felt more real to her right then than any of the men she'd known her entire life. And that was trouble, because she needed to bond with her consort, not someone she just thought was attractive.

Not attractive, she chided herself. *Totally smoking hot.*

As if this wasn't hard enough already. She let out a groan of exasperation, then got up from her bed and headed into the en suite bathroom. Although she had a feeling sleep would be a long time coming that night, she might as well get herself ready for bed.

As she got out her face wash and moisturizer and toothpaste, she wondered what Evan was doing right at that moment.

This place was...well, he should have known that Luz Trujillo wouldn't put him up at the local Motel 6, but as the front desk clerk handed Evan the plastic key card for his hotel room, he couldn't help thinking that he would have been perfectly happy with something just a little less upscale.

It was probably his imagination, but he got the distinct impression that the other guests at the CopperWynd resort were staring at him as he made his way to the elevator, giving his worn boots and jeans and untucked henley shirt the side-eye. All right, he definitely was out of place here, among these smooth, polished-looking people in their chinos and polo shirts and perfectly tailored dresses, but he couldn't do much about that now.

Thank the Goddess, no one else was in the elevator. Its doors shut, closing out all those quietly disapproving stares. Evan stood there, beat-up duffle bag clutched in one hand, and waited for the elevator to take him up to the top floor. He had to hope that Luz hadn't booked his shabby self into the penthouse suite. That would have been a bit much.

When he entered his room, even though it wasn't the penthouse, he saw at once that it was still far nicer than he needed, with a big king bed covered in expensive linens, a little sitting area off to one side, even a fireplace—the last thing you'd think a person would need in Phoenix, he observed with a shake of the head. The bathroom was all gleaming black granite, and almost as big as the flat he owned in Jerome.

But he knew he couldn't protest. If this was how Luz Trujillo wanted to play things, so be it. He dropped the duffle bag on the little folding stand in the closet and then went back out to the main room, heading for the sliding glass doors that let in an amazing view of this desert suburb. Off to the east, beyond a range of jagged mountains—the Superstitions? Evan wasn't clear enough on the geography of the area to know for sure—a large yellow moon had just begun to rise.

He wasn't watching the moon, though. For some reason, his gaze moved toward the lights that covered the hilly suburb, as if his eyes could somehow pick out Zoe's house from all the others clustered there.

Which was just stupid. For one thing, he wasn't even sure if he could see her house from the resort, considering the way the terrain undulated here. The Sandoval residence could very likely be hidden behind a hill. And anyway, he'd been in the house twice and didn't have that clear an image of its exterior, only that it had been pale beige stucco with a red tile roof, and some kind of palm trees planted in the front yard.

Definitely not the kind of place you'd find in Jerome, or probably not even in Cottonwood. Maybe Sedona; he knew the resort town boasted a fair number of upscale houses, even though he hadn't personally seen any of them. No McAllister witches lived in Sedona, since it hid its own powers, and one of the only things the McAllisters and the Wilcoxes had agreed on back in the day was that neither clan could call it home. That would have been giving too much of an advantage to the witch family that claimed the small desert town as its own.

His stomach rumbled then, and Evan realized it had been a good eight hours since the sandwich he'd hastily assembled around noon and then eaten one-handed as he fiddled with the Barracuda's engine. He and Zoe had been so busy chasing around that they hadn't bothered to eat anything. They could have ordered some food at BJ's, but they'd both been shaken by their encounter with the monster, and had been much more interested in having a drink to steady their nerves than choosing something to eat.

No way was he going downstairs and eating alone in the resort's restaurant, though. He could only imagine the looks he'd get then. Instead, he picked up the room service menu, winced a little at the prices, and then decided on a burger, since it was hard to go wrong with that.

Luckily, the kitchen was still open, and the woman who took his order promised it would be up in no more than fifteen minutes. Evan resisted the urge to have a beer along with the burger; while one beer wouldn't do that much to impair him, he was feeling tired and sluggish, and realized he'd be better off without it. He couldn't risk not being at his best if he got a call in the middle of the night and had to go back out on the monster's trail.

As he waited for his food to arrive, he went back to the window and looked outside. Several floors below, the resort's swimming pool shimmered blue-green in the darkness. He even thought he saw people in the water, which seemed crazy to him. But this was Phoenix, not Jerome, and maybe it was still warm enough outside that you could go for an evening swim without completely freezing your ass off.

His fingers found the piece of black tourmaline that he'd stowed in his pocket. He pulled it out and turned it over in his hand, watching as the flat edges of the crystal caught the lamplight in his hotel room. Strange to think that this hunk of rock could be anything except a bauble that should have been hanging from a necklace, or maybe a keychain. In this coolly elegant room, the world of witches and spells and creatures from other dimensions seemed very far away.

But Evan knew better.

He didn't get any sort of vibe from the stone. It felt completely neutral. That didn't necessarily mean anything. It could be working on protecting him, and he wouldn't even know it. What Jack Sandoval had said about it also acting as a tracking device—well, Evan wasn't so sure about that. He wasn't getting even the faintest tingle from the tourmaline crystal. Which meant…what? That the monster was too far away for the stone to detect it, or that, for whatever reason, he just wasn't capable of picking up the stone's signals?

A knock came at the door, and he went to open it. A Hispanic kid who didn't look old enough to vote, let alone drink, stood outside in the hall with a room service cart. He wheeled it in and put the covered silver tray on the table by the window, then paused. "Anything else, sir?"

Oh, right, the tip. It had been so long since Evan had stayed in a hotel—in fact, the last time had been his honeymoon with Kelly—that he'd pretty much forgotten about that part of the ritual. He dug in his pocket and pulled out his wallet, then retrieved a ten-dollar bill. That was probably way too much, but otherwise all he had was twenties stuffed in there, and he knew twenty bucks was definitely overkill.

The kid looked thrilled with the tip; he grinned and said thanks, and then informed Evan he could put his empty dishes and their tray out in the hallway when he was done. After Evan thanked him, the kid pushed the cart back into the corridor and took off.

Well, overpriced or not, the burger smelled delicious, and his stomach told Evan that he'd better sit his ass down and eat it before it got cold. So he did, taking a seat at the window with its perfectly framed view of the rising moon.

The first few bites told him this was exactly what he needed, and he ate some more before he allowed himself to slow down and really savor the food he was consuming. When he paused to take a sip of water from the bottle he'd found in the welcome basket, he found his gaze moving around the room once again. This really was quite a place. He had to wonder what Luz Trujillo had been thinking when she sent him here. Were the fancy accommodations just a courtesy, as the de la Paz clan would never consider putting a guest up anywhere that wasn't the best? Or was it a more subtle way of showing the difference in wealth between her clan and his, and letting him know that her niece deserved better than a scrubby McAllister warlock?

No, that was ridiculous. For one thing, Luz had reached out to the McAllisters to invite several men of eligible age to see if they were Zoe's consort. Normally, that wasn't the sort of thing Evan would pay much attention to, except that the younger brother of his cousin Travis, one of Evan's closer friends among the clan, had been one of those who'd gone down to share what turned out to be a not-so-fateful kiss with Zoe Sandoval. Donny had struck out, of course, but Travis and Evan had still discussed the situation a bit while drinking beers in Evan's garage. It had been strange to contemplate that a McAllister might be the consort of a de la Paz, since in general clans liked to have their *prima*'s match be a member of the same family. Kept things stronger, or whatever.

So clearly Luz Trujillo didn't have an issue with McAllister warlocks in general. Those dark eyes of hers seemed to miss very little, which meant she'd probably noticed a certain kind of chemistry between him and her niece. Evan had been doing his best to seem completely uninterested, but he'd never been that great an actor. He knew he was attracted to Zoe. That in itself felt strange, because after Kelly had bailed out on their marriage, he hadn't paid much attention to other women. A few dates with more distant cousins from the Prescott branch of the family, and even a weird sort of "friends with benefits" arrangement with Tina, one of the civilian waitresses who worked at Grapes restaurant up in Jerome. At least with Tina he didn't have to hide what he was, since Jerome's civilian population knew there was a little something extra about the McAllister clan, but even so, he'd known that relationship wouldn't work in the long run. He liked Tina, and they could laugh and share a beer together, and have some fairly satisfying sex afterward, but the spark hadn't been there. Their breakup had been amicable, and she didn't seem to harbor any ill will toward him after the relationship ended.

But this weird pull he felt toward Zoe…it was just wrong any way you looked at it. He would be thirty in June, and she wasn't even twenty-two yet. To some people, that might not be that much of a difference, but that wasn't how these things were done in witch families, where most couples got together young and were generally fairly close in age. Also, Zoe would be her clan's *prima* one day. The last thing she needed was someone nearly eight years her senior, a man with the millstone of a very conniving ex-wife around his neck—an ex-wife who could expose them all with some spitefully ill-timed words. Not that Zoe's clan would ever allow the two of them to get close enough for that to happen.

Did Luz Trujillo know anything about his history? He had a feeling she must, just because during the last few weeks, he'd heard through the grapevine that the de la Paz clan had begun reaching out to unmarried warlocks older than twenty-five, which was the usual cutoff for a *prima's* consort. But no one had contacted him. Even if he'd thought to offer himself, which he hadn't, that sort of thing just wasn't done. It was up to the *prima*-in-waiting's family to decide who was suitable and who wasn't.

Evan ran a hand through his hair and wished he'd ordered that beer after all. But he ignored the temptation to pick up the phone and call room service again, and instead methodically finished the rest of his burger and the parmesan truffle fries that had come along with it. He figured afterward he'd sit up in bed and watch TV, give himself time to digest. Then he'd go to sleep, and pray that he didn't dream of Zoe Sandoval. And he wouldn't let himself think of what it might be like to have her lying in that big king-sized bed next to him.

Following the room service waiter's instructions, Evan put the silver cover back on his plate, then went and deposited the tray with his dirty dishes on the floor outside his room. Afterward, he untied his boots and took them off, and reached into his pocket to remove his keys so they wouldn't dig into his hip as he sat there on the bed.

When he took out the chunk of black tourmaline, it felt warm in his hand.

What was that supposed to mean? Had it become active because the enemy was somewhere close by? Evan had a sudden flash of that misshapen monster tearing through the lobby of the resort and prayed he was mistaken.

But....

He hefted the stone in his palm. A weird tingling sensation moved up his arm, while at the same time something seemed to whisper in his mind, *East.*

For a moment, he stood there, wondering whether he should call Luz Trujillo, or maybe Zoe's house. Luz had given him the number. But he was feeling conflicted enough about Zoe that he didn't think that was a very good idea. Besides, he'd been called down here to take care of the problem. He and Zoe had tried working together earlier today, and that hadn't gone very well. Wouldn't it be better for everyone concerned if he could just slip out, confront the monster using the techniques Jack Sandoval had shown him earlier that afternoon, and then go back to Jerome once the situation was handled?

That way, he could leave Zoe to find her consort, and he...well, Evan told himself he'd forget her soon enough. They'd only spent a few hours together. He wouldn't deny the attraction he felt for her, but neither would he allow it to ruin relations between the de la Pazes and the McAllisters. Stepping in when he hadn't been invited was probably the fastest way to put the Phoenix witch clan on the warpath.

Well, when he put it that way….

Mouth grim, he went to retrieve his boots. It looked like he'd be heading out for a nighttime drive.

CHAPTER EIGHT

Zoe sat up in bed, heart racing. What had awakened her, she really couldn't say...but she supposed that didn't matter. She was definitely awake now, eyes straining into the darkness. Actually, the room wasn't all that dark, since a soft glow from the nearly full moon made its way in here, allowing her to see the outlines of the furniture, the way the drapes at the window moved gently in the night breeze. It had been a warm day, but since it was still only early March, temperatures had cooled enough that, once the sun was down, her parents turned off the central air and made sure the windows were opened instead.

All was quiet. Zoe glanced at the clock on her nightstand and saw it wasn't really that late, only a little past ten-thirty. Her parents were probably still up, although if they were watching television, they must have been doing so in their own room, rather than out in the family room where the big 60-inch TV was located.

Without thinking, she pushed back the covers and went to the window so she could look outside. Maybe the sound that had woken her had been a car pulling up in front of the house; heart beating a little faster, she wondered if it might have been the deep bass rumble of the Barracuda's engine.

But the street was empty, everyone's cars safely tucked away in their garages for the night. No sign of Evan, or his car.

And yet....

Zoe went to her dresser and pulled out a pair of jeans and a plain dark V-neck T-shirt. She grabbed a scrunchie and pulled her hair back, then dug out some tinted lip balm from the top drawer of her nightstand and applied a thin layer so she wouldn't feel completely bare-faced. After that, all she needed was a pair of socks and her running shoes, and she was ready to go.

Well, almost. Acting mostly on instinct, she picked up the piece of tourmaline Uncle Jack had given her and slipped it into her pocket. The stone felt warm to the touch, which meant it must be picking up on something wrong, something that shouldn't be prowling the safe neighborhoods of Fountain Hills.

No wonder she'd woken up. A little tremor went through her, and she wondered if she should go tell her parents what she was experiencing.

No, this was her mistake, her fight. Besides, she didn't know how much they could actually do to help her. Her mother was one of the clan's mediums, but no spirits of de la Pazes past had yet appeared to give any guidance on Zoe's predicament. And while Luis Sandoval was a silver-tongued devil in the court-room, his own magical powers were not all that strong. He was something of a weather-worker, but more that he could sense when storms were coming than actually possessing the ability to change their paths, or to summon them when the sky was clear. With his talent, he probably would have made a great meteorologist, but he'd always been interested in the law instead.

Anyway, their powers weren't anything close to the gifts their daughter possessed. Better to keep them out of this. Aunt Luz would be a great help, but she was fifteen minutes away, and Zoe had the feeling she had to act now, or the opportunity to catch up with the creature might slip away.

What she really should do was call Evan, but he'd neglected to give her his number. She doubted that was an accidental oversight, and wanted to curse his caution. Yes, she knew where he was staying, and so she could always call the CopperWynd and have the front-desk operator there transfer her to his room, but....

Forget it. She touched the unnaturally warm tourmaline in her pocket, just to reassure herself that she wasn't imagining things, then picked up her purse from where it rested on top of the dresser and slung it over her shoulder. This was her problem, and she should be the one to fix it. Anyway, as much as she'd enjoyed spending time with Evan today, she'd really been the one doing the heavy lifting when it came to dealing with the creature. She could handle this without him.

Moving as quietly as possible, she tiptoed down the stairs. As she'd thought, once she reached the first floor, she could hear the faint murmur of the television coming from the slightly open door to her parents' bedroom. The background noise should serve to cover up any sounds she made, but she still crept along until she reached the laundry room off the kitchen, and went from there into the garage.

Would they hear the garage door opening? With the television on, maybe not. She could always hear it whenever someone entered or exited the garage, but that was because her bedroom was right on top of it. Her parents' bedroom was toward the back of the house.

She'd have to risk it.

After setting her purse down on the passenger seat, she pushed the button for the ignition and simultaneously activated the garage remote with her free hand. As soon as the door rose enough for the little Fiat to clear it, she backed out onto the driveway, sliding under the half-open garage door. Then she was away from the house, which remained quiet and dark, except for the lights that flanked the front door, which her parents almost always left on.

Even through her jeans, she could feel the heat of the stone, acting as a sink for whatever negative energy might be surrounding her. At the same time, she sensed that she needed to head east. There wasn't much out there, except the Indian casino just south of Fort McDowell, but she wasn't going to question the impulse that was guiding her away from the safety of the suburbs.

She needed to stop this thing before anything truly bad happened. The image of the girl she and Evan had found outside the apartment complex in Superstition Springs swam up behind her eyes, and Zoe wondered what would have happened if they hadn't appeared then, if no one had been around to stop the creature from doing whatever it had planned to do.

What did it want? After that first encounter, Zoe would have said that it seemed to be pursuing other girls who looked like her, but the spot where they'd tracked it down at the golf club had been deserted—thank God. At least no one had been around to witness that particular confrontation.

The problem was, Zoe knew she didn't have enough information to draw any conclusions. She needed more than two encounters with the creature to begin to see any kind of a pattern. On the other hand, she certainly didn't plan to sit back and just observe while the creature went from place to place in Phoenix, at the very least drawing unwanted attention, and at the worst....

Well, she really didn't want to think what its worst might be.

She dropped down to Highway 87 and kept driving. The lights of Fountain Hills dwindled behind her, and she repressed a shiver, right before she reached out and switched the A/C in the car over to vent only.

It was so dark out here. No, she wasn't the only person on the highway, because people appeared to still be coming and going toward the turnoff for the casino. Once she passed that exit, however, the night seemed black as pitch, the only illumination the reflective signs on the side of the road, and the gleaming paint that marked the lanes of the highway. The moon was up, but now it was almost overhead, and the glare from her headlamps seemed to erase any light it might have cast.

This was crazy, wasn't it? She glanced down at her cell phone where she'd propped it up against the console so she could plug it into the charger, and saw that she only had one bar of 4G left. Pretty soon that would be gone, and she'd be out here in the middle of nowhere with no cell reception, no weapons, no nothing.

Except yourself, she told herself fiercely. *You're the next* prima *of the de la Paz clan, and you've beaten this thing twice already. You don't need anyone's help.*

Although she really would have liked to have Evan there....

She bit her lip and kept driving. Good thing she'd filled up the car just that morning, since God only knew how far she'd have to go until the tourmaline or her witchy sense or whatever it was told her to stop. She knew if she stayed on the 87, eventually she'd come up on the mountain town of Payson from underneath. McAllister territory, so she'd be safe enough there. But how many miles was that? At least sixty, she thought, but she didn't know for sure. She'd never driven up that way. Sixty miles didn't sound that far until you realized it was sixty miles of desert wilderness, along twisty mountain roads.

No, she had to be going someplace closer than that. At least she hoped she was.

Up ahead, Zoe saw a sign that said "Mesquite Staging Area." She didn't know what that even meant. However, the twinge told her the staging area was where she needed to go, so she pulled off the highway onto an access road that was paved for only short distance before it turned to rutted dirt.

Shit. She slowed down to a crawl and turned on her high-beams, illuminating the cloud of dust blowing all around her. Too bad her witch sense hadn't told her to steal the keys to her parents' Audi, which at least had all-wheel drive, even though it wasn't a true off-road vehicle, not like her Uncle Jack's Wrangler. She bumped along on the washboard road, teeth gritted and hands clenched on the steering wheel. Then she came to an open area, one crisscrossed with all types of tread marks.

This must be a place where people could come to offload their ATVs before they headed up into the hills into really rough terrain. Why the creature had come out here, she had no idea, but better here than back somewhere in Phoenix. Out in the middle of nowhere like this, she sure as hell wouldn't have to worry about there being any witnesses.

She left the headlights on and unbuckled her seatbelt. No, she didn't have any weapons, but she had a big Maglite flashlight in the trunk, something Jack had given her a while back.

"Don't leave home without it," he'd told her with a wink. At the time she'd only been somewhat mystified—her usual haunts were shopping malls and restaurants and hair or nail salons, not places out in the wilderness where she'd even need a flash-light—but at the moment she could only be glad of his prescience.

Moving carefully, eyes darting all around her as she went, she headed toward the rear of the Fiat and opened the trunk. There was the flashlight, along with the emergency kit she always carried, with basic first aid supplies, road flares, that sort of thing. Hidden underneath it all was the spare tire and the tire iron. For a moment Zoe contemplated getting out the tire iron, since it would make a heck of a club, but then she decided the Maglite would work nearly as well. Besides, she wasn't sure whether she'd be able to manage both the flashlight and the tire iron at the same time.

She got out the Maglite and turned it on, let-ting the bright beam move around the area where she'd parked. As she'd thought, this was clearly a spot where people would trailer their ATVs or dirt bikes. Several trails, narrower than the access road she'd driven in on, cut through swaths of mesquite and manzanita before they headed off into the hills somewhere. But the combination of moonlight and the much brighter illumination from the Maglite didn't show her anything else. Yes, she supposed the creature could be hiding behind one of those clumps of manzanita or mesquite, but the stone in her pocket, while warm, hadn't heated up to the point where she thought the monster she'd summoned could be anywhere close.

Instead of reassuring her, though, the utter emptiness of the place only served to set her nerves on edge that much more. While she wasn't exactly looking forward to a confrontation, she also didn't want to think her powers had failed her so utterly that she couldn't even tell when the creature was around, especially since the tourmaline was supposed to be helping her.

Great.

Zoe stopped in the middle of a largish circular area, probably a favorite spot for turning around big trucks with trailers, judging by all the overlapping tread marks in the sandy dirt. The wind began to pick up and she shivered, wishing she'd thought to bring a jacket with her. Phoenix's hot, dry days tended to make you forget that it could get damn cold out in the open desert once the sun went down.

Another flick of the flashlight around the clearing revealed absolutely nothing. And yet....

She could feel the tourmaline heating up in her jeans pocket, despite the thick fabric that prevented the stone from touching her bare skin. After transferring the Maglite to her left hand, she reached into her pocket and retrieved the tourmaline, then winced slightly at its heat against her bare palm.

Was it *glowing?*

No, that wasn't possible. She knew about black tourmaline's psychic properties, but nothing she'd ever read had told her it could start to shine from within, a deep, dark red appearing at its very heart.

That alteration startled her so much she almost wanted to drop the stone, but she knew better than that. If it was glowing this intensely, then that meant something bad was coming, even if she couldn't see it yet.

Everything in her was screaming at her to shove the tourmaline back in her pocket and make a run for the car. She even took a step in that direction before she stopped herself. What was the point in coming all the way out here if she'd only intended to drop everything and flee at the first sign of danger?

Instead, she swallowed and stood her ground, then moved the Maglite in careful arcs calculated to show as much of the open area as possible. If the creature really was about to descend on her, she wanted to get as clear a look at it as possible when it approached.

But still she saw nothing, even though the tourmaline now felt as if it was about to burn a hole right through her jeans. The wind died away suddenly, the leaves on the manzanitas and the mesquite trees going dead calm.

Was that a good sign, or—

Something grabbed her wrist in a grip like iron. Startled, every nerve ending coming alive with a massive jolt of adrenaline, Zoe dropped the Maglite. It hit the ground and rolled away a couple of feet… but not far enough away to keep it from showing exactly what had accosted her.

It towered over her, somehow even bigger than it had appeared when she'd confronted it at the golf course. Or maybe that was just her fear talking. She didn't know for sure, only saw that it had to be well over a foot taller than she was. The fingers wrapped around her wrist burned hot against her skin, hotter than the tourmaline in her pocket, which now felt like a live coal had somehow lodged itself in there.

And its face—it had inched a little closer to something resembling normal human features, and yet was still distorted enough that it wasn't anything like the *telenovela* star she had hoped to conjure into being. Its eyes were pale yellow and glazed with fury as it pulled her closer.

Her body broke out in a cold sweat, her heart hammering in her chest, but Zoe knew she couldn't let herself fall apart now. Gritting her teeth, she made herself recall the words of the spell she'd dutifully repeated over and over just a few hours ago.

"To any spirits who threaten me in this place,
Fight water with water and fire with fire

Banish their souls into nothingness
Remove their powers to the last trace
Let these evil beings flee
Through time and space."

The creature let out a howl, as if the words of the spell had hurt it somehow, but it did not let go of her. If anything, its grip increased, grinding the fragile bones of her wrist together. Zoe couldn't help crying out in pain, even as she tried to ignore the throbbing in her limb. She had to stay focused, but....

Why hadn't the spell worked? Uncle Jack had said it should work. Had she said it wrong?

Frantic, she began to babble her way through the words again, but just as she got to the word "banish," the monster pulled her closer, then brought its distorted face down closer to hers.

Oh, God. It wasn't...no, that wasn't possible. This couldn't be happening.

The thing was trying to kiss her.

Zoe screamed.

CHAPTER NINE

HE'D HEADED OUT ON HIGHWAY 87, BUT WHEN HE CAME to a turnoff for something called Bush Highway, Evan took a hard right, following the road as it climbed up into the hills. The way was winding and narrow, and he had to turn on the high-beams. So far he hadn't seen another soul here, which made sense. Who else but a crazy man would be out driving around on this forgotten highway in the middle of the night?

Okay, not exactly the middle of the night, just a little past ten-thirty. But still.

To his surprise, he saw a sign pointing to a marina, of all things. Was there a lake hidden up here in the hills somewhere? There had been that artificial lake at the apartment complex where they first saw the monster...and that golf course had its own ponds and waterways as well. Maybe something about the water attracted the creature.

Evan turned down the access road leading to the marina. A minute later, he pulled into a parking lot with an illuminated sign that told him he was at Saguaro Lake Marina. Okay...now what?

Just as he slowed almost to a stop, the tingle that had been guiding him disappeared abruptly, and the warmth of the tourmaline stone in his jeans pocket evaporated as well.

What the hell?

He sat there with the engine idling, looking around the empty parking lot. The moonlight was bright enough to tell him that Zoe's little powder-blue Fiat was nowhere to be seen.

So why was he here?

Cold washed over him then. Shit. *Shit.*

He'd been suckered. He'd trusted the power of the stone to guide him where he needed to go. But he'd never stopped to think that maybe, just maybe, the monster Zoe had brought into this world had powers of its own, including the ability to manipulate the tourmaline's energies so it would send him in exactly the wrong direction.

Which meant that it might be with her right now. Someplace far away from here, no doubt.

Think, Evan, think, he told himself.

But panic was sending spikes of adrenaline all through his body, and he didn't seem capable of logic right then. Angrily, he reached into his pocket, pulled out the tourmaline, and flung it onto the floor next to the car's passenger seat.

That burst of rage didn't make him feel any better, though. He'd come down here to Phoenix to help Zoe, keep her safe, and so far he was doing a pretty miserable job of it.

He gripped the steering wheel and made himself focus. Clearly, Zoe wasn't here. So he'd need to rely on his own strength, his own talent, to find her. Closing his eyes, he visualized her face, those big brown eyes in their frame of astonishing lashes, eyes that could glint with humor or turn sly at a moment's notice. The straight, elegant shape of her nose. That mouth....

The tingle that hit the back of his neck right then was so sharp, it felt more like someone had just stuck a pin in him. But that was good, because it was as if the part of his gift he needed the most had suddenly decided to wake up.

And it was telling him he needed to go back the way he'd come, down to the 87, and then head north.

His foot mashed down on the accelerator, and the Barracuda roared forward. Good thing it was late at night and the marina was deserted, or he very likely might have crashed right into anyone coming down the access road.

Evan took the curves of Bush Highway far too fast. But he knew his car, knew what it could do. It squatted down on the hairpin bends like it had been invented for that kind of maneuver, and in a very short amount of time, he was down on Highway 87, accelerator pressed to the floor as he sent the Barracuda like a shining black bullet northward.

Past a hundred miles an hour, and he had to hope like hell there weren't any local cops or Arizona Highway Patrol vehicles cruising these roads at the moment. Getting a ticket would slow him down far more than going the speed limit.

But he couldn't make himself go any slower than that. His witch senses were telling him that he was now on the right track, and he could only pray that the monster couldn't interfere with his inborn talents the way it had messed with that tourmaline. How it had even figured out how to do such a thing, Evan had no idea, but they were well outside charted territory now, off in the kind of zone that used to be marked "here be dragons" on old-timey maps.

Once he had to zig into the slow lane to get around someone cruising along in the left lane, a driver in a Prius who was clearly offended by the Barracuda's insane speed and had no intention of moving out of the way. Evan cursed under his breath but didn't waste any more time than that, rocketing back in front of the offending vehicle and then speeding away so quickly that soon its lights had all but disappeared from the rearview mirror.

That was the only other car he encountered, though.

A sign appeared at the side of the highway—*Mesquite Staging Area*—and Evan stomped on the brakes, feeling the Barracuda skid slightly before it got back on track and pivoted onto the highway exit. That exit led to a short access road, one that quickly turned to dirt. He gritted his teeth as the car bumped its way over the washboard surface, but he couldn't worry about what the road might be doing to his suspension. He had to get to Zoe.

Thank the Goddess—there was her car, the dust covering it visible even in the moonlight. A single glance was enough to tell him that it was empty, so he stopped and turned off the Barracuda's engine. Once its throaty roar was gone, he heard it right away.

A woman screaming.

He flung open the car door and ran toward the screams, thankful for the bright moonlight, since it did well enough to illuminate his way. As he came around a curve and past the stand of scrubby manzanita that blocked his view, he could see Zoe—and the creature. It had its oversized hand around her fragile wrist and was dragging her toward it, its hideous face bending down toward hers.

Oh, hell no.

Zoe could use her *prima* gift to throw balls of light at the monster, but Evan knew he didn't have that kind of ability. And he had a feeling that she must have already tried the banishing spell to get rid of it, but clearly it was still here.

Well, where magic failed, human strength might prevail.

He launched himself at the creature, praying that the muscles he'd built up working on the car and hefting heavy pieces of metal at his father's shop might stand him in good stead now. And don't forget the element of surprise—the monster's attention was all on Zoe, and Evan was coming up from behind it. He had to stand at least a ghost of a chance.

Running into the creature felt more or less like running straight into a brick wall. The impact knocked the breath from his chest, but he couldn't let that stop him. Because the monster stumbled and let go of Zoe, and she backed away immediately. Her right hand hung at a strange angle, and her full mouth was taut with pain. Clearly, though, she wasn't about to let that deter her, because she raised her other hand and flung white fire at the creature.

It howled, an ear-splitting sound that had become all too familiar to Evan lately. He took advantage of its distraction to recite the spell Jack Sandoval had taught him. Maybe it wouldn't work this time, either, but he knew he had to do something, and trying to tackle the creature while Zoe was throwing fireballs at it sounded like a recipe for getting his own ass blasted off.

The words flowed out of him, laced with power, his voice sounding strange to him, as if something was amplifying it far beyond what even a normal shout would have sounded like. The monster put its hands to its ears and backed away, its pale, feverish gaze darting from him to Zoe and back again. White fire glared around her hand, and the promise of that additional assault seemed to be enough. It released a final cry of anguish—or anger—and then disappeared, fading into the night as if it had never been there.

Evan pulled in a breath and then ran over to Zoe, who stood there cradling her injured hand and staring at the place where the creature had stood. Her eyes were wide with fright and pain, but incongruously, she smiled at him and said, "Thought you'd never get here."

"I almost didn't," he replied. Then he glanced at her right hand. "Are you okay?"

"Not really," she said, sounding almost cheerful. "I think it broke my wrist. I'll have to have Alba patch me up."

"Alba?"

"The de la Paz healer in Phoenix."

Oh. He wanted to sag with relief at Zoe's words. The McAllisters had been without a healer for so long that he'd forgotten this kind of injury didn't have to mean weeks of being in a cast. Zoe would be good as new soon enough.

So because he didn't have to worry about her wrist, he let the wave of anger flow through him. "Then can you tell me what the hell you thought you were doing, coming out here all by yourself? That thing could have—" He stopped there, because he really didn't want to think about what the creature might have done to her.

Apparently, those same thoughts had passed through her mind, because the pale oval of her face in the moonlit darkness looked positively stricken. "I thought I could handle it. I'd beaten it before. But then Uncle Jack's spell didn't work...." She stopped there, eyebrows lifting. "Why did it work for you and not me?"

"I don't know," Evan said. "Magic can be weird sometimes. But we can leave that for later. Right now I need to get you home."

"Home," Zoe repeated, looking less than thrilled. Probably she was thinking about the recriminations she knew waited for her. Then she shifted slightly, and bit her lip. "I don't think I can drive with this wrist."

"Then don't. We'll leave your car here, and come back for it tomorrow when it's daylight and your wrist has been healed." He paused for a moment and looked around, realizing this was probably a kind of day-use area for ATV enthusiasts. Zoe's car should be safe enough here for a while; you couldn't even see it from the highway.

"All right." She sounded resigned, but at least she didn't seem inclined to argue with him.

"Come on." Evan turned toward the place where he'd left the Barracuda and began to walk. Part of him rebelled, because what he really wanted to do was take her and hold her and tell her everything was going to be okay, but he didn't dare trust himself to take that kind of a liberty. No, he'd just have to keep walking and hope she'd follow without protest.

Which she did. She stumbled once or twice on the uneven ground, but she didn't say anything, just kept going, and caught up so she walked next to him. At least she'd had the sense to wear running shoes and jeans for this outing, as if some part of her had known she was headed into rough territory. Her long black hair was pulled back into a ponytail, and it didn't appear as if she wore a lick of makeup. Somehow, however, even though the ensemble should have made her look more like a kid, she appeared older and harder, her face drawn with pain, as if the purity of her features in the moonlight had momentarily transformed her from the girl she was into the woman she was becoming.

Evan thought she was probably the most beautiful thing he'd ever seen. He didn't stare, though, but just kept walking to the car. In silence, he went over to the passenger-side door and opened it for her, then waited as she sat down. She began to reach for the seatbelt with her left hand but clearly was having some difficulty.

So he said, "Let me get that for you," and reached down and stretched it across her. It was harder than he'd thought, being this close, catching that faint sweet scent from her hair once again. The seatbelt locked in place and he stood up quickly, almost hitting his head on the roof of the car in his haste.

Her full mouth began to curve in a smile, as if she knew exactly why he was trying so hard to get away from her.

Without comment, he walked over to his side of the car and got in. Still without speaking, he started up the engine and turned around so he could get headed in the right direction on the access road. He drove slowly, but he saw how Zoe's lips tightened in pain whenever they went over a particularly bad bump.

Well, the healer would take care of the injured wrist for her. And after that...he just didn't know.

Her parents were very quiet as the healer worked on Zoe. Oh, they were angry—she didn't know if she'd ever seen them this angry. But, unlike some of the other members of the clan, they weren't the type to explode in front of others. They'd wait until Alba was done, and then they'd let their daughter have it.

Or maybe they wouldn't. Zoe's gaze strayed to where Evan stood off to one side, watching as Alba passed her hands over Zoe's broken wrist. He hadn't said much on the drive here, and she'd been fine with that. Her mind was racing in so many directions, she didn't even know if she would have been able to carry on a rational conversation.

When he'd bent so close to fasten her seatbelt for her—despite the pain she'd been in, she'd wanted nothing more than for him to lean in even closer, to place his mouth on hers. But of course he was far too careful, too in control of himself, to do anything like that. Only specially selected candidates were allowed to kiss the *prima*-in-waiting, and Evan clearly was well aware of that fact, knew that trying to kiss her without being invited would cause all sorts of trouble.

Speaking of which...as much as her mind wanted to rebel at the thought, she had to analyze the creature's actions as it had assaulted her. For some reason, she had the impression that it really hadn't intended to hurt her, more that it didn't know its own strength. Her broken wrist had just been an unfortunate result of its desire to pull her close.

To kiss her. Her stomach churned at the idea, but she couldn't put it out of her head. After all, hadn't she brought the creature here because of her need for a true consort? Maybe it was just trying to pursue what it thought its true purpose in life must be.

God.

She gritted her teeth as Alba closed both hands around her wrist. This was the necessary final step—she'd seen Alba do the same thing when Zander broke his arm after he fell off his skateboard—but knowing it was just part of the way the magic worked didn't make it hurt any less. Her earlier movements had served to get the bones to line up, and now Alba held Zoe's wrist so she could send her healing energy within and make the break knit itself together. Having it in a cast would accomplish the same thing, but why be incapacitated for weeks when you could brute-force your way through a little pain and then be good as new again?

Alba had knelt while she used her healing powers on Zoe. Now she stood up and smiled. "All better. It will feel a little stiff for a few hours, but when you wake up tomorrow, it will be good as new."

"Thanks, Alba," Zoe said, and meant it. Her wrist still ached, but she could get back to monster chasing tomorrow, no problem. Well, unless her parents decided to confine her to her room for the next three years. Not that they could really get away with such a thing. A *prima*-in-waiting led a restricted life, true, but Zoe was still an adult. She could invoke her powers as the clan's heir, threaten to leave.

Yeah, right. If Zoe tried anything like that, her Aunt Luz would put her foot down so fast, it would probably create a small earthquake.

"Yes, thank you, Alba," Andrea said, getting up from the couch where she'd been sitting. "And thank you for coming over so late at night."

"Healing knows no hour of the day," Alba responded. It was something Zoe had heard her say more than once.

"Still," her father put in. "We do appreciate it."

Alba smiled and retrieved her purse, and Zoe's parents went to see her out. They'd barely shut the door, however, before someone knocked on it. Alba, returning for something she'd forgotten?

But then Zoe saw the grim glance her parents exchanged, and knew that wasn't Alba at the door.

Luz Trujillo came into the house and stalked straight into the living room, her slender form practically vibrating with anger. Although she usually wore her long, dark hair pulled back in a clip or in a low bun on the back of her neck, right then it flowed loose over her shoulders, indicating that she'd been relaxing at home for the night and had come straight here without bothering to make herself more presentable.

Crap.

She paused in front of Zoe, arms crossed, apparently oblivious to Evan McAllister's presence only a few feet away. Or maybe she simply didn't care that an outsider looked on while she upbraided her niece and heir. "What on earth were you thinking, Zoe?"

"I—"

"To sneak out like that without telling anyone where you were going? To go after a dangerous and unknown creature, all by yourself?"

"I—"

"This recklessness has got to stop! You aren't just endangering yourself—you're endangering the future of the clan. Did you ever think about what would happen if you were hurt, or worse?"

No, she really hadn't. Oh, of course she had no intention of getting injured while tracking down the creature, but intentions couldn't always keep the bad stuff from happening. She herself was a sort of insurance policy in case anything happened to Luz. That was why witch clans always made sure there was a *prima*-in-waiting, should the worst occur. But so far a successor hadn't appeared who could take

Zoe's place if she herself suffered a fatal accident or injury. Such situations were very rare, of course, but the de la Paz clan hadn't survived and prospered this long by taking chances.

Zoe knew she was in the wrong. Maybe even as recently as a few days ago she would have made a sulky reply and pointed out that nothing bad *had* happened—well, beyond her injured wrist—and so there wasn't much point in getting all bent over the situation. But she could feel Evan's gaze on her. She didn't want to sound like a spoiled brat. She wanted to be someone he could admire.

"I'm sorry," she said quietly. "I could feel something pulling me there, and since we'd been having such a hard time finding the monster, I didn't feel as if I could waste any time in going after it. Also, I'd been able to defend myself against it before. Twice. I didn't think it was that big a risk."

Her words didn't seem to mollify her aggrieved aunt, whose arms remained crossed. "Of course it was a risk. Just going out alone like that in the middle of the night was a risk. What if your car had broken down? What if you'd run into someone who wanted to take advantage of a young woman all on her own in the middle of nowhere?"

"Okay," Luis said, stepping forward as he sent a warning look at his sister-in-law. "I really don't think it's necessary to jump directly into worst-case scenarios."

"I'm the *prima*," Luz shot back. Her dark eyes glinted with anger. "I have to consider worst-case scenarios. It comes with the territory."

"We know that," Zoe's mother said quietly. "But Zoe is safe now. Evan got there in time to save her. Thank you for that," she added, her gaze finding Evan where he stood off to one side, his expression almost too blank, as if he was expending a lot of effort to prevent everyone from guessing what might be passing through his mind. "I don't think we really had thanked you yet."

"It's fine," he said. "The important thing was getting Zoe healed."

He barely looked at her, but Zoe didn't mind. They'd already traded a few heated glances, and the last thing she wanted was for either her parents or Aunt Luz to pick up on any of that.

But that didn't mean Zoe didn't want to be alone with him so they could talk. She wanted to discuss her latest insights about the creature with him, get his take on why he'd gotten the banishment spell to work when she'd failed so dismally.

All right, and also see if he might be tempted to lean in toward her once more, to maybe risk their lips touching....

No, he'd never do that. He knew he wasn't intended to be her consort, and he'd never muddy the waters while there was still time to find her true match.

"Anyway," Luz went on, "you are absolutely *not* to go after this creature—or anywhere else—unless you have someone with you."

At any other time, such a commandment would have made Zoe grit her teeth and push the argument further. Yes, she was used to having members of the clan watch over her from a distance, but that was a far different thing from being stuck with a glorified babysitter. Now, though, she thought she had the perfect bodyguard in Evan McAllister. He'd just proved to all of them that he could protect her, and would, at serious risk to his own life and limb.

And if anyone complained, well, she'd just point out that she wasn't the one who'd sent for him, was she?

"That's fine," she said, in tones so sweet that her father sent her a suspicious glance, as if he guessed she was up to something, even if he couldn't quite figure out what it might be. "I know you and Mom have things to handle at the office, and Zander's powers are still developing, so I don't think he'd be much help. But maybe Evan can keep an eye on me? I mean, that's why he's here, right?"

Aunt Luz's lips pressed together. Clearly, she'd just figured out her niece's angle and was trying to decide how best to circumvent it. "We asked Evan to come down here to help reverse the spell, not play bodyguard. He—"

"It's okay," Evan broke in. He stepped away from where he'd been standing by the wall and came a little farther into the room so he could face Zoe's family members. "Part of figuring out how to reverse the spell involves being near the creature, and the best way to do that is to be with Zoe, since it seems to be drawn to her—or she's being drawn to it. I haven't quite decided yet."

That remark didn't seem to go over well with anyone there—Luz frowned, and Zoe's parents exchanged worried glances, as if they feared the monster was going to show up on their doorstep next. Which Zoe supposed could be a valid concern. After all, they really didn't know why its movements followed the patterns they did, or if there was really any pattern at all. She should probably just be glad that it hadn't decided to appear right in the middle of the mall, or in the center of Phoenix's downtown district. That would require a hell of a lot of explaining...and covering up.

"So it just makes sense," she said quickly, before anyone could present another argument as to why Evan shouldn't play bodyguard. "Unless there's a reason why you need to be back in Jerome right away, Evan?"

A shadow seemed to pass over his face. Since Zoe really didn't know that much about him, she couldn't hazard a guess as to why he wouldn't be eager to return home. But he only shrugged and said, "No real reason. The elders knew I might have to be down here for a while, that this might not be an easy fix. So we can take it day by day."

Day by day. Zoe liked the sound of that. She'd just experienced one of the fullest days of her life.

She knew a lot could happen in a day.

CHAPTER TEN

IT DIDN'T TAKE A ROCKET SCIENTIST TO FIGURE OUT THAT neither Zoe's parents nor her *prima* aunt were completely thrilled by the idea of Evan hanging around, although he could tell that Andrea and Luis were grateful to him for coming to the rescue the way he had. At least his gift hadn't failed him when he needed it most, sending him the twinge that let him know where to find her. However, Evan also noticed how Zoe's parents hadn't put up any further arguments, with Andrea even unbending enough to say that she'd be happy to have Evan come by for a late breakfast before she headed off to help with supervising a remodel she and her husband were having done on his office.

Evan had accepted her invitation because it would have been churlish to turn down the offer. And better to do that than hang around here and keep ordering room service on the de la Paz clan's dime. Now, though, as he lay in bed and stared up at the unfamiliar ceiling of his hotel room, he wondered just how the hell he was going to get through another day in Zoe's company without doing something that might lead them both down exactly the wrong path. He wanted to think he had plenty of self-control, but....

Wasn't this exactly his problem, though? He'd fallen just as hard for Kelly, and almost as immediately, although otherwise the two women couldn't have been more different. You'd think he would have learned his lesson after that first disaster. And it wasn't as if he couldn't be casual about his love life, because his fling with Tina, the waitress from Grapes, had proved that it was possible for him to be intimate with a woman without being crazy in love with her. But it seemed that when a woman with the right chemistry—whatever that was—appeared, his common sense flew right out the window.

Well, at least Zoe was a witch and not a civilian.

The next prima, he told himself. *Off limits. So very off limits.*

He had to wonder, if her parents and her aunt really had started to sniff out something not entirely kosher between him and Zoe, why they'd agreed to this whole bodyguard thing in the first place. Surely the most logical thing to do would have been to thank him for his help and send him packing back to Jerome.

But they hadn't. He had noticed how they'd been very cagey with the healer about how Zoe had broken her arm, hadn't said a single word about the creature their daughter had conjured. That omission seemed to indicate that they really, really didn't want the story getting out to the clan at large. He could see why, as the situation not only showed that their future *prima* was capable of some pretty epic screw-ups, but also that such magic still could be worked and hadn't been relegated to a grimoire, forgotten with the passage of time. Like most witch clans, the de la Pazes were all about maintaining the status quo. They didn't want anything going on that might attract the attention of the non-magical community.

So it seemed mum was the word, and he'd do his best to keep it that way. He certainly had no desire to cause problems for Zoe's family, or for her. One day she'd have to lead those people, and the last thing she needed was a black blot on her reputation before she even got started.

That all sounded very noble. When he shut his eyes, though, all he could see was Zoe's face, the tilt of those dark, dark eyes, the determined set of her mouth as she'd ignored her injured hand so she could confront the monster again. She certainly didn't lack courage, no doubt about that.

Evan knew he'd have to be equally strong. About all he could hope was that they'd come up with a way to get rid of the creature once and for all…and that he'd be safely back in Jerome before Zoe met up with the man who was truly intended for her. Evan thought he could put up with a lot, but he really didn't want to be around to witness her happiness when she eventually found someone else.

That would hurt too damn much.

Saturday morning. Zoe was extremely relieved that it was the weekend, because that way she wouldn't have to worry about manufacturing a reason to miss her classes so she could be with Evan instead. It also meant that Zander would probably take his sweet time coming home from his friend Brad's house. With any luck, she and Evan would be out for the day before Zander even showed up.

Normally, she would have had to worry about her parents being underfoot, but her father was in the middle of a big remodel of his office, and her mother felt the need to be there to help oversee things. Because Luis didn't want his place of business torn up any longer than was strictly necessary, he was paying a lot extra to also have the construction crew come in on Saturdays and keep the work going. So that meant she'd have the whole day unsupervised.

Well, unsupervised except for being with Evan, but that was basically the same thing.

Since she wasn't sure what they might end up doing, she decided to wear jeans and a girly sleeveless top with embroidery around the neckline, and a pair of flats. That should get her through most situations, and she figured she could throw her running shoes and some socks in the trunk of the car, just in case she needed to change into something a little more wilderness-worthy than ballet flats.

The car. What with everything else that had been going on, she'd almost forgotten about her Fiat, still sitting out in the ATV staging area forty minutes from her house. Well, they'd just have to go up there after breakfast to retrieve it. She hoped the Fiat was okay. Evan had sounded convinced that nothing would happen to the car, but he couldn't know for sure. If she'd stopped to think about it, she maybe could have cast an illusion spell to make it look like an old junker, something no one would want to steal, but at the time she'd been too rattled and in too much pain to do much besides get in Evan's car and have him drive her home.

She pushed her worries aside as she finished putting on her makeup and then used a large curling iron to set loose waves in her hair. Nothing too much, just "done" enough that she would look good for Evan.

Stop thinking like that, she scolded herself, but she knew it was only the truth. If she'd only planned to spend her Saturday hanging around the house, she certainly wouldn't have spent so much time on her appearance. But she wanted to look good for him. She wanted him to notice her.

With a sigh, she unplugged the curling iron and set it to one side so it could cool down. One last look in the mirror told her she appeared ready to face the world or, more to the point, Evan McAllister.

Zoe took in a breath then. She had to look cool and unconcerned, or her mother would be sure to pick up on something. Why her parents had even agreed to let her keep working alone with Evan, she wasn't sure, but she had a feeling that they didn't want to make a stink because if they did, they'd only be drawing attention to something they wanted to pretend didn't exist.

After turning off the bathroom light, she went back into her bedroom to pick up the pair of silver filigree earrings from Mexico that she'd gotten on her last birthday, and slipped them into her ears. They were dangly and fun, and she hoped they might catch Evan's eye. Or at least, catch his eye after her mother wasn't around to keep scrutinizing his reactions.

The smell of frying chorizo drifted upward, and Zoe's stomach growled as she hurried down the stairs. She loved the breakfast scramble her mother made with eggs and Mexican sausage and peppers and cheese. It could be on the spicy side, though, and Zoe wondered if Evan would be able to handle the heat. Yes, he was one of the best-looking guys she'd ever seen, but he was clearly pretty white bread, too.

Well, she supposed she'd find out soon enough.

The doorbell rang then, and she felt her heartbeat speed up. That had to be Evan. Almost unconsciously, she reached up to smooth her hair, then hurried over to the foyer so she could answer the door.

Yes, Evan McAllister stood just outside. The morning sun caught his dark red hair and made it look almost as if he had a halo of fire around his head. He'd traded the henley for a plain dark T-shirt, and now Zoe could clearly see the bulge of his biceps beneath the short sleeves.

She swallowed, then said quickly, "Hi, Evan. My mom's just finishing up with breakfast."

A smile that seemed almost as incandescent as the sun. "I can tell. It smells amazing. Is that chorizo?"

"Yes," she replied. "You like it?"

"Oh, yeah. They have some pretty decent stuff at one of the supermarkets down in Cottonwood, but this smells even better."

He came inside then, and she closed the door behind him. Feeling suddenly awkward, she went on, "We'll be eating in the nook off the kitchen. Just the three of us, because my father left a while ago so he could open up his office for the remodeling team. He's not that big on breakfast anyway."

"Seriously?" Evan looked like he didn't quite want to believe her. "When your mother makes food that smells that good?"

"I don't get it, either. But he's always been a toast and coffee kind of person."

A shake of the head, but Evan didn't say anything else as he followed Zoe over to the breakfast nook. Her mother had already set three places on the table, and a pitcher of water and a pitcher of orange juice waited there as well. "Do you want coffee?" Zoe asked. "We made some earlier, but I can start a fresh pot if you want." There. That sounded nice and neutral and hospitable. At least, she thought it did.

But Evan said, "No, thanks. I had two cups at the hotel before I came over here, and that's my limit for the day. Some orange juice would be great, though."

She picked up the heavy blown-glass pitcher with its cheerful speckles of blue and red and yellow, and poured some juice into one of the matching glasses. Just as Zoe was handing the glass to him, Andrea appeared, a big bowl of the egg and chorizo scramble in her hands.

"Good morning, Evan," she said casually, as if having warlocks from other clans over for breakfast was something she did every day. "Did Zoe ask if you wanted coffee?"

"She did, but I'm fine," he replied with one of those smiles that made Zoe's heart go all melty. "Thank you, Mrs. Sandoval."

"Andrea," she responded, looking a little flushed. She set down the bowl of eggs and chorizo, and appeared to gather herself. "So what are you and Zoe planning to do today?"

"Well, first we need to get her car and bring it back here," he said. Clearly, he also thought that task was the most important one to get out of the way. "But after that, I was thinking maybe we should see if it's okay to go up to her Aunt Luz's house so we can look through the books on magic there, see if there's anything we can find that might help us."

Good one, Evan, Zoe thought then. It probably would be helpful to scour the library, look for any precedents, as her father might put it. Also, her aunt's house had to be probably the safest destination Evan could have suggested. All right, Zoe's last visit there had ended in disaster, but if Luz was home, then there definitely wouldn't be a repeat of that particular incident.

And no chance of anything happening between Evan and Zoe. She wasn't happy about that, but at the same time she knew that her wistful fantasies of what it might be like to have him hold her in those strong arms of his, to have him press his mouth against hers and create the spark that would bond them forever, were just that—fantasies. Nothing could ever happen between them.

"That sounds like an excellent idea," Andrea said. "I can call Luz, if you like. Just to make sure she'll be there."

Evan didn't blink. "I'd appreciate that, Mrs.—Andrea."

She smiled, although whether in response to the slip-up over her name, or because she was glad he hadn't tried to argue about going over to the house even if Luz Trujillo wasn't home, Zoe couldn't tell for sure. Her mother could keep her cards pretty close to the vest when she wanted to.

They were silent for a moment as the eggs were dished up, along with homemade pinto beans and sliced fresh fruit. Evan took a bite of his breakfast and nodded in appreciation. "This is amazing," he said. "Thank you so much for inviting me over for breakfast."

"You're welcome, Evan," Andrea said. Something about her expression softened just a bit; she always was a sucker for compliments about her cooking. "I don't do big breakfasts as often as I'd like, since Luis really isn't into that sort of thing. But I thought it would help you two to get off to a good start today."

"It'll probably take about an hour and a half round trip for us to get the car," Zoe put in. She was glad to see the two of them getting along this morning; even though she knew her time with Evan would be short-lived, she'd rather have her mother look favorably on him while he was around. Everything that had happened the day before was not his fault. "So I guess that means we should get to Aunt Luz's house around one or so."

"I'll let her know."

They went quiet again after that, each of them apparently consumed with their own thoughts. Zoe had to keep herself from chattering nervously, of bringing up inane things like what the traffic might be like that morning, or whether her Uncle Jack might return for some more magical defense training. Well, maybe that last wasn't so inane; considering her failure the night before, it seemed obvious enough that she needed a little more help in that department.

She did appreciate that Evan wasn't someone who needed to fill up the silence with chitchat; he ate calmly, helped himself to more food, then asked her mother about the chorizo. If he'd intentionally meant to butter her up, he couldn't have picked a better question to ask, since the chorizo came from a *carniceria* that a de la Paz cousin owned, and a number of the local clan members made it a point to get their specialty meats there when they could.

But at last they'd eaten their fill. Andrea set down her napkin and said, "Well, I told Luis I'd be at the office by ten-thirty, and I'm already running late. Zoe, do you mind cleaning up?"

"No," she replied, although the last thing she wanted to do was postpone driving off with Evan just so she could do the dishes. However, she also didn't want him to see her protest doing a few chores, so she added, "Go ahead, Mom. I'll take care of everything."

Andrea smiled. "Thanks, *mija*. I'll call Luz from the road, let her know you're coming. And thank you, Evan, for taking Zoe out to get her car." She paused, as if she'd meant to say something else and then decided not to. Zoe had a feeling she'd been about to mention how they wouldn't even have to fetch the car if it weren't for her daughter's foolish actions the night before, but luckily Andrea held her tongue.

"No problem," he said. "Glad to help."

She nodded, said her goodbyes, and picked up her purse from where it sat at the end of the counter and headed out to the garage.

After the door had closed behind her, Evan cocked an eyebrow at Zoe. "*Mija*?"

"It means 'daughter,'" she replied. "A term of endearment, I guess."

He nodded. "It's pretty."

Zoe wasn't sure how to respond to that comment, so she said, "Well, I guess I'd better get this cleared away so we can get on the road."

"Let me help." He picked up the mostly empty bowl that had held the chorizo scramble, as well as his empty juice glass, then took them over to the kitchen counter.

"You don't really have to—" she began to protest, but he only shrugged.

"I don't think it's fair to sit here and watch you clean up."

Deciding it wasn't worth the argument, she gathered up the empty plates and her own glass, and deposited them on the counter next to the items Evan had already brought over. He fetched the platter with the cut-up fresh fruit, and she got out the plastic wrap so she could cover the leftovers and put them in the refrigerator. After that, the only task remaining was to rinse the plates and glasses and set them in the dishwasher, which didn't take much time at all.

"Thanks," she said as she wiped her damp hands on the towel that hung from a hook next to the sink.

"How's your wrist?" he asked as he watched.

Had she winced? She didn't think so, because, just as Alba had said, her injury had finished healing itself as she slept. The warmth of the hot shower she'd taken earlier that morning had helped that much more, so Zoe thought she really was good as new.

"It's fine," she said. "I'd almost forgotten about it, actually. But I'll still try to be careful with it."

He nodded, but something about his expression looked vaguely troubled, as if he thought there should be something more to the process. Well, the McAllisters didn't have a healer of their own. They didn't really understand how all this worked in the real world.

"Anyway," she continued briskly, "I need to run upstairs and get my purse, but then we can head out."

"Okay." He hesitated, looking as if he wanted to ask her something else but was vaguely embarrassed to.

She guessed the reason for his diffidence, since that was a matter she also planned to attend to when she went up to her room to fetch her purse. "The guest bathroom is just down the hall, past the living room."

"Um…thanks." He headed in the direction she'd indicated, and she followed him, then kept going to the stairs.

Guys could be so funny sometimes. After all, everyone had to pee from time to time—even witches and warlocks.

There was some Saturday traffic headed toward the casino off Fort McDowell Road, but once they passed that exit, the volume of cars on the 87 northbound dropped a good bit. In direct contrast to his last trip out here, Evan stayed right around the speed limit, knowing that his car attracted enough attention on its own without going like a bat out of hell.

In the passenger seat, Zoe watched the dry landscape go past and didn't seem inclined to say much. Was she replaying her actions of the previous night and trying to justify what she'd done? Or was she trying hard to forget?

He'd noticed the way she'd massaged her wrist a few times as she sat there, as if it still pained her somewhat, even though she'd said she was completely healed. She had pretty hands, small and slender, just like her. Actually, everything about her was pretty, which only served to complicate matters. He liked the way her dark hair hung in long, loose curls, the way the coral-colored top she wore warmed her olive skin.

And he knew he'd better not think about the way her legs looked in those skinny jeans she was wearing....

Her phone *bing*ed, and she pulled it out of her purse and unlocked the screen. "My mom," she said after she'd checked her text messages. "Luz is home today and expecting us, so we can head on over there after we've dropped off my car."

"Sounds good," he said, even though part of him was secretly disappointed that Zoe's disapproving aunt was going to be hanging around. But then, that really had been part of his plan. He'd wanted her there, partly to show everyone that he didn't have any hidden intentions where Zoe was concerned, and partly because he figured that having a chaperone on the premises would keep him from doing anything he might regret later.

She was silent for a moment as she replaced the phone in her purse. Then she said, "So how fast were you going last night when you came to find me?"

"Too fast. About a hundred and five, I think."

Her dark eyes widened. "How fast will this car go?"

"I'm not sure," he admitted, then smiled slightly as he recalled one time he wanted to put the Barracuda to the test. "We don't have a racetrack in Jerome or anything. But one time I was driving from Cottonwood to Sedona—the highway is fairly flat there for a while—I opened her up, just to see. I got up to almost a hundred and twenty before I thought better of it and slowed the hell down. That would've been a pretty expensive ticket."

"That's for sure. Don't you have any McAllisters in the local police, though...just in case?"

"No. We've discussed it, but decided we'd rather just stick to being low profile instead of manipulating the police department from inside."

She didn't seem to like that reply very much; her full mouth pursed slightly, and she lifted her chin as she pretended to be looking out the window again. "So you think we're manipulating things, just by having some of our clan's members in the police?"

Shit. He'd really stuck his foot in it there. "Well, maybe not exactly manipulating. I get it that you're a much bigger clan and have a lot more on the line. And you're in a big city. So...." He pulled in a breath and risked a sideways glance at her. One eyebrow was tilted at an ironic angle, so clearly she wasn't buying what he was selling. "I mean, I know the Wilcoxes do the same thing."

"So now you're comparing us to the Wilcoxes?"

Oh, great. True, the Wilcoxes had come a long way toward redeeming themselves over the past few years, but.... "That's not what I meant—"

She snickered, then shifted in her seat so she could face him. "I'm teasing you. I don't have a problem with the Wilcoxes. I mean, a few of them even came down here to see if they would be my consort."

Even though he knew he shouldn't go there, the words slipped out anyway. Stupid of him to be jealous of those Wilcox candidates, since they obviously weren't Zoe's intended partners, either. But at least they'd had a chance to kiss her. "I guess that didn't work out so well."

Her eyes narrowed. "Maybe not, but it wasn't because they were Wilcoxes."

"I know. Look, sorry I mentioned it."

She lifted her shoulders and settled back in her seat. A few miles passed before she spoke again. "So what's your deal, anyway?"

"My 'deal'?" he repeated, not sure what she meant.

"Well, if you McAllisters are anything like us de la Pazes, you tend to marry pretty young. So why are you unattached?"

The question made him want to wince, even though he knew it was a valid one. Also, he'd detected more than just idle curiosity in her tone. Or at least he hoped he had. "I was married," he said, the words coming out clipped, just this side of angry. He knew he should have controlled his reaction better than that, but Zoe had managed to touch on a sore spot that didn't want to heal. "Now I'm divorced."

"Oh." Her fingers tightened on her purse. "Does that happen a lot in your clan? Just wondering, because we de la Pazes are pretty Catholic about that sort of thing. I mean, my *abuela* never divorced Grandfather, and he—" She cut herself off there, mouth tight. "Well, anyway, it's not really a thing for us."

"It's not really a 'thing' for us, either," Evan said, wondering what had gone on between Maya de la Paz and her husband. Didn't sound good, whatever it was. Strange, because wasn't the marriage of a *prima* and her consort supposed to be all perfect bliss and stuff? "Witches and warlocks tend to stay married. I married a civilian, though."

"You did?" She sounded surprised, although he knew that sort of thing had to happen in the de la Paz clan, just as it did with the other witch families. They needed to bring in new blood so they wouldn't get inbred. "What happened?"

Goddess. He clenched his jaw, then relaxed enough to reply, "It didn't work out. End of story. Okay?"

"Okay," she responded, although she didn't sound okay. Without looking at him, she settled against the seat and crossed her arms.

Perfect. This trip down to Phoenix was just getting better and better. Then again, maybe it was a good thing that they were at odds right now. At least if she was annoyed with him, she would be less likely to act on the attraction that had begun to spark between them.

They drove in silence until he got to the turn-off for the Mesquite Staging Area. He pulled off the highway and headed down the same access road that he'd traversed the night before. Today, though, he saw a couple of dirt bikes zip past, and then when he came to the place where Zoe's Fiat was parked, he had to maneuver around a heavy-set guy in a *Duck Dynasty* ball cap offloading an ATV from the back of his half-ton pickup.

"I was wondering about that," the guy said as Evan and Zoe climbed out of the Barracuda. "Not the best place in the world to leave your car."

"It died on me last night," Zoe said. "So I had to leave it here."

The guy at the truck looked her up and down in a way that Evan didn't like very much. Even though it was barely noon, the man smelled of stale beer. "Well, I suppose that's what happens when you buy that foreign crap."

Zoe's dark eyes began to blaze, and Evan said hurriedly, "It just needed a fuse. So we got one at the dealership this morning and drove back out here. Pop the hood, would you, Zoe?"

She nodded, although her expression was still somewhat stormy. But she didn't say anything as she unlocked the door and got into the driver's seat, then pulled on the hood release. Evan made a show of leaning into the engine compartment, then pretended to fish something out of his pocket and fiddle with the fuse box.

The guy with the ATV watched for a few seconds before he shrugged and went back to his truck, where he closed the tailgate. But apparently Zoe and Evan were putting on a more interesting show; the stranger propped himself up against the rear fender of the truck so he could watch further.

Fine, then they'd continue with this little farce. Thank the Goddess that Zoe knew how to play along. "Okay, try starting it now," Evan said.

She pushed the ignition button. Of course the Fiat fired right up, because there hadn't been anything wrong with it in the first place. "We're good," she called out the open window.

"Great," he told her. "I'll follow you home."

He turned to go back to the Barracuda, only to find ATV Guy blocking his way. "Something I can help you with?" Evan asked. He did what he could to keep his tone as mild as possible, but seriously, right then he was thinking he had had just about enough that day.

"Nice car," the guy said, his gaze moving past Evan to the Plymouth. Then it flicked over to where Zoe sat in the idling Fiat, the sun catching warm sparks from her dark hair as it shone in the open window. "That one, too. Where did you find her? Because she's one hot tamale."

"What?" Evan gritted. Who the hell did this guy think he was? That was the future *prima* of the de la Paz clan this mouth-breather was talking about.

"Your girl. I'm not much for Mexicans, but I think I might make an exception in her case. That mouth of hers looks perfect for—"

Evan's entire body went tense. If this guy didn't quit it, he was going to find out exactly what happened to lowlifes who had no respect for women. "You know, I think you'd better shut up."

The guy rolled his eyes. "Come on, man, I'm paying her a compliment. She's obviously built for it, if you know what I'm saying. Just the thought of that *chica* over there wrapping those lips around my—"

Evan's fist came up before he could even stop to think about what he was doing. It connected with the guy's mouth with a *crack* that seemed to resonate all the way up and down Evan's arm. The guy staggered backward, slamming into the side of his Dodge pickup. Blood trickled down from his split lip.

"Wha da fuck—?" he began, rage blazing in his eyes as comprehension began to trickle into his pea-sized brain. "Ash-hole!"

Well, since he was in it already—Evan swung again, this time catching the guy in the jaw just as he started to push himself away from his truck. The bastard went down this time, that stupid *Duck Dynasty* hat flying from his head.

"Drive!" Evan shouted at Zoe, who'd been sitting there in her idling Fiat, eyes wide as she watched the confrontation go down.

"But—"

"Get out of here!"

He saw her jaw clench, and then she hit the gas, the car's tires throwing out dust in every direction as she peeled away. As soon as she started to move, he ran for the Barracuda and threw open the car door, foot hitting the accelerator before he'd even closed the door behind him. The car leaped forward, tires grinding at the dusty earth and leaving a plume behind him.

Shit. Shit. Goddammit. The members of his clan usually swore by the Goddess, but sometimes you just needed to let a good old-fashioned "goddammit" fly.

At least there hadn't been anyone around to see him take out Mr. Duck Dynasty, but Evan wasn't terribly reassured by that fact. His car was just too damn distinctive. It wouldn't be that hard to describe to the cops. This might be a case where Evan would have to rely on the de la Paz family's connections with the authorities to keep his ass out of jail. He had to hope they had some people in the county sheriff's office, too, although he wasn't even sure which county he was in at the moment.

Out on the access road, and moving fast down the 87—but not too fast. He caught sight of Zoe's Fiat a little bit ahead and let out a relieved breath. She, too, was speeding slightly, although not enough to attract the attention of anyone except the most zealous of state troopers.

Evan scrubbed a hand over his face and then placed it back on the steering wheel. Where the hell had that come from? Yeah, the guy was being a complete ass, but Evan could have just walked away. It wasn't as if he had a history of getting into fistfights.

Well, except for one notable occasion, not too long after Kelly had walked out, when Evan's cousin Dean had taken him out drinking. Some crappy dive bar down in Dewey, which was technically McAllister territory, although no actual members of the clan lived there. Maybe that was why Dean had taken him to the place to begin with. Anyway, a couple of drunk cowboys had started hassling one of the waitresses, and Evan had just exploded. Yeah, part of his rage was probably fueled by the waitress looking just a little too much like Kelly for comfort, blonde and pretty and with the kind of figure that any straight guy would want to stare at. But the cowboys wouldn't leave her alone, and Evan had punched one right in the face before Dean dragged him out of there, casting a spell in his wake that made everyone conveniently forget what either of the two McAllister warlocks actually looked like.

Dean's magic had saved his ass that time. Evan worried he might not be so lucky on this go-round.

CHAPTER ELEVEN

ZOE FELT HERSELF RELAX SLIGHTLY WHEN EVAN'S BIG black car appeared behind her on the highway and then settled in at a comfortably safe distance. Even so, she still couldn't quite believe what she'd just seen.

Obviously, that jerk had said something to set off the McAllister warlock, but she'd been just far enough away—and had the Fiat's motor running—that she hadn't really been able to hear the exchange. She could guess, though. She might not have been able to hear his words, but she'd seen the leer on his fat face as he stared at her. Besides, even though she'd led a pretty sheltered life, it wasn't so sheltered that she hadn't been on the receiving end of comments that ranged from racist to sexist to a particularly vile combination of both.

Clearly, Evan had been defending her honor, and she didn't know quite what to do about that. He wouldn't have done something like that if he didn't feel something for her…would he? She didn't know. He seemed like an honorable person. She had a feeling that he would have punched that guy regardless of his relationship with her, even if they were strangers to one another, because decent guys didn't let jerks get away with crap like that.

Either way, it had been like watching something out of a movie, Evan's fist coming up so fast and hitting that guy right in the mouth, and then in the jaw a few seconds later. It had been so…physical. She wasn't used to that sort of thing.

Her breathing steadied the farther away they got from the ATV staging area. She kept flickering her gaze toward the rearview mirror, certain that she'd see flashing blue and red lights pulling up behind her and Evan. But no cops appeared. True, she'd taken a few measures of her own before driving away, subtle spells that would help to keep Evan safe and make sure he didn't suffer any consequences from his outburst. However, she'd been so panicked that she now worried she hadn't cast the spells correctly.

Eventually, though, they got to the turnoff from the 87 that would lead them back to her house. Zoe eased off the accelerator and drove carefully, making sure that Evan was always behind her. It seemed as if he'd started to figure out his way around, but even so, she didn't want to lose him because of going through a yellow light at the last minute, or whatever.

A few minutes later, they had pulled up to the house. She went ahead and parked in the garage, since she knew they'd be taking Evan's car to her aunt's house. He waited for her at the curb, engine idling in a low, throaty growl. She had no idea that a car's engine could sound so sexy.

Then she climbed into the passenger seat and closed the door behind her. Almost immediately, he had the car moving away from the house, going back the way they'd just come.

For a few seconds, neither of them said anything. Since Evan looked tense and unsmiling, his fingers wrapped tightly around the steering wheel, Zoe figured she'd have to be the one to speak first.

"You want to tell me what happened back there?"

His shoulders lifted slightly, but he didn't relax his death grip on the steering wheel. "The guy was being an asshole, and he wouldn't shut up. I lost my temper. That's all."

"So I guess it's true what they say about redheads," she quipped, although she had a feeling he wouldn't much appreciate the joke.

Another shrug. "Maybe. I really don't make it a habit to go around slugging random people." One side of his mouth quirked the tiniest bit. "It's kind of hard to do that whole witchy 'fly under the radar' thing if you keep getting in fistfights.'"

"You're probably right," Zoe said, relieved that he seemed to be relaxing just a little. She shifted her purse on her lap and added, "And I don't think you need to worry about Mr. Duck Dynasty making any kind of a report. I sort of took care of that."

Now Evan swiveled his head so he could send a quick glance in her direction before returning his attention to the road. "What do you mean?"

"Just a little illusion. Luz is really good at that sort of thing, so she's been showing me how to do it. If that guy was even thinking straight enough to remember our license plates—which I kind of doubt—he would have seen plate numbers that were wrong. Also, I made your car red instead of black, and this one brown instead of blue. So I don't think anyone's going to be able to track us down."

He let out a breath, and a certain tension appeared to leave his shoulders. "Thanks, Zoe."

"No problem," she replied, a little thrill going through her at the appreciation she saw in his expression. Finally she'd managed to do something right. Maybe covering up assault and battery wasn't the best use of her talents, but Evan had only been trying to protect her. He certainly didn't strike her as a violent person in general. Anyway, she thought it was probably a good idea to change the subject. "Do you remember how to get back to my aunt's house?"

"Onto Shea Boulevard from here, right?"

"Right. And then a right onto 120th Street when you get into Scottsdale."

He nodded, and drove in quiet again for a few more miles. Traffic was pretty thick, with people from Fountain Hills heading down into the greater Phoenix area to shop or eat or go to the movies. Right then, Zoe wished she could be indulging in some of those ordinary activities with Evan—maybe a movie, where they could sit next to each other, and maybe she could reach over and take his hand.

Yeah, right. Like that would ever happen in a million years. She supposed she should be glad that they were having such a hard time dealing with the creature she'd summoned. At least this way, continued failure meant continuing to spend time with Evan McAllister, and she sure wasn't going to complain about that.

They'd been so occupied with other matters this morning that she really hadn't stopped to think about it, but she realized she hadn't gotten any sense of the creature today. Even though Evan had intimated the stones couldn't be trusted, she'd still put the lump of black tourmaline in her jeans pocket this morning, just in case. But she hadn't gotten any twinges from it, no sense of where the monster might be.

"Have you felt it?" she asked abruptly.

Evan didn't bother to ask her what she meant by "it." "No," he said. "Nothing. This morning when I first got up and had some coffee, I tried sitting by the window for a while, reaching out to see if I could sense it anywhere, but I got nothing. I'm not sure what to think about that."

"Maybe Jack's banishing spell really did work," she suggested, hoping with all her heart that might be true. But then, if the monster actually had been sent back to its own plane of existence, then Evan would have no reason to be here. So maybe she should only hope for its disappearance with half a heart.

"I don't think so," he said. "I mean, yeah, the spell worked in terms of getting it away from you. But the only way to get rid of it permanently is to reverse the original spell you cast. Otherwise, it's just going to keep coming back." He stopped then and lifted his right hand from the steering wheel to flex it, as if it pained him.

"Did you hurt yourself when you hit that guy?" she asked, unable to keep the worry out of her voice. If he was hurt, he should really see Alba...but then, that would only invite a whole round of questions as to why he'd injured his hand in the first place.

"No, I'm okay," he responded immediately. "It's just a little stiff. It's not going to keep me from doing anything I need to in terms of helping you out, though."

"Good," she said. "I mean, I'm glad you're not hurt." She paused for a second or two, wondering if she should say anything else. But she thought she should really let him know how much what he'd done had impressed her. "That was pretty amazing back there," she added. "I've never had anyone do something like that for me before."

He gave a grim shake of his head. "It was a pretty Neanderthal thing to do, really. It just pissed me off so much when I heard that crap coming from his mouth. Sexist pig."

Her estimation of Evan McAllister went up a whole bunch of notches, even as curiosity spurred her to ask, "What did he say?"

"I'm not going to repeat it. But—you know how it is with witch-kind. We have women in charge of our clans. We respect women's strength. We don't act like women are objects."

"Well, unless you're a Wilcox, I guess."

A grim-sounding chuckle. "Maybe. No, that's not being fair. They have a man in charge, true, but now that Damon Wilcox has been gone for a couple of years, a lot of things have changed with them. I haven't met that many of their clan, but the ones I have met seem like decent enough people. But even Damon Wilcox at least understood that women had their own power, or he wouldn't have tried to kidnap Angela. Or had a female cousin as his confidant for so many years."

Zoe could only nod. She'd heard the stories, of course, but her clan never had that much to do with the Wilcoxes, out of both necessity and choice. Even now that Damon, a dark warlock if she'd ever heard of one, was gone, there still wasn't that much inter-mingling going on between that clan and the de la Pazes. Reaching out to the Wilcoxes to see if one of their men would be a fit consort for her had been pretty much an act of desperation.

She could tell Evan really didn't want to talk about the confrontation, so she decided to let it go for now. She did have one more question, though.

"Do you think that guy learned his lesson?"

Evan's mouth twisted. "Guys like that never learn their lesson."

Luz Trujillo's house looked serene and elegant, with its carefully arranged native plants and palm trees in the front yard. Evan pulled up in front and parked the car, then turned off the engine. As he'd been forced to admit to Zoe, his right hand did feel a lit-tle stiff, but not enough that it should get in his way. Even if it had hurt more than it did, he still wouldn't have complained unless it was outright broken. He really didn't want to be forced to explain to the de la

Paz healer how he'd punched some redneck in the mouth because he was being disrespectful to her clan's *prima*-in-waiting.

Zoe climbed out of the car and Evan followed, glad she was taking the lead. He still felt off-balance from that encounter at the ATV staging area, jangly and not quite himself.

Then again, one could say he'd felt pretty much that way ever since the moment he met Zoe Sandoval.

She rang the doorbell and waited. He stood slightly behind her, not too close, his expression studiously neutral. Luz Trujillo had already been giving him the side-eye, so he didn't see the point in providing her with any more ammunition when it came to her niece.

The door opened. Luz Trujillo looked out at both of them, her expression far more pleasant than the last time he'd seen her. That might have even been a trace of a smile on her mouth as she said, "Hello, Zoe, Evan. Come on in."

They followed her inside, Zoe shooting him a slightly mystified glance over her shoulder as they did so. Clearly, she wasn't quite sure what was going on with her aunt's change of attitude, either.

As they walked, Luz continued, "I brought some water into the library for you. Are you hungry, though? It's past lunchtime."

That whole mess with the redneck had pretty much killed Evan's appetite. He gave a half-hearted lift of his shoulders, and Zoe said quickly, "We ate breakfast pretty late, so I think we're good for now."

"All right, but just let me know if you need anything."

She let them into the library, which was a longish room with bookcases lining the wall and a large light fixture made of wrought iron hanging directly over the round table at the center of the space. Off to one side stood a well-worn leather chair and matching ottoman, and next to it another, smaller chair that didn't quite match, seeming to indicate to Evan that it had been brought in here from somewhere else in the house.

The water Luz had mentioned sat on a tray on the circular table. It did look good, because the bottle of water he'd had in the car had been drunk hours ago.

Zoe said, "Thanks for this, Aunt Luz. I'll let you know if we need anything else."

Her words were friendly, but they were also a dismissal. Luz didn't seem offended, though, but only nodded and went back out into the hallway. Evan could hear the sound of the high-heeled sandals she wore clacking on the tile floors until it eventually faded away.

He also couldn't help noticing how she'd left the door standing open.

Zoe had obviously seen it, too; her eyes flicked there and then back to him, and she shrugged. "Well, we'd better get to work. I figured we could start with going back to the spell I used."

She went over to one of the bookcases and extended a hand. One of the books there came loose from the shelf and floated down into her outstretched fingers, and Evan had to keep himself from shaking his head in disbelief. Yes, he was from a witch fam-ily, same as Zoe, but McAllister talents tended to be subtler ones, the sort of thing you wouldn't notice unless you were really looking for it.

He made sure he kept his expression impassive as Zoe set the book down on the table and then began leafing through it. She went almost all the way to the back before she spread the book open a little wider and pointed to the right-hand page.

As he'd seen before, the handwriting was ornate, almost calligraphy, with a fancy drop capital on the first line. Now, though, he noticed that the leaves in the intricate pattern bordering the spell had been drawn as hearts. Pretty. Really, the whole thing looked very innocuous, like something you'd see on a wedding invitation, but Evan knew better.

"So you know how to speak Latin?" he asked.

"No," she replied. "And it's not like knowing some Spanish helped me any. I had to get one of those language learning courses on my phone to figure out the pronunciation. But now I wonder if that's part of where I screwed up, like I said something wrong and that's why the spell didn't work the way it was supposed to."

Evan supposed that was possible. His clan's spells were a lot more freeform, and so when they went wrong, it was usually more due to intention than because a certain usage wasn't rigidly adhered to. And maybe that was the real problem here. Maybe Zoe had thought she was focusing all of her energy on conjuring the perfect consort, but some part of her had been conflicted, leading to the emergence of the disfigured creature he'd seen instead of the ideal man she wanted.

However, bringing up that hypothesis could be tricky. He'd done his best to avoid talking about her consort search, mostly because the topic was already a sore one with her, and frankly, he didn't like to think about it all that much, either. The last thing he wanted to do was admit to any kind of jealousy, since it was stupid to feel that way about kisses she'd exchanged with men before she'd even met him, but there it was. He did feel jealous, even though he knew he didn't have a chance in hell with her.

But they weren't going to solve this problem by being cautious. If there were hard questions to be asked, then dammit, he'd ask them.

"How about we sit down?" he suggested, and although the request clearly surprised her, from the way her eyebrows lifted, she didn't protest.

"Sure. Want some water?"

That sounded great. He nodded, and she poured him some water from the pitcher Luz had left for them. After he'd taken the glass from Zoe, he went over to the less comfortable-looking of the two chairs and sat down. His choice elicited another raised eyebrow, since the big leather chair would have fit his frame better. But apparently she decided not to protest, because she went to the other chair and sat without comment, her water glass held in both her hands.

He drank, because his mouth suddenly felt dry. Zoe followed suit, her dark eyes curious as she waited for him to speak.

Well, he might as well get to it. "I was just thinking about that spell...what you said about possibly mispronouncing something in it."

"Do you think that's how we'll fix it? By getting it exactly right?"

She sounded hopeful. He really didn't want to dash those hopes, but he also didn't want to lead her on. "Not exactly."

"How do you mean?"

"I mean that what we put into a spell is just as important as the spell itself. I'm starting to wonder if that's where the real problem lies."

His comment made her brows pull together, and she set her water glass down on the small table that separated the two chairs. "So, what...you're saying I screwed it up *on purpose?*"

"No," he replied quickly. Damn it, he'd been afraid she might react this way. "Sort of the opposite, actually. More like...consciously you wanted the spell to work, but underneath there was some part of you that didn't. And because those two parts of your mind and spirit weren't in alignment, something went wrong."

She didn't like that explanation at all. Her entire body stiffened, and her big dark eyes narrowed as she considered the implications of what he had just told her. "I *did* want it," she said, the words clear and cutting. "I would never have tried something so crazy if I hadn't wanted it very badly."

Oh, boy. Evan resisted the urge to run an exasperated hand through his hair. "I know you *thought* you wanted it," he said carefully. "I'm not disputing that at all. But...this was a very powerful spell, one that would require every ounce of your being— mind, body, and spirit—to make it work correctly. Have you ever done anything like this before?"

Her gaze wouldn't quite meet his. "Of course not. No one in my clan's done anything like this for—well, for longer than I can remember. Back in the day we used to be more adventurous, I guess, but with the way things are now, people watching, using cell phone cameras, everything being filmed... it's just not safe. We're witches, but we use the smallest part of our talents, the little gifts that help us get along from day to day but won't attract much attention. I'm guessing everyone in their various clans does more or less the same thing."

"We do," Evan said, in the hope that she'd think he was sympathetic. Well, he was. Hiding their particular talents wasn't necessarily fun, but definitely a better alternative than having their magical natures exposed to the world. "It's just how it is."

"Right. So yeah, it wasn't as if I could ask anyone for help. I read the books here, heard what Aunt Luz had to say about the responsibility of a *prima*, of bonding with the power that lives within me." Zoe put a hand to her chest, as if indicating that was the place where the *prima* gifts dwelled. "I thought about it for a long time. And I decided that I'd be letting down my clan more by not having a consort than by trying to use magic that's forbidden. If it worked, it would have been fine, right?"

"The end justifies the means?"

"You say that like it's a bad thing, but yes."

And in her case, he supposed the end result would have justified whatever methods she'd used to achieve it. If she really had succeeded, she would have had a consort and ensured that her powers would reach their full potential. Evan still couldn't quite figure out how anyone could have a meaningful relationship with a being that had been conjured out of nowhere and had no past, no history, nothing to shape its personality. However, he hesitated to press Zoe on that one point. She'd shown a lot poise and resourcefulness so far in his dealings with her, but she was still very inexperienced when it came to relationships. How could she be anything else? The whole point was to keep the *prima*-in-waiting cloistered and away from any male temptations.

"Okay," he said, choosing his words with care, even though he didn't know if the world's most diplomatic response would be enough here. "I understand what you're saying, Zoe, but I've had to come in and fix a lot of spells gone wrong. In just about every case, it was because the person casting the spell didn't have their energy and intentions focused enough. So that's why I had to ask you about it."

For a long moment, she didn't say anything. She reached over and retrieved her glass of water, took a sip. With the glass cradled once more between her hands, she gazed down into it as if she could use the still waters within as a scrying mirror to help her find the missing creature. When she looked up, the worry in those big eyes with their frame of sooty lashes was almost overwhelming.

"I know," she said quietly. "And maybe that is where I messed up. I wanted to deny it, but…I just don't know. I was so scared. I was standing there"— she pointed toward the table in the center of the room where the spell book lay open—"and for the longest time I just looked at the book and the spell, not sure I could really go through with it. I almost did put the spell book back and leave. But then I thought about how my birthday was less than two weeks away, and how my consort was nowhere to be found, and what would happen if he never showed up…how I'd probably be forced to marry one of my cousins and how I'd never develop all my powers. And so I went ahead and said the spell."

She looked so stricken that once again Evan had to put aside the urge to go over and wrap his arms around her, hold her close and tell her everything would be okay…even if that would be nothing more than a comforting lie. He knew he couldn't do such a thing, though.

Somehow he managed to remain in his seat and meet her gaze, praying the whole time that she wouldn't be able to see anything of the conflict within him. "Well, what you just told me now seems to prove what I was worried about. You thought you were resolved, but some part of you wasn't ready to do this, knew it was wrong. And a spell that powerful has to be committed to completely. It's not your fault," he hastened to add, as her dark eyes began to snap. "You couldn't have known, because no one in your clan had used any magic like this in your lifetime. The things your aunt has been teaching you wouldn't have been enough to prevent it from happening."

Those words seemed to mollify her; she relaxed against the back of her chair and sipped again at her water. "So…if you think that's really the issue, then what can we do now to fix it?"

Good question. He rose from his seat and went back over to the table so he could stare down at the spell again.

Ab umbra ad lucem,
Ad diem ac noctem,
De somnium est re,
Id quod dico

His mind stumbled over the Latin, picking its way through the unfamiliar words. He didn't try speaking them aloud; what he really wanted to do was stare at them, imprint them on his mind, so his own talent could begin to pick away at the Latin phrases and begin to formulate a counter-spell.

A soft waft of perfume, and he realized Zoe was standing very close to him, gazing down at the page as well. She'd never stood this close before, and he could feel himself go still, forcing himself not to react. It would be all too easy to turn slightly, to bend down and touch his lips to hers, run his hands over the long, loose curls in her glossy dark hair.

She said, "It's kind of crazy that something so simple could cause so much trouble."

"I know," he said, the words coming out way too strained. He cleared his throat. "Magic isn't always predictable. That's why it's magic and not science. But I think I'm starting to get an idea of how to fix this."

"But we need the creature."

"Yes." That sounded crazy, but it was the truth. Without the monster she'd summoned right in front of him, he wouldn't be able to use a counter-spell to get rid of it.

Zoe sighed. Trying to act casual, Evan moved away from her and went over to the nearest bookcase so he could inspect the volumes there. He had to hope she'd think he was only looking for another book of magic that might help him in creating a counter-spell. But no way could he keep standing that close to her, even with the door open, presumably to ensure that nothing except research happened in the library.

For that matter, how did he know Luz hadn't been eavesdropping on his and Zoe's entire exchange? No, that didn't seem like her style. Anyway, with those high-heeled sandals she'd been wearing, Evan would have heard her coming back down the hall.

In a way, he would have welcomed a chaperone. Then maybe he wouldn't have been such a mess around Zoe.

She came over to him, but he noticed how she stopped a few paces away, a much more respectable distance than the one she'd put between the two of them just a few moments earlier. "Looking for something in particular?"

"I'm not sure," he said, thinking quickly. "I think I'm getting an idea of where to go, but without the creature around, that's not going to help us much. So I guess I was looking for a book that might have a summoning spell in it."

"That would be back in the same grimoire," she replied, looking over her shoulder to the spell book on the tabletop. "But do you really think summoning it is such a good idea?"

No, he really didn't. He couldn't think of anything else to do, though. The creature had led them on a wild goose chase the day and night before, but today it seemed to be lying low, for whatever reason. Maybe they really had hurt it during that last encounter.

"I don't know," he admitted. "But we need to try something. Otherwise—"

He broke off there, because this time he did hear a pair of high heels clacking down the hallway toward them, moving fast.

Zoe heard it, too, and turned toward the open doorway. In the next instant, Luz appeared there, looking worried and slightly out of breath.

"Jack just called me," she said. "There's been a sighting in downtown Scottsdale, and all hell is breaking loose."

CHAPTER TWELVE

ONCE AGAIN ZOE FOUND HERSELF IN THE PASSENGER SEAT of Evan's car as they drove toward the latest catastrophe. This time, though, her Aunt Luz was following them in her silver Lexus. Zoe would have preferred that she and Evan handle this on their own, but she knew there was no way to prevent the clan's *prima* from coming along to help with damage control.

Jack hadn't said much, only that calls had been coming into dispatch about some kind of deformed-looking man appearing out of nowhere and aggressively approaching young women who had long dark hair. So it sounded as if Evan's first guess had maybe been right, that the creature was trying to get to Zoe and kept going after the wrong targets.

Only…the evening before it hadn't had any problem drawing her out when she was alone. So why hadn't it come for her directly?

She didn't know, and she wasn't sure she wanted to. It was entirely possible that the creature really didn't have any kind of logical game plan, and only kept lurching from one stratagem to another. Last night it had lured her out but had been driven back by a combination of hers and Evan's magic, so maybe it had thought to try again and go back to assaulting helpless young women.

Her cell phone rang, and she dug it out from inside her purse. Her uncle's number showed on the screen. "Hi, Jack," she said. "We're almost there."

"Slight change of plans," he told her. He sounded brisk but not worried, although Zoe knew that had to be a façade, and that inwardly he was probably freaking out. Supernatural goings-on in public places was every witch clan's worst nightmare. "Last sighting was outside the Museum of Contemporary Art. Off Second Street. Can you find it?"

"Yes," she replied. "I'll look it up on my phone."

"All right. Damn thing keeps appearing and disappearing. I don't know what the hell its game is. I guess I should just be glad that so far none of the civilians out there have looked at it as anything except a man with a facial disfigurement and a taste for brunettes."

"I'm sorry—" she began, but he cut her off, saying,

"Don't be sorry. Just get here."

He ended the call, and she hurriedly went to the map application on her phone so she could have it look up the exact location of the museum and guide them in. Luckily, they were less than five minutes away.

"In half a mile, turn right on Second Street," the phone instructed, and Evan gave it a quick glance.

"Where are we headed?"

"There's a museum. That's where Jack said the monster was last sighted."

"Got it."

He sped up, but just a little; they both knew that getting a ticket would delay them far more than obeying the local speed limit. They didn't get too far before they came to another red light, and Zoe cursed under her breath. Behind them, she could see Aunt Luz tapping her fingers on the steering wheel in impatience.

"It's okay," Evan said. "We'll get there."

"I know," she replied. "But will we get there in time?"

His jaw tightened, but he didn't answer. How could he? He didn't have any way of knowing that they wouldn't arrive on the scene before the monster decided to take off again. It could go up the street just a block, or to a different part of town entirely. Maybe it would decide that the hunting might be better at the local mall, not too many blocks away.

In the meantime, all they could do was head toward the last place it had been spotted.

Zoe's phone remained silent, which had to be a good sign. If the creature had taken off, then Jack would have called her with an updated location. If he had one, that is.

They passed restaurants and shops, and then Zoe could see the museum approaching on the left-hand side. She'd been there once on a school field trip years ago, and so she recognized the big blocky building with the distinctive curved wing off to one side.

"There's no street parking," she said, hearing the sharp worry in her tone. "But if you turn right and go around the block, you can park at the civic center. Or you can try. Parking always sucks around here."

His jaw set. "I'll park in front of a damn fire hydrant if I have to. No worries."

He took the corner too fast, wheels squealing slightly. Zoe doubted that anyone noticed, though, because across the way at the museum she could see people running in all directions, fleeing for the street or down the sidewalks.

Looked like the creature was still here.

Luck was with them, because there were two parking spaces right next to each other as soon as they pulled into the civic center parking lot. Evan killed the engine, Zoe stowed her purse under the passenger seat so it wouldn't be in the way, and the two of them took off in the direction from which all the other people seemed to be fleeing. Out of the corner of her eye, she could see her aunt pulling into the empty spot next to the one they'd just occupied, but Zoe didn't have time for anything more than that one quick backward glance. Luz would just have to catch up as best she could.

Parked illegally at the curb in front of the museum was a black Taurus—Jack's unmarked police car. In fact, he climbed out of it as they approached, expression grim.

"I'm doing my best to keep the rest of the department from descending, but if we don't get this contained fast, there won't be much I can do to stop them."

"Got it," Evan said. "Where is it?"

"Down the walkway that leads between the museum and the performing arts center," Jack replied.

"We'll go check it out," Zoe told him, although right then she didn't know exactly what they were supposed to do. Well, all right, by this point they were pretty good at getting rid of the creature, if only temporarily. However, hurling balls of light and reciting spells out loud in such a public place wasn't exactly the best way to avoid attracting attention.

She began to hurry in the direction Jack had indicated, Evan right beside her. As they jogged away, she thought she heard her aunt's voice, and her uncle responding. Zoe couldn't stop to see what else they were doing, though, because she had far more important matters to keep her occupied.

The area ahead of them was empty...almost. Everyone else appeared to have scattered, but she came skidding to a stop when she realized the creature stood there, holding a girl of about Zoe's age by the arm. She hung in his grip like a rag doll, eyes shut, and Zoe gulped in a breath. No, the creature couldn't have—

"I think she probably fainted," Evan murmured as he came to stand close to her. "Just like the first girl."

Zoe had to hope so. She didn't want to let herself think it could be anything worse. For the moment, she could only be somewhat relieved that any potential onlookers had fled the scene. They'd be carrying crazy stories with them, true, but at least Zoe wouldn't have to worry about them watching her throw white fireballs at the monster.

Without really thinking about what she was doing, she stepped forward a few more paces. "Put her down."

The creature, which had been turned slightly away from Zoe, pivoted so it could look her directly in the face. She swallowed but stood her ground. Gazing at it, she saw that the monster had changed again. Really, she didn't know if she could keep calling him a monster at all—yes, his face was still twisted, not yet normal, and yet it was completely distinguishable as human. He stared at her with bright blue eyes full of baffled rage, the unearthly yellow glare of the day before now apparently gone.

"Zho...."

He was trying to say her name again. She knew it. Ignoring Evan's sound of muffled protest beside her, she took a step forward, then another.

"Yes, I'm Zoe," she said. "You were looking for me, weren't you?"

The creature didn't respond, only kept gazing at her. He let go of the girl he'd been holding, and she fell to the ground in a boneless heap, her dark hair spilling across the sidewalk.

Far off in the distance, sirens began to wail. They didn't have much time.

"It's all right," she went on. "No one wants to hurt you. I'm sorry that we had to last time, but we didn't have any choice. It's just—" She faltered there, because she wasn't sure what she should do. He wasn't making any move to attack her, so she certainly didn't feel justified in confronting him physically. And he'd let go of the girl. Zoe hoped with all her heart that she was all right.

The creature's gaze shifted from her, and its twisted mouth pulled into a scowl. In the next second, she knew why. Evan had moved closer so he stood by her side, although he had made no threatening movements.

That seemed to be enough, though. The creature's eyes were blazing. It hated that Evan was there. Because he had helped to dispel the thing the night before? Or was it because its mind had flared with jealousy at the sight of the McAllister warlock?

She had to hope it was the first option.

"You don't belong here," she said quietly. "I'm sorry I brought you here. It was wrong. But now we have to send you back where you came from before anyone else gets hurt."

The creature shook his head. "No."

The syllable sounded almost normal. Zoe shivered, but knew she had no choice but to press on. Next to her, Evan was tense, intently watching the exchange. She guessed he would step in the moment things started to go sideways, but she really hoped that wouldn't be necessary.

And then it moved forward, one hand stretched out to her. "Zho...mine."

She'd shivered before, but now it felt as if someone had just pumped a load of liquid nitrogen into her veins.

"Zoe...." Evan murmured, her name a warning.

"Wait, Evan," she replied in an undertone. But she knew she couldn't make him hold off much longer, especially not with those sirens growing ever closer. She hadn't seen any sign of her aunt, and so Zoe guessed she must have stayed back with Uncle Jack, probably to perform her own subtle spells of damage control.

The creature took another step forward. Now less than a yard separated them, which meant he could easily reach out and grab her if he wanted. Her right wrist twinged, as if in memory of the last time they'd met up.

"No," she said. "That was a mistake. I'm not yours. I'm not—I'm not anybody's."

His distorted features twisted even further as he frowned. She saw the way his chest rose and fell under the ragged dress shirt he wore. Zoe wondered where he'd gotten it, because the last time she'd seen him, he'd had on a pair of too-short dark pants, and that was it.

"Brah...brought me here. You did. For me."

Oh, God. Guilt washed over her then, for what she'd already done to the poor creature, for what she knew she would have to do. She could never be his, but she didn't know how to make him understand that. And although the words were hoarse, uttered in a slurred mumble, as if the tongue that shaped them was too thick for the task, she had understood him well enough.

"I know," she said. "It was wrong of me to do that. This isn't your world. You aren't meant to be here. You need to go back where you came from."

Another of those fearsome scowls, and that penetrating blue gaze shifted to Evan. "His?"

At first Zoe didn't understand the question. Then she shook her head, knowing she had to convince the creature that the McAllister warlock wasn't a threat. "No. Not like that. Just…a friend."

"Friend?" The creature's head tilted to one side, as if he was trying to figure out exactly what a friend was.

"Zoe," Evan said in urgent whisper, "those sirens are getting damn close. You think your uncle is really going to be able to hold back half the Scottsdale P.D.?"

Of course he couldn't. Zoe knew Jack was a high-ranking detective on the force, but even his status would only go so far toward deflecting the situation. With a swallow, she shook her head.

Apparently wishing to take advantage of her distraction, the creature moved forward again. From the corner of her eye, she saw it reach out for her, and Evan swore.

And then his voice boomed with the words of the banishing spell, and the creature took a step back, his face twisted with fury. Zoe really didn't want to hit him with her magic, but she knew she didn't have much choice. She lifted her hands.

"No!" he cried out. "No!" His eyes met hers, despairing.

In the next instant, he was gone.

Evan couldn't let himself relax, because he could hear the crackle of police radios and the sound of heavy feet moving toward them. He grabbed Zoe by the arm and said, "We've got to go. Now."

"What about her?"

All this time, the girl the creature had captured lay unmoving on the ground, still apparently passed out. Without answering, Evan let go of Zoe, then went to the girl and touched her on the wrist. Right away he could feel her pulse, steady and slow and strong.

"She's fine," he said. "She's just passed out. The cops will find her and take care of her. Come on!"

He took off running in the opposite direction from where he'd heard the police radio. Zoe pounded along next to him, although he could tell she was having a hard time keeping up because his legs were so much longer than hers. They kept running along the narrow walkway that separated the museum from what Jack Sandoval had referred to as the performing arts center, then eventually emerged into a parking lot.

"This way," Zoe said. "I know where there's a bar the next street up. We can hide there until the coast is clear."

A bar. Yeah, Evan thought he could use a drink right about then.

He followed her another block, and then into a brick-fronted building. Inside were a few tables, most of which were occupied. But Zoe kept going, to a secluded spot off in a corner. The table hadn't even been bussed yet, the empty glasses from its former occupants still sitting there, but Evan really didn't care. Someone would be along to take care of it, and in the meantime, Zoe had found them a great place to stay under cover until the police left.

"What the hell was that back there?" he asked.

She didn't pretend to misunderstand. "I was hoping I could reason with him—I mean, it."

Evan didn't like that particular slip of the tongue. Yes, the creature had looked even more human this go-round, which meant...what? That Evan's fears of it becoming completely human, and therefore the consort Zoe had wanted to conjure in the first place, might actually come true? "You can't reason with a monster," he said, his tone flat.

"I—"

She was forced to stop there, because the waitress, a woman around Evan's age with flaming red hair, came by. "Sorry about that. Let me take care of it." She gathered up the empty glasses and ran a damp rag over the tabletop. "What can I get you?"

"Cuervo gold margarita on the rocks," Zoe said promptly.

"Cuervo for me, hold the margarita," Evan said.

The waitress smiled. "Got it." Her smile faded, however, as she glanced back over at Zoe. "I.D.?"

Shit. Evan knew Zoe didn't have her identification on her because he'd seen her slide her purse under the seat before they left the car, presumably because she didn't want to be weighed down with it during whatever confrontation might ensue.

But Zoe only offered the woman a smile of her own, right before she said, "You don't need to see my identification."

The waitress blinked, her expression turning glassy. "Oh, that's right. Sorry. I'll go get your drinks now." She turned and walked away, even as Zoe let out a small giggle.

"I always wanted to do that."

Evan stared at her. "Did I just see you pull a Jedi mind trick on that waitress?"

"More or less."

"So…you can control people's minds?"

"Well…." She paused, as if trying to figure out the best way to reply, then said, "It's just a variation of making that redneck out at the ATV area think he saw a red Plymouth Barracuda instead of a black one. Harmless. It's not like I could order that waitress to jump off a roof or something. But when you just need a little misdirection…." The words trailed off, and she shrugged.

"Is that a *prima* thing?" he asked. "Because I know I've never seen Angela pull anything like that."

"Maybe she never had to. But it could be a de la Paz *prima* sort of gift. Powers can vary slightly from clan to clan."

Evan supposed that was true enough. While everyone had their own talents, and there existed a variety that seemed to be shared equally among witch-kind, no matter the clan they'd been born into, each clan also seemed to have its own flavor. The Wilcoxes didn't seem too concerned with whether the magic they worked impacted others, while the McAllisters were all about staying in tune with nature. He hadn't quite figured out the de la Paz angle on things, but it did seem clear enough that they relied more on traditional spells than performing magic in the loosey-goosey way the McAllisters did.

The waitress came back with their drinks. Evan couldn't miss the glint in Zoe's eyes as she thanked the woman for her margarita. The only answer she got was a "sure," so clearly the little mind trick she'd pulled didn't fade away all that fast.

He allowed himself an internal shake of the head, then sipped at his tequila. Part of him really wanted to just bolt the entire contents of the shot glass, but then he'd be left with nothing to drink. Ordering another one wasn't really an option, since he needed to stay functional. This drink was just to settle his nerves after their latest go-'round with the creature.

And the way it had looked at Zoe....

No, he hadn't liked that at all. Not one bit. Yes, she'd brought it here to be her consort, but deep down Evan had thought it would never actually see her as a partner. But he'd heard the longing in its voice.

Damn it, now he really wished he could have more than just the one shot of tequila.

Across the table, Zoe sipped at her own drink, eyes closing in apparent ecstasy as the margarita hit her system. "Mmm, that's good."

"I'll bet. So are we going to talk about what happened?"

Her eyes opened, and she took a quick glance around the bar. For two-thirty on a Saturday afternoon, it really wasn't that crowded, but still, he could understand her reticence. If anyone overheard them....

"Not here," she said frankly. "I just want to have this drink and get my brain together, and then after that I guess we can go back to my aunt's house if you think there's anything you might find in the library that would help."

"I doubt it," he said. "I mean, yeah, I could give it a shot, but I saw the original sp—that is, I saw what you used. I've memorized it. Probably what I really need to do is starting picking it apart, figure out if there's some way to reverse-engineer it, for lack of a better term."

"Okay," Zoe responded, looking somewhat relieved that he didn't want to return to Luz Trujillo's home. "Then it's back to my parents' house, I guess... or maybe we could go to your hotel? It would be more private."

That was for sure. All sorts of red flags went up at the thought of having Zoe alone in his hotel room. As little as he liked the idea of taking her home, he knew he couldn't risk being with her at the hotel. He was tired and on edge, and even though he'd like to think that his self-control could stand up to the challenge, he just didn't know for sure.

"Well—" he began, but didn't get any further than that because his cell phone rang. He dug it out of his pocket, frowned at the unfamiliar number, and decided he'd better answer it anyway.

"Where the hell are you?"

Jack Sandoval, sounding pissed off as hell. "Hi, Jack," Evan said. Zoe sat up a little straighter and wrapped her hands around her margarita glass, looking worried. "We're in a place a few blocks away. We're fine. We just thought it would better to put some distance between us and…you know."

A pause. "You're at a bar."

Was Zoe's uncle psychic? Or maybe he just knew the area really well. "Um, yeah. I figured we'd hang out here for a while, and then I'd drive Zoe home."

She didn't look too thrilled with that comment. One eyebrow lifted, and she mouthed, *Oh, really?* at him and took another swig of her margarita.

"Okay, I'll pass that along to Luz."

"How's the girl?"

"She's fine. The paramedics took her to the hospital for observation, but it looks like she just fainted."

As Evan had thought, but he couldn't help exhaling in relief before he allowed himself another sip of his Cuervo.

Jack went on, "We searched the area but didn't find anything. Got a few statements from eyewitnesses, but so many had fled the scene that there weren't too many people to talk to. And what they said was so contradictory that I'm pretty sure the whole incident is going to get written off as some kind of mass hysteria."

"So we dodged a bullet."

"More or less." The detective's tone sharpened slightly. "But that's no excuse to brush off what happened here. We might not be as lucky next time. That thing has got to be contained before it causes any more trouble."

Evan had to suppress the urge to reply with, *Yes, sir!* Instead, he said, as calmly as he could manage, "We're working on it. I got some valuable information from your *prima*'s library, so I'm sure it's only a matter of time before we get rid of that thing permanently."

"Good. Tell Zoe to take her damn phone with her next time, all right?"

"Um, sure—"

The call ended there, however, saving Evan from having to say anything else. He replaced the phone in his pocket and gave Zoe a sour look. "Your uncle doesn't sound very happy with us."

"Probably just jealous. I'm sure he'd rather be in here having a drink instead of going back to the station and filling out a report."

Well, when she put it that way…. "Maybe you're right. But he's also worried that this is going to escalate if we don't stop it soon."

The half-smile she'd been wearing disappeared. "I'm worried about that, too. You think I want to be the one responsible for the whole world finding out about us? Um, no. But if you have any ideas for how we could be handling this better than we already are, I'm all ears."

She had him there. At least they were able to get rid of the creature every time it showed up. Only… this last time it had almost looked as if the thing had made itself disappear. Yes, Evan had spoken the words of the banishing spell, but Zoe hadn't yet powered up her fireballs. Had the monster taken off because it didn't want to be on the receiving end of a nasty attack from its lady love?

Okay, Evan *really* didn't like the sound of that.

He picked up his shot glass and drained the rest of his tequila. Not bothering to reply to her last remark, he said, "We should get going."

Zoe gave him a pained look. "I haven't finished my margarita."

"Then finish it while I take care of the check."

Her dark eyes flashed fire at his tone, but she didn't reply, only picked up her glass and took a long pull through the straw. He got off the stool where he'd been sitting and went in search of the waitress, who was hanging out on the patio and chatting up a couple of guys in shorts and Sun Devils T-shirts. She looked less than happy about being interrupted, but she did get the check from the receipt book in her apron, then went to ring up the tab at the cash register.

By the time he got back to the table, Zoe's margarita glass had been drained, and she was standing there, arms crossed, as she stared out at the street.

"See something?" Evan asked.

"Not really. I'm just looking at all those people out there, shopping and looking at gallery windows. Having fun." She tilted her head up at him, dark eyes meeting his. Her gaze awoke an unwelcome warmth in him, and he crossed his arms, willing the unruly flush of desire away. "Wouldn't you like to have fun, Evan? You know—go out and act like normal people?"

"We're not normal people," he pointed out, and her face fell.

"No," she said, her voice tight as she turned away and began to move toward the exit. "I guess we're not."

CHAPTER THIRTEEN

ON THE DRIVE BACK TO HER HOUSE, ZOE FORCED HERSELF
to stare out the car window. If she didn't keep her gaze
fixed outward—if she allowed herself to look back
over at Evan—she had the unfortunate feeling that she
might burst into tears.

Some kind of *prima* she was going to turn out to
be.

She tried to tell herself that she was just exhausted
from all this running around, and that this particular
confrontation with the creature had been a lot more
unsettling than she'd bargained for. The last thing
she'd expected was that he—it, whatever—would actually be able to speak to her. Plead with her.

Crap.

And then to have Evan shoot her down like that....
Well, what had she expected? He hadn't come down

here to Phoenix to socialize. He'd come here to clean up her mess.

It was all the margarita's fault. They mixed them pretty strong at that bar, and the tequila had hit her nearly empty stomach like a ton of bricks. If she'd been more in control of herself, she wouldn't have reached out to Evan that way, would have kept things casual the same way they'd always been so far in their interactions.

Problem was, maybe it had been the tequila talking, but she did want to be with Evan like that. She wanted to walk with him in the sunshine, have him hold her hand. Go into a gallery and talk about which paintings they liked and which ones they didn't. She really didn't know all that much about art, but she knew that one day in the not-too-distant future she'd have her own house with her consort, and she'd be able to decorate it as she liked, and that might include choosing the art which hung on the walls.

That is, if she ever managed to end up with a true consort. She very much feared that her family would force her to marry some halfway suitable cousin, even if he wasn't her soul mate, even if he wasn't the one to make her heart sing and her blood hot with hidden fire, just because it wasn't safe to have an unattached *prima*-in-waiting hanging around. Her powers could still be bound to a different clan if she was snatched up the way Angela McAllister had been by Damon Wilcox, or like Matías had tried to kidnap Zoe herself. There was just far too much risk involved to allow a *prima*-in-waiting to remain alone and unattached.

The tear had dripped its way past the end of her nose before she even realized she'd started to cry. In horror, she reached up to wipe at her eyes before any more betraying drops could fall.

Of course Evan chose that moment to glance over at her. His brows pulled together behind the black Ray-Bans he wore. "Zoe, are you okay?"

"F-fine," she managed, but that was all she could get out. She turned her head to look back out the window, where the landscape had dissolved into a smeary blur of tears.

"Zoe."

"I said I'm fine, Evan!" she burst out. "Anyway, what do you care?"

Dead silence. She risked the quickest, tiniest peek at him and saw that now he faced straight forward, his hands clutched on the steering wheel so hard his knuckles showed white. When he spoke, his voice was tight with anger. "That's a hell of a thing to say."

Because she couldn't help herself, she shifted in the seat so she faced forward as well. She couldn't quite bring herself to look straight at him. "It's the truth, isn't it? I mean, you just came down here to help out my clan. My personal problems aren't any of your business, right?"

Another long pause. "Zoe, I know this had been hard for you—"

"'Hard'?" she repeated scornfully. "You don't know the first thing about it. Everybody watching you all the time, making sure you don't do anything that could jeopardize your standing as the *prima*-in-waiting. Having to tell your friends that you belong to some weird religion that doesn't allow you to date, and that's why you couldn't go to prom and why you couldn't have a boyfriend. Everyone on your case so you're Little Miss Perfect, a shining beacon for the clan. It fucking sucks, that's what it does."

During this outburst, he remained quiet and didn't try to interrupt. In a way, Zoe was glad of her anger, because it helped to dry up the flow of tears before they could completely destroy her makeup. She lifted the back of her hand to her eye to mop up the last bit of moisture.

As she did so, Evan said, "I'm sorry. I didn't— well, I didn't know how it was for you. I'm not saying it wasn't tough for my cousin Angela, but she didn't have to go through all that."

"Probably not," Zoe said, repressing a sigh. "Things are a lot more structured in my clan, I think. And for the past year, I've tried so damn hard to be what they wanted me to be. I got rid of the pink in my hair—"

"You had pink hair?" he interrupted, his tone a mixture of surprise and amusement.

"Just a streak. And I stopped wearing my Doc Martens and those band T-shirts my mother hated so much, and I tried to be the good girl they wanted me to be, and what did it get me?" She crossed her arms, glaring out the windshield at the BMW in front of them. It had a vanity plate with the legend "BMRBOY" on it, and right then she wished she was wearing her Docs again so she could plant her booted foot right in the middle of that stupid license plate. "All that, and I still couldn't even get a real consort, just a bunch of guys who didn't know how to kiss."

This time Evan shot her a sideways glance. "They were *all* bad kissers? Every last one of them?"

"Well...." All right, maybe she was being a little melodramatic there. Problem was, she didn't even know how to judge. When you were looking for your consort, either the kiss was a total dud or the next thing to a nuclear explosion. There wasn't a lot in between. "Okay, I don't have much basis for comparison. But is it any wonder I got so desperate? I thought I'd fulfilled my side of the bargain, but the universe sure backed out of its end of things."

"I'm not sure that's how the universe works."

"Maybe not. But...." She let the words trail off there, since she wasn't even exactly sure what she'd meant to say. "Anyway, I'm sorry I lost it. You didn't do anything wrong."

"It's all right. I get it." He paused, then added, "I think we've both got low blood sugar. Why don't we get something to eat before I take you back to the house?"

His tone sounded contrite. And she liked the olive branch he was holding out. That margarita had only woken up her stomach, and she knew she should eat something. Besides, maybe all was not lost. She could have him take her to her favorite place in Fountain Hills, which was pretty and romantic without being too obvious about the whole thing.

Then who knew what might happen?

"We can go to Sofrita," she said.

The restaurant wasn't big, but what it lacked in space it made up in charm. The walls were painted a warm terra-cotta color, and hung with crosses and tin mirrors and wrought-iron candle holders. Since it was the middle of the afternoon, none of the candles had been lit, but Evan saw how it was probably a very romantic space in the evening.

So romantic, actually, that he couldn't help wondering at Zoe's motives for bringing him here, even if it was still broad daylight. But she just chattered away about how she loved the food here, and how it was nice to have something decent here in Fountain Hills so they didn't always have to drive down into Scottsdale to get a good meal.

She ordered sangria, and promptly produced her I.D. when the waitress asked for it. Evan wasn't sure about the wisdom of drinking wine on top of the tequila they'd just had, so he asked for water.

Zoe gave him the side-eye after he made that request. "It's just sangria," she said. "It's not even as strong as drinking plain wine."

"Maybe," he allowed. "But I'm driving, and I can only imagine the look I'd get from your parents if I gave even a hint of being intoxicated when I dropped you off."

"I doubt they'll be home yet," she said. Now that they were seated in the restaurant, she appeared far less tense than she had in the car. He really didn't blame her for breaking down like that, since he couldn't imagine the pressure she'd been under for almost the past year. "When they go to ride herd on the contractors, they usually don't even leave the office until after six."

And it was only three now. Was this Zoe's oblique way of letting him know that they'd be allowed some alone time in the house, in case he wanted to take advantage of that? But no. No way. He wasn't stupid enough to try messing around with the de la Paz clan's *prima*-in-waiting in her own home.

Actually, scratch that. He wasn't stupid enough to mess around with Zoe, period.

No matter what his baser instincts might be trying to tell him.

"Even so," he said. "It wouldn't be very responsible."

"And are you always responsible?"

He shrugged. "Some days more than others."

The waitress showed up then with Evan's water and Zoe's sangria. Because this restaurant was a favorite of hers, he went ahead and let her order, since he wouldn't have even known where to start. She asked for *ropa vieja* tacos and *elote* and a couple of other things he didn't recognize, but it all sounded good.

After the waitress left, he remarked, "That's a lot of food."

"It's tapas-style. Small plates. Anyway, I'm hungry. Facing down that—well, I guess it took a lot out of me."

Evan couldn't argue with that. Now that the adrenaline rush had subsided, he was feeling starved himself. They couldn't talk about what had happened with the monster, since they needed a far more private venue for that, but Zoe's breakdown in the car still bothered him, even if she was now acting as though everything was okay.

He picked up his glass of water and took a large swallow before asking, "Are you going to be all right, seeing this thing through to the end?"

Her brows drew together. "Of course I am!" But her gaze shifted away from him as she lifted her glass of sangria and sipped from it. Her chest rose and fell as she drew in a large breath. Then she went on, "I'm sorry about—about in the car. It won't happen again."

"It's okay if it does," he said, and her dark eyes flared with surprise. "You may be the *prima*-in-waiting, but you're also human. It's okay to flip out every once in a while."

"Not according to my parents or my aunt, it isn't." She fiddled with a corner of the cocktail napkin that had come with her drink. "I'm supposed to be Polly Perfect. And then to screw up this badly—"

"We'll fix it," he assured her, but from the way her full mouth twisted, he had a feeling she didn't believe him.

"So you say. And I know we have to keep trying, but...." She sipped some more sangria. "My birthday is just nine days away now. Nine. That's not a lot of time. And while we're running around trying to fix this problem, I'm not available to meet any candidates."

"There are more?" Evan asked, trying to sound casual. He really hated the idea of Zoe having to kiss a bunch of random guys, even though he knew she didn't have any choice.

"Of course. I mean, she hasn't given me any specific names, but Aunt Luz said something about reaching out to the Castillo clan in New Mexico. I just don't know if she actually did anything about it, because all this crap happened. And I know there are some older cousins from other parts of our territory that she's planning to circle back to, even though she skipped over them before."

Zoe didn't sound happy about any of that, and Evan couldn't blame her. The cousins thing could be strange, but there was nothing wrong with it as long as the relationship was attenuated enough. And of course there were de la Paz cousins down in the Tucson area and along Arizona's southern border with Mexico, people she probably didn't know very well, if at all. It wouldn't be like asking her to marry someone she'd grown up with.

The Castillo comment did surprise him, just because he'd always heard that the New Mexico clan was in bed with the Wilcoxes, for whatever reason. But now that relations with the Wilcoxes had changed so much, maybe the Castillos weren't off limits anymore. Obviously, because of what had happened with Matías Escobar, the Santiago clan in

California was off the table when it came to possible consorts.

Of course, Evan didn't like the idea of any of them being with Zoe, no matter what her aunt or her parents might think of the new candidates they were trying to find. But he knew he couldn't say that, couldn't act as if he had a vested interest in whoever her consort turned out to be.

"But," she went on with a sigh, "I don't think Aunt Luz wants to approach any of them until our little problem gets fixed one way or another. Too much explaining. I know she's trying really hard to keep the other members of the clan from finding out."

"Except your Uncle Jack."

"Well, he was sort of necessary, especially since he needs to be around to help keep things contained as much as possible. Anyway, he's a cop. He knows not to go spreading stories."

Probably not. Jack struck Evan as a no-nonsense kind of guy, definitely not the sort of person you'd ever suspect was actually a warlock. "He seems cool."

Zoe's face lit up, erasing some of the strain that had lent too taut an edge to her features. "He is. He's my favorite uncle. Even though he's a cop, he doesn't take things too seriously, you know? It's kind of a relief when so many other people want to act like the fate of the world is resting on my shoulders or something."

Maybe not the weight of the whole world, but definitely that of her clan. Luz Trujillo was a vibrant woman in the prime of her life, but accidents could happen. He thought of Angela's mother dying in that motorcycle accident, leaving his own clan without a *prima*-in-waiting for years until Great-Aunt Ruby declared that Angela would be the one. But if something had taken Ruby away from them before Angela's status was determined...well, he really didn't want to think about that. A clan without its *prima* was vulnerable to outside attack. Such things hadn't happened for years, but they had in the distant past, back before the McAllister clan had even settled in America. So he could see why Zoe felt as if she carried far too heavy a burden.

He also thought that Jack Sandoval seemed serious enough, but Zoe was his niece; she knew him far better than Evan did. Also, it was distinctly possible that Jack had put on his no-nonsense cop face around Evan because he wanted to make it abundantly clear that he didn't have much patience for McAllister interlopers messing with his clan's future *prima*.

"I'm glad he's on your side," Evan said, hoping that sounded neutral enough.

If Zoe detected any subtext to the comment, she didn't show it. She only nodded and sipped at her sangria.

And then the waitress was there with their food, and Evan was able to fall into a companionable silence while he and Zoe dug in, sending their over-taxed bodies the fuel they so desperately needed. After a few minutes had passed, though, she slowed down and wiped her fingers—greasy from the tacos—on her napkin and looked across the table at him, expression earnest.

"Thank you," she said. He lifted an eyebrow, and she went on, "For everything. For sticking with this. For not freaking out when I freaked out. For...not thinking I'm a complete loser."

"I don't think you're a loser," he said. It felt so hard to hold her gaze, but he knew he couldn't look away, that any evasion might be far more telling than looking at her directly now. "I think you're doing the best you can in a very difficult situation."

A small flush colored the warm olive skin of her face. "Even though I caused that situation in the first place?"

There was a thornier question. He dug a tor-tilla chip into the *elote*—corn dip with spicy mayo and crumbly Mexican cheese—and took a bite so he could sort out his thoughts before he replied. "Do I think it was the best idea in the world? No." Her mouth tightened, and he quickly added, "Do I get why you did it? Yeah. I do. When you feel like you're backed into a corner, you don't always make the right choices."

"Were you backed into a corner with her?" Zoe asked.

For a few seconds, Evan couldn't understand what she was talking about. Then he realized she must be asking about Kelly. He'd avoided the subject ever since Zoe's one abortive attempt to bring it up, but he could tell she was curious.

What the hell. He wouldn't lie. Zoe had been more than honest with him, and so he thought she deserved to have the favor returned.

"No," he said, wishing right then that he'd ordered some sangria for himself. Since at least it would help with his suddenly dry throat, he swigged some water. "I walked right into that of my own accord. I fell for my ex, even though I knew that relationships with civilians could be tough. You have to be so, so sure of them, you know? Because it's not just your relationship at stake, but the safety of your clan."

"Because if things go south, then they could tell everyone what they know."

"Right. Well, things did go south—Kelly's from Phoenix, and she didn't like living in the Verde Valley. Oh, at first she was enthusiastic about how different everything was, but when she realized she couldn't go to what she referred to as a 'real mall,' or drive down to Phoenix whenever she felt like it to hang out, then she started to get resentful. She started trying to convince me to move, which of course was impossible. None of us are free to go wherever we want, whenever we want."

Zoe gave a sympathetic nod. "Don't I know it."

"Right. So when she realized she couldn't get me to move out of Cottonwood—and I'd done that for her, bought a house there and everything because my flat in Jerome was way too small—she started just taking off for Phoenix whenever she could. Said that maybe I was stuck in the Verde Valley, but that didn't mean she had to follow those same rules." He drained the water in his glass and hoped the waitress would be back around soon for a refill. His throat was parched. "Turns out she was seeing a divorce lawyer down in Phoenix. And sleeping with him."

Eyes wide, Zoe said, "Oh, God, Evan. I'm so sorry."

He shrugged. The pain now felt far away and mostly scabbed over. "In the end, I think she did me a favor. At least she bailed out early before we'd started a family. But it cost the clan a lot to make sure she wouldn't talk about us, and that's the part that really sucks."

For a long moment, Zoe didn't reply, only sat there in sympathetic silence. Then she said, "My grandfather cheated on my grandmother. A lot."

It was Evan's turn for his eyes to widen. "On *Maya?*" Maybe that was a stupid question, but his brain couldn't quite grasp the notion of a consort cheating on his *prima*. That sort of thing wasn't supposed to happen, was it? What about their soul-bond?

Zoe nodded. "Yes. They tried to hide it as best they could, of course. Divorce was out of the question. *Primas* don't get divorced. So my *abuelo* had I don't know how many girlfriends, almost right up to the point when he died of a heart attack. He didn't even live with my grandmother—he moved into his own house as soon as my Aunt Luz made her match with Uncle David, which was way before I was born, obviously." She picked up a chip and scooped up some *elote,* but just held the tortilla chip between her fingers, as if she wasn't sure what she'd meant to do with it. Her shoulders lifted, and she added, "So I guess what I'm trying to say is that all our clans have had some weird relationship stuff go on. I don't think Grandfather ever said anything about being a warlock to any of his girlfriends, though. He was indiscreet, but not *that* indiscreet."

Evan wondered if anyone in his own clan knew about Maya's history. He doubted it, though, because it certainly wasn't the sort of information the former *prima* of the de la Pazes would have wanted to get out in the world. From what he'd heard, she was one tough woman, and admitting that she was married to a serial philanderer would have seemed like a sign of weakness.

"I'm sorry, Zoe," he said.

"It was a long time ago. It didn't really affect me that much. Just sort of the way things were, you know?" Finally she did eat the chip and *elote*, chewing contemplatively. "Aunt Luz and her husband— they're happy. My parents are happy. So I know it was just one of those things that happen. But...." She trailed off, mouth pursing as if an unpleasant thought had just occurred to her.

"But?"

Those dark eyes of hers were so deep that he wondered if he might drown in them. "But I can't help thinking that might have had something to do with what I did. That in the back of my mind, I knew this custom of matching a *prima* and her consort wasn't infallible, and that's just another reason why I decided to take matters into my own hands."

Not sure what he should say, Evan only offered a grim nod. Because when she put it that way, who could really blame Zoe for what she had done?

CHAPTER FOURTEEN

WELL, MAYBE IT HADN'T BEEN QUITE THE ROMANTIC MEAL she had hoped for, but Zoe felt a thousand times better as she climbed into Evan's car so he could drive her home. Her sense of well-being didn't just come from a full stomach, but from a feeling that they'd done a lot to clear the air between them. He'd told her the truth about his ex-wife—and what a wench she sounded like—and Zoe had spilled a few secrets of her own.

And even with all that, he was still here, hadn't shown any sign that he planned to take off for Jerome and leave her to sort out her own mess. No, it was clear to her that he would stick by her until they sent the creature away for good.

During the meal at Sofrita, she'd been half expecting her phone to ring again, to have her uncle call and tell her that there had been another sighting and that she and Evan had to drop everything and come take care of it. She'd also worried that Aunt Luz might call to find out where she was, but that hadn't happened, either. No, they'd been left blessedly alone to enjoy their meal. Maybe her aunt was still busy dealing with the aftermath of the creature's appearance in downtown Scottsdale and didn't have time to be checking on Zoe every damn minute.

Evan pulled into what she now thought of as his usual place in front of the house. She noticed how he never drove up into the driveway, even when he must know there wasn't anyone at home for him to be blocking with his car.

"Well," he said, and paused.

"Well," she echoed. This was awkward. Should she invite him in? No, she knew he wouldn't come inside, not when it would be just the two of them alone in the house. It was one thing to be off together in fairly public places, but.... "Thanks for the margarita."

He grinned, hazel eyes lighting up. She liked to see him like that, because a lot of the time he looked too damn serious, as if he was the future *prima* with the weight of the world on his shoulders, not her. "Thanks for lunch."

Because she'd insisted on paying, since it was her idea to go to that particular restaurant. The only reason she'd let him pay for the margarita at the bar in

Scottsdale was because she'd left her purse shoved under the passenger seat in his car. "No problem. So you're going back to the hotel?"

A nod. "If that's okay. Your aunt made it seem as if my reservation there was kind of open-ended...."

"Oh, that's for sure. She wanted to make sure you'd have someplace to stay until this was all settled. So I guess...call me if you get a twinge, and I'll do the same." Back at the restaurant, they'd made sure to get each other's numbers safely stored in their phones. And he also had the number for the land line at her house, just in case.

"Sounds like a plan."

Since she knew it would only feel weirder if she lingered, she smiled, said, "'Bye," and shut the car door behind her. She'd expected to hear him drive away immediately, but instead he idled there, watching to make sure she got inside the house okay. Only then did the sleek black car move away from the curb and head back down the hill.

Zoe watched until he was gone, and then she locked the front door behind her. Her footsteps echoed on the tiled floors, the house silent around her. So, as she'd thought, her parents were still down at her father's office. When they got home, they'd probably get more takeout, maybe pizza this time. Her mother never felt like cooking after a marathon with the contractors.

And Evan would go back to the hotel, and...
what? Watch TV? He didn't seem like a television
kind of guy. Hang out by the pool? The weather
was definitely warm enough for that, but she kind
of doubted he'd packed any swim trunks for his trip
down here. Even so, she couldn't help imagining
what he might look like with his shirt off. His chest
and stomach must be just as well-muscled as those
arms of his. A delicious little thrill went through her
at the thought, and she sighed.

"Hey!"

Adrenaline shot through her and she whirled,
only to see her brother Zander leaning up against
the opening off the main hallway that led into the
kitchen. "Goddamn it, Zander!" she snapped. "Do
you always lurk around like that so you can sneak up
on people?"

"I wasn't sneaking," he said, grinning, clearly
pleased that he'd gotten the jump on her. "You were
staring off into space, all moony-eyed."

She wanted to tell him he didn't know what he
was talking about, but she had a sinking feeling that
she'd probably looked exactly the way he'd described
her. Moony-eyed, and thinking of Evan.

So because she didn't have a proper rejoinder,
she just said, "Whatever," and pushed past him into
the kitchen so she could get a glass of water. Maybe
Zander would decide she wasn't worth baiting and

would head up to his room, or at least to the family room so he could turn on the TV.

Unfortunately, he didn't do either of those things. Instead, he followed her into the kitchen and leaned up against the counter, watching her. Leaning. He did a lot of that, like he didn't have the energy to stand up under his own power. For all she knew, he didn't. He'd shot up something like five inches in the last six months, and that had to be exhausting.

"Who was in that car?"

"What car?" she asked, playing dumb.

He raised an eyebrow. She hated that now he was a lot taller than she. In the past, she'd been able to intimidate him with the big-sister thing because she was so much older and could look down at him or at least meet him eye to eye, but no more. "The car that just dropped you off, *pendeja.*"

"Mom'll kill you if she hears you talking like that."

"Maybe." He shrugged. "But she's not here right now. So what's with the car? I don't know anyone in the clan who has a car like that."

He would know, because if there was anything Zander was more obsessed with than video games, it was cars. Since she knew it would come out eventually, she said, "It's not anyone from our clan. The car belongs to Evan McAllister."

"McAllister, huh?" Zander crossed his arms and gave her an inquiring glance. "What's he doing here?"

"Helping," she said shortly, then went to the cupboard and got down a glass.

"Helping with what?"

"Clan business." She shoved the glass under the water dispenser in the refrigerator door, then pushed the button so water would begin to flow.

"What kind of clan business?"

"The kind of business that isn't any of your business."

"Says who?"

"Says me," she retorted. God, she hated how almost all of her conversations with Zander seemed to devolve into her acting like a fourteen-year-old as well. Talk about bringing people down to your own level. "And since I'm the *prima*-in-waiting, that means you need to leave it alone."

"Huh," Zander said. "Big deal. A *prima* without a consort."

She turned away from the refrigerator so she could glare at him properly. "Shut. The. Fuck. Up."

Then she stalked past him, glass in hand. He was giving her his best icy stare of death as well, but since she was used to that, she ignored him and headed up the stairs so she could lock herself in her room and get herself some privacy. Thank God Evan hadn't been around to hear that particular exchange—he'd be counting himself extra lucky that he didn't have a chance of getting involved with someone so immature.

She slammed the door and touched her hand to the knob, willing it to lock itself in place until she was ready to release the spell. Her parents hadn't been too pleased with that particular trick, especially since neither of them was a powerful enough user of magic to break through the minor enchantment.

A quick glance at the clock on the wall told her it wasn't quite five. So her parents probably wouldn't be back for at least an hour. She could open up her laptop, surf around, see if Amber was on Facebook so they could chat or something. Yes, she could have done all that on her phone, but it was so much easier with a bigger screen.

But the idea of passing the time with such mundane activities wasn't very appealing. She felt like she should be doing something. Anything. Unfortunately, she really didn't have an idea as to what that "anything" should be, since the creature had disappeared back there in Scottsdale, and she hadn't gotten a single twinge as to its whereabouts since.

Okay, but where was it written that she had to wait for it to appear again? She'd brought the thing here—surely there had to be some way she could reach out to it on her own.

No, that was dangerous. She didn't have any idea what would happen if she attempted that kind of spell. With her luck, she wouldn't even draw the creature to her, but instead would bring a whole other monster to this particular plane of existence.

That idea made her shudder. No, they definitely had their hands full enough already. Hard as it was, it seemed as if waiting was her only option.

She just wished she could be waiting with Evan.

Her phone chimed, a new text message coming in, and she pounced, hoping against hope that it was Evan reaching out to her to let her know he was just as bored as she was.

Of course not. The text was from her Aunt Luz. Zoe frowned a little at that, because in general, her aunt was the type of person to call, not text. When she read the message, though, Zoe's frown only deepened.

So sorry—with everything going on, forgot that I'd set up your cousin Carlos to meet you and see if he would work out. He just called to say he was almost to the house. I'm on my way, too—I'm trying to get there before he does. Hang tight.

"'Hang tight'?" Zoe repeated out loud in disbelieving tones. "Why didn't you just tell him to turn around and go home, that I was sick or something?"

Her words hung in the empty air, because of course no one else was there to hear them. She started to text back angrily that she wasn't going to see anyone, least of all this Carlos person, but then stopped herself. Getting into an argument with Luz via text message wouldn't change anything. Besides, if he was almost to the house, there wasn't that much they could do except let matters run their course.

Since she didn't know of a Carlos in either the Phoenix or Tucson branches of the family, Zoe assumed he had to be one of her distant cousins from the southern part of the state. That actually made her feel a little better, since at least Luz wasn't scraping the bottom of the barrel by trying to make her kiss a guy she'd known since kindergarten.

But still…Zoe didn't want to kiss anyone who wasn't Evan McAllister. The mere thought made her flesh crawl, although she knew she would do what was expected of her. A *prima*-in-waiting didn't have any choice.

So she texted back a short *okay,* and then went into the bathroom to brush her teeth and smooth her hair, as well as to repair any damage her outburst earlier might have done to her makeup. She wondered if she should change out of her jeans, then decided she was tired and didn't feel like worrying about it. This Carlos person would just have to deal with her looking a little more casual than usual.

Because Luz hadn't really given her a timeline, Zoe decided she'd better wait downstairs. The last thing she needed was Zander being his usual jerk self to the latest in a very long line of candidates. He seemed to find the situation entirely too amusing.

When she descended the staircase, however, she was relieved to find that he'd disappeared. Probably went up to his own room to play more of his useless video games, once he realized she wasn't going to hang around and get teased unmercifully.

The house was immaculate, as usual, and so Zoe didn't have to worry about tidying up. Just as well, because she had plenty of other matters to keep her worried—having to deal with cousin Carlos, whoever he was…she briefly thought about trying to find him on Facebook and abandoned the idea once she realized she didn't know for sure if de la Paz was also his last name; stressing because now that she'd met Evan, she didn't even know if she would have the guts to kiss another candidate; the low-lying fear in the back of her mind that the creature might get brave enough to appear in her own house, although she wouldn't know why he would do such a thing now when he seemed to be making a habit of cruising around the greater Phoenix area instead.

And the thing that bothered her the most right now, besides having this latest candidate show up at all, was that Zoe might very well have to meet him alone. Yes, Luz had said she was on her way over, but she hadn't been terribly specific about her arrival time. Since a *prima*-in-waiting always lived at home until she met her consort and got married, it was easy enough to make sure that someone was around during these meetings. But Luz wasn't here yet, and Zoe's parents were half an hour away at her father's office in downtown Phoenix. All right, she couldn't say she was completely alone, since Zander was upstairs in his room. However, Zoe didn't really consider him an effective chaperone, and although she didn't *have* to have someone overseeing her meeting with a prospective consort, one of her parents had always been present before. It felt weird to have a candidate coming over now when both of them were gone.

At that inopportune moment, the doorbell rang. She sucked in a breath, then ran her hands over her shirt front to help smooth away some of the wrinkles she'd gotten from the seatbelt while riding around in Evan's car. Then she went to answer the door.

She didn't recognize the man standing outside, of course, but she knew he must be Carlos. Older than most of the other candidates, as she'd expected, just because she'd already run through every eligible warlock who was under twenty-five.

He was attractive enough. Not drop-dead gorgeous like Evan McAllister, but if she'd met Carlos before she'd met Evan, she would have thought he was just fine. Definitely above the median when it came to her consort candidates. No, Luz hadn't sent her anyone who was downright ugly, but Carlos was tall and well-built and had nice, regular features, the kind of good looks you might see in a TV commercial or in a local television reporter.

"Hi," she said, and offered a smile, just because she knew she had to appear pleasant and friendly, even if she really wanted to flee to the garage, climb in her car, and speed off to where Evan was staying at the CopperWynd resort. "I'm Zoe."

"Carlos Reyes," he replied, although he didn't smile back, only looked her up and down like something displayed in a glass case.

Uh-oh. Not the sort of response she'd been expecting. A creepy-crawly sensation began somewhere at the base of her neck, although Zoe tried to tell herself that she was already on edge, and so was probably overreacting. Maybe this Carlos Reyes just wasn't the friendly type. Or maybe he'd been pushed into coming up here to see if he might be her consort, even though he had no real desire to do so. She had to wonder why he was still single. In general, witches and warlocks married fairly young because of their ability to recognize their own soul mates, and so to have someone who was still unattached in their late twenties tended to be unusual, if not entirely unprecedented.

"Come on in," she told him, since she couldn't exactly leave him standing there on the doorstep.

He entered the foyer and gave it a quick, unsmiling glance. Zoe had no idea what that dispassionate inspection meant. Was he impressed? Turned off by the mini-mansion style of the house?

Well, when in doubt, forge ahead.

"So, where did you drive up from?" she asked.

"Sierra Vista," he replied, which didn't tell her much at all. She knew the town was way south of Phoenix, down near the grape-growing areas that supplied so much of Arizona's wine, but that was the extent of her knowledge when it came to Sierra Vista.

But since she at least could guess that he'd driven a couple of hours to get here, she ventured, "Do you want some water, or some iced tea?"

"Water would be great."

Thank God. Something to occupy the next minute or so, during which time she prayed fervently that Luz would show up. Yes, Zoe knew she'd have to kiss this unsmiling stranger eventually, but she really, really didn't want to do it without the *prima* around.

She made a show of fetching a glass and filling it partway with ice, then dispensing water so the glass was mostly full. Still wearing a fake smile that she knew she would have hated if she'd been able to see it for herself, she handed it to Carlos. "So, what do you down in Sierra Vista?"

He shrugged. "Grow grapes. We sell them to a bunch of the wineries around there."

As she'd suspected. He didn't sound very thrilled about it, though. Was he hoping that by becoming her consort, he'd be able to come here to Fountain Hills and live a life of relative luxury?

She couldn't tell. Most of the time she could get a read on people by watching their expressions, paying attention to the tone in their voices, but this guy was like a blank wall. Evan was intense, not exactly what she'd call lively, but she could still tell that he cared about things—probably cared too much, which was why his ex had done such a number on him.

And she knew she shouldn't be comparing Evan to Carlos. She'd just met Carlos. Some people didn't let it all hang out on first meetings, even if that meeting did involve kissing someone who was next thing to a stranger.

"Luz should be here soon," Zoe said quickly, and something changed in his expression, something she couldn't really put her finger on but made that creepy sensation return to the base of her neck. "Why don't we go into the living room?"

"Sure," Carlos replied, and followed her as she led him out of the kitchen and around the corner to the living room.

It was a formal-feeling space, with cream leather couches and glass and bronze tables and light fixtures. Every time Zoe went in there, she worried she might leave a smudge, but she figured Carlos couldn't do too much harm with just a glass of water, even if he did commit the cardinal sin of setting his glass down on a table without using a coaster. Anyway, she hoped that the uptight vibe of the room would keep him on his best behavior until Luz showed up.

Shouldn't she have been here by now? Zoe wondered if she could come up with an excuse to run upstairs and get Zander down here. Her little brother was annoying as hell, but better some kind of buffer than none at all. It was a sign of Luz's desperation that she'd allowed Carlos to come over even though she knew Zoe would be alone, except for her brother's presence.

"Um, we can sit down here," she ventured, but Carlos shook his head.

"That's all right," he said. "I've been driving and sitting down for the past couple of hours. Mind if I take a look outside?"

"No, it's fine," she replied. Was that better or worse? At least outside she wouldn't have to worry about messing up her parents' living room, but on the other hand, it felt as if they'd be more isolated out there. Would she be able to hear the doorbell from the backyard?

To cover up her unease, she went over to the sliding glass door and unlocked it, then closed it again once both she and Carlos were outside in order to prevent any of the air conditioning from escaping. After the cool confines of the house, it felt uncomfortably warm outside, although she knew it wasn't really that hot yet, nothing like how it would be in a few more months and the brutal Phoenix summer really descended.

At least it wasn't too bad out on the covered patio, which protected her from the worst of the sun, although Carlos wandered out into the sunshine so he could walk along the edge of the infinity pool. Zoe had to admit it was sort of impressive the way it seemed to just drop off to the edge of the sloped yard, even though she knew it was only an optical illusion.

He paused down near the end with the spa, then lifted his hand to shield his eyes from the sun as he looked across the pool to the casita she used as her lab. "What's that?"

Since he was really too far off for her to have a casual conversation with him, she reluctantly stepped out from the shelter of the patio's roof and went over to where he stood. "The pool house, but I use it for my workroom."

"Workroom?" His dark eyes were intent as he studied her face. Thank God she wasn't the type to blush easily.

"My talent is potions," she explained. Obviously, he didn't know anything about her. Although, why should he? It wasn't as if he lived someplace where he would have many interactions with the branches of the clan here in the Phoenix area. Probably he knew her name and that she was the *prima*-in-waiting, and that was about it. "I sort of took over the pool house so I'd have a place to work."

"Ah." He seemed to mull over that response, then asked, "Can I see it?"

Zoe didn't know why the question would make her uncomfortable. Really, she should be happy to show him her workspace, since that would kill some more time and give Luz more of a chance to appear. And she hadn't minded having Evan in the lab....

Because it was Evan, she thought. *Even though you'd just met him, you knew there was something special about him.*

But she shouldn't be letting herself think things like that. Mooning over him definitely wouldn't help her right now.

"Sure," she replied, and hoped Carlos hadn't noticed the way she'd hesitated. "Come on. I'll show you."

She went over to the door to the pool house and laid her hand on the knob so it would unlock itself. Inside, the air was stuffy and hot; since she'd known she wouldn't be working in here today, she hadn't bothered to turn on the A/C. The remote for the ductless unit lay on the worktable closest to her, so she picked it up and powered on the air conditioner, even though she wasn't sure they'd be in here long enough for it to make a difference.

Carlos stepped inside and looked around, although his expression didn't betray any particular curiosity. "What kind of potions?" he asked.

"A little bit of everything," she replied with a shrug. "Cures for colds, the flu. Draughts for arthritis, to regulate blood sugar levels for clan members with diabetes. Hangover cures," she added with a grin, hoping maybe he'd finally smile back at her.

But he didn't. He just gave a small nod, his attention apparently fixed on the bunches of herbs hanging from the walls. Who knows—he worked in agriculture, if in a sort of specialized branch of it, so maybe he was trying to identify some of the plants. Then he turned toward her, eyebrows raised slightly. "Love potions?"

Yikes. Was he asking in case he needed one to warm up to her? So far he hadn't shown any signs of attraction at all. Not that she'd really expected him to drop to his feet and declare himself overwhelmed by her undying beauty, but still....

"No," she said. "That sort of thing is off limits. So much can go wrong." She stopped there, mouth twisting slightly. Too bad she hadn't heeded her own advice when it came to conjuring that creature. Yes, the spell she'd used wasn't exactly a love potion, but it did have basically the same desired outcome, when you stopped to think about it. "I think some people still make their own, but if they do, it's not the sort of thing they advertise, if you know what I mean."

"I suppose so." He didn't say anything for a moment, just stood there, still watching her with that vaguely unsettling expression on his face.

Madre de dios, they'd really scraped the bottom of the barrel with this one. Zoe cleared her throat and said, "Well, I guess we'd better go back inside. It's a lot more comfortable there. I—"

She'd been about to say, *I'm sure Luz must have gotten here by now,* but the words didn't have a chance to escape her lips, because Carlos grabbed one of her hands and propelled her toward him, and then his mouth descended on hers.

By that point she'd kissed so many guys that she was more or less inured to the process. She'd known Carlos couldn't be the one, so she figured she'd let him kiss her and get it over with. His behavior was abrupt and more than odd, but oh, well.

To her dismay, however, when she went to pull away from him, his grip on her wrist only tightened. His tongue was probing her mouth, and she wanted to gag. She managed to tear away for a second or two, just long enough to gasp, "Let go of me!"

But he didn't. He grabbed her with his other hand, and he kissed her again, forcing her mouth open. Did this *pendejo* have any idea what kind of trouble he was going to be in, manhandling his clan's future *prima* like that?

Obviously, he didn't care. As disgusted as she was, Zoe really didn't want to resort to the kind of force that might hurt him permanently, but she didn't think she had much choice. Physically, she was no match for him, but she had her own powers, and she knew she was going to have to use them.

Even as she felt the *prima* energy begin to boil within her, however, a horrible shrieking noise assaulted her ears. As if he'd emerged from a tear in the world, the creature was there, mouth open wide with rage as he screamed at her attacker. Carlos' eyes widened in sudden fear at the unholy apparition, but he didn't have any time for more of a reaction than that, because the creature took Carlos by the shoulders and hurled him away from Zoe with such force that he hit the door to the pool house and actually knocked it down, then went sprawling onto his back on the gravel walkway outside.

That apparently wasn't enough for the creature, though. As Zoe watched, paralyzed in horror, he picked up Carlos and threw him another three yards or so, far enough away that he landed on the concrete swimming pool surround. Moaning and gasping, he tried to push himself up onto his hands and knees so he could try to get away, but the creature was having none of it. He grabbed the hapless man by the neck and then dragged him to the pool before thrusting his head under the water. At once Carlos began to struggle, thrashing away in the creature's iron grip.

At last Zoe recovered herself enough to cry out, "No, don't. Please, don't!"

The creature lifted Carlos' dripping face from the water. As her would-be consort choked and gasped, the creature said simply, in its deep, raspy voice, "Why?"

"Because—because he didn't really hurt me. I'm all right. Please…let him go."

No response at first. The creature maintained its grip on the back of Carlos' neck and stared at her with its head tilted slightly, apparently ignoring the struggles of the man he held. "But he could have hurt you."

Scary how much its speech had progressed. One part of Zoe's mind didn't want to accept that she was standing here and having a conversation with the thing she had summoned. Seeing it in broad daylight like this was also somewhat shocking, because she could clearly tell how far its transformation had progressed. The mouth was still slightly twisted, and one eye sat just a bit higher than the other, but otherwise, it had advanced much further toward the ideal man she'd thought she was conjuring.

Zoe didn't quite know what she should think about that.

"But he didn't hurt me," she said quietly. "Thank you—thank you for protecting me. But I don't want you to hurt him. Let him go, and then he'll go home and leave me alone. Isn't that right, Carlos?" she added, fixing him with what she hoped was the sort of glare that would convince him he needed to let this whole thing go.

"R-right," he gasped, although behind the fear in his eyes, she could see thwarted fury at being overpowered like this.

"If you wish," the creature said, letting go of Carlos so suddenly that he almost pitched head first into the pool, and only caught himself at the last minute by grabbing on to one of the pavers that surrounded it.

"What the hell is going on here?"

Zoe whirled away from the creature at the sharp sound of her aunt's voice. Luz was hurrying from the house toward the swimming pool, her usually elegant and serene features now showing a combination of shock and worry.

"I—" What the hell could she possibly say to explain the situation?

And the creature was no help, because it saw Luz striding toward it like an avenging angel, and clearly decided it was time to flee. Before she could get too close—and presumably use her own powers to try to dispel the thing—it disappeared, leaving a gasping Carlos by the side of the pool. He pushed himself up to a standing position. Livid bruises were already beginning to appear on the warm brown skin of his throat.

Luz's eyes were practically shooting fireballs on their own. "Zoe!"

"What?" she demanded, furious at Carlos, furious at her aunt for summoning him here...furious at the creature for disappearing on her like that, although Zoe supposed she probably would have done the same thing if she'd been in its shoes. "This is all his fault!" And she pointed at Carlos, who had one hand placed up against his neck, as if trying to reassure himself it wasn't broken.

"My fault?" he sputtered, voice hoarse from the abuse he had just suffered. "What—what was that thing?"

"Nothing you need to concern yourself with," Luz said smoothly. Obviously, she'd shifted into damage-control mode. It was exactly what a *prima* was supposed to do, but all the same, Zoe couldn't help experiencing a flare of frustrated rage.

"It came to protect me," Zoe snapped, "when you wouldn't get your hands off me."

Carlos' eyes narrowed in anger, even as shock registered on Luz's features.

"Yeah, that's right," Zoe continued. "This stupid candidate that you tried to force down my throat wouldn't leave me alone, even when it was obvious he wasn't my consort. So instead of trying to blame me, maybe you should do a better job of choosing the people you're sending my way, instead of grabbing anyone nearby with a pulse!"

And since she didn't think she had anything to add besides that last retort, she stalked past her aunt and into the house, ignoring Luz's warning, "Zoe—"

Screw that. She was sick of the whole thing. Her purse was still in her room, and the last thing she wanted was to have to go upstairs to retrieve it. Her rage must have been fueling her powers, because no sooner had the thought crossed her mind than her purse appeared right in front of her, sitting on the kitchen counter. She scooped it up and hurried to the garage, and pushed the button to open the garage door. An unfamiliar pickup truck sat in the driveway, blocking her exit, and she swore.

"Oh, no, you don't," she muttered, and raised a hand. At once the pickup began to roll backward into the cul-de-sac. It missed the front bumper of Luz's Lexus by mere inches and came to a rest against the curb directly across from the house.

Good. Zoe slid in behind the wheel of her Fiat and backed out of the garage, fuming the entire way. She had to get out of here. Right then, it felt as if she would explode if she had to deal with any of her family members ever again.

Time to get away. And she knew exactly where she should go.

CHAPTER FIFTEEN

EVAN SAT OUT ON THE PATIO AT THE COPPERWYND RESORT, nursing a Kilt Lifter ale. Since he figured he didn't have anywhere to be right then, a beer sounded like a damn good idea. And it did help to sit here in the shade of the covered patio, to watch the kids splashing in the pool and basically try to disengage his brain for a little while. He still couldn't believe that only a few hours earlier, he and Zoe had faced off against the monster once again, but the memories were sharp enough. That confrontation did seem like something that had happened in another world from where he was now, though.

Who knew how much fallout there would be from that particular incident. It did seem as if Luz Trujillo and Jack Sandoval were doing their best to cover up what they could, that they'd do everything in their power to deflect attention away from the one place they wanted it the least—the de la Paz clan—but would it be enough?

It didn't help that no matter how hard he tried, he couldn't get the image of Zoe speaking to that monster out of his head. Evan had found the creature a lot easier to deal with when it was a misshapen lump straight out of a nightmare. Now, as it seemed to inch closer and closer to looking like a real human being, he didn't know what to think.

He took another swallow of beer, watching as a chunky kid in neon green swim trunks cannonballed almost on top of a girl with the same sandy brown hair, probably his sister. She screamed, but more in outraged delight than anything else. Evan could tell they didn't have a care in the world. What they were doing here, he had no idea. It was too early for spring break, but, based on his experience of spending his entire life in a tourist town, time of year mattered less than you might think when it came to family vacation time.

His phone rang. For a second or two, he considered ignoring it, just because the combination of the beer and the warm sunlight was making him feel extraordinarily mellow. However, because of all the crap that was going on, he knew he really didn't have the luxury of blowing off a phone call. That could be Luz Trujillo, or Jack Sandoval. Hell, it could be one of the McAllister elders checking in to see how things were going, although that was more of a long shot.

Or it could be Zoe on the other end of the line.

That settled it. Evan dug his phone out of his pocket and touched the screen to accept the call. Although he only glanced at the number displayed there, he could tell from the area code that it had to be a Phoenix number. "Hey."

"Hey yourself." Zoe's voice, although she sounded shaky and not entirely herself. "Where are you?"

"At the hotel," he said, wondering as he replied just exactly where else she'd thought he might be. "What's up?"

"Can I come over?"

Yes, that was definitely a tremor in her voice, even though he could tell she was doing her best to hide it. Although warning bells started to go off in his mind, Evan knew he couldn't refuse a girl who sounded like that. Especially Zoe.

"Sure," he said. "I'm out on the patio by the pool. Do you want to meet me here, or should I come inside the hotel?"

"Is there a bar inside?"

"Yes."

"Then I'll meet you there. I'm about five minutes away."

The call ended abruptly, leaving Evan to stare at his phone for a few seconds before he shrugged and put it back in his pocket. Obviously, something had happened in the hour or so they'd been apart, but what? Had the creature returned?

No, Evan didn't think that was it. Or rather, it wasn't the whole story. Zoe had faced the thing down enough times by now that it really shouldn't have rattled her that badly, even if she'd had to go it alone this time.

As to why she wanted to meet inside, well, he supposed if she was upset, she'd rather talk in a dark corner of a bar rather than out here in the sunlight with plenty of people looking on. He signaled the waitress to bring him the check, even though he knew he could have just put the beer on the room tab. Somehow that didn't feel right, though. Luz Trujillo might be paying for his hotel room while he was here, but damned if he was going to make her buy his beers, too.

After slipping a ten-dollar bill into the little leatherette case with the check, Evan wandered into the hotel, blinking at the contrast between the bright sunlight outside and the moody lighting in the lobby. Since he figured it would be easier for Zoe if he'd already secured a booth in the bar, he went in there and found a place off in a corner where they wouldn't be disturbed. It was almost five, and time for people to start thinking about drinking, but the bar wasn't all that crowded, just a few people occupying several more of the booths, and a mixture of couples and singles at the bar itself.

The waitress came by and asked him if he wanted anything, and he told her he was waiting for a friend but that he could use some water. She nodded, flashing him a brilliant smile and what he hoped he had incorrectly interpreted as a glance containing just enough interest to make him feel less than comfortable.

Before the waitress could return with the water, though, Zoe appeared at the entrance to the bar. She stood there for a second, her face strained, before she saw him and came over and took the empty seat across from him.

"Are you all right?" he asked, just as soon as she set her purse down on the cushion next to her.

"No," she said shortly. "But I don't really want to talk about it until I've had a drink."

"Okay," he replied. "The waitress is getting me some water, but I'm sure she'll be back in a minute. Then you can order something."

"All right."

They lapsed into an uncomfortable silence then, Zoe tapping her fingers impatiently on the tabletop, Evan watching her in some mystification. Obviously, something had gone down, and curiosity was almost killing him, but he knew he'd have to let her get around to it in her own time.

The waitress did return with the water, and appeared vaguely disappointed that Evan's companion was female, and attractive. But she sounded professional enough as she took their orders—another beer for him, and a glass of white wine for Zoe.

"I really wanted a margarita," she said. "But since I had that sangria last, I figured I'd better stick with wine."

"Okay," he allowed, somehow knowing she was mentioning such inconsequentials because she didn't want to get into anything too sensitive until the waitress had brought their drinks and they could be assured of being left alone for a while to talk.

Luckily, they didn't have to wait too long; only a minute or so later, their drinks arrived and the waitress disappeared. Clearly, her interest in Evan had only lasted until she determined that he wasn't as unattached as she'd hoped.

Well, actually, he was unattached…even though right then he kind of wished his personal status could be different.

Zoe took an over-large swallow of her chardonnay and then gusted out a breath. "That's better." But from the way she ran a nervous finger up and down the stem of her wine glass, Evan wasn't sure how much the wine had really steadied her nerves.

"You want to talk about it?" he asked, his tone gentle. Maybe she didn't. Maybe she had only needed to get away from…whatever it was that had upset her so.

Her shoulders lifted. "Do I want to? Not really. But I probably should." She swallowed some more chardonnay. At that rate, she was going to need another glass in just a few more minutes. "My aunt dug up this stupid candidate and had him come over. Said she was sorry, it had totally slipped her mind, but he was already on his way, and there wasn't anything she could do about it."

"Well, that was shitty timing," Evan remarked, although he tried to keep his tone neutral. Inwardly, though, he could feel himself tensing up at the thought of Zoe kissing yet another candidate. It was obvious enough that it hadn't worked out, or she wouldn't be sitting opposite him now in this booth, but….

"Yeah, just about what I thought. But I knew I wouldn't even bother to argue with her, because she'd start lecturing me about my duty and all that crap." An impatient flick of her hair off her shoulder, and she sighed. "He was a creep. Wouldn't stop kissing me, even though it was obvious he wasn't my consort. And I was both scared and angry, because I knew I might have to hurt him to get him to stop, and then…."

"Then?" Evan asked, expecting the worst. *Had* she hurt the bastard, whoever he was? That could cause a lot of headaches, even if Zoe was able to prove that she'd only been defending herself.

"Then...*it* came. Just appeared in my lab and threw Carlos through the door like he was a doll. Pushed his head into the swimming pool and probably would have drowned him if I hadn't been screaming for it to stop."

Goddess. Evan hadn't taken a sip of his beer yet, but he lifted it then and took a swallow that lowered the level of alcohol in the glass by nearly an inch. No wonder Zoe looked so shaken. It seemed clear to him that the creature must have sensed her distress, and had come to her rescue. So had they been linked all this time, or was its bond with her growing stronger as its appearance became more and more human?

Neither possibility was terribly appealing.

"But it did stop."

"Yes." She pulled in a breath, fingers wrapped around the stem of her wine glass, although she didn't make a move to drink. "It wanted to know why I asked it to stop. I tried to explain, but I'm not sure how much it understood. It only stopped because I told it to, not because it saw anything wrong with trying to kill Carlos."

Damn. That the creature had come in like some kind of avenging angel…Evan didn't know what the hell to think about that, except that clearly its mind had been evolving along with its form. A chill went over him, but he knew he had to sound as calm and reassuring as possible as he said, "Well, I guess the important thing is that it did stop. So…did you send it away?"

"No. It took off when my aunt showed up. I think she frightened it. But I was so angry and scared that I basically told her to fuck off, and then I left. I think she's texted and called at least five times since, but I turned off my phone when I got to the parking lot here."

He nodded. He couldn't really blame her for that. The last thing you wanted when you were trying to calm down was to keep getting harassed by the person who'd pissed you off in the first place. "Do you think they'll guess you're here?"

Another shrug. "Maybe. I don't care. Or maybe she and my parents will think I went to my friend Amber's house. In a way, that would have been a smarter thing to do, because they'd never make a scene in front of a civilian."

"Does your friend know?"

Zoe didn't bother to ask what he meant by that question. "Yes. We've been friends forever. I told her the truth in sixth grade, made her swear not to tell, or

I'd get my *abuela* to put a hex on her. Not that Maya would have ever done such a thing, but Amber didn't know that. Anyway, she's kept my secret this whole time, but even though she knows, her parents don't, and she still lives at home like I do. So going there would be safe, since Luz and my parents wouldn't be able to follow me and make a big stink about it."

It made sense. Which begged the question why Zoe had come here, when it would have been better for her to go to Amber's house.

Problem was, he had a pretty good idea as to why Zoe had come to the CopperWynd. He just wasn't sure if he wanted to acknowledge that truth yet.

"But...." he said, and Zoe wouldn't quite look at him.

"But I remembered that Amber was working this afternoon, and so that's why I didn't go over to her place." The words came out quickly, as if Zoe wasn't sure he'd believe them.

He didn't know if he did. That is, it did sound perfectly plausible that her friend might be working today, since he assumed she must be in college and so had to take work hours that didn't conflict with her classes. But the excuse had sounded a little too glib.

Better to let it go. If he probed too much, then Zoe might admit to things he wasn't ready to hear. "Besides, you needed a drink, right?"

"Right." She was quiet for a moment before adding, "Really, I'm not as much of a lush as it seems. I have days go by when I don't drink anything at all. I'm just really stressed right now."

That made two of them. Evan couldn't blame her for wanting to take the edge off, not when he'd just been doing basically the exact same thing.

His phone buzzed then. Zoe's eyes widened in dismay. "Don't answer it," she said. "I know it's got to be my aunt trying to track me down."

"Probably," he agreed as he took out his phone and looked at the display. Sure enough, that was Luz's number. "But I can't blow her off forever, Zoe. She's only going to figure it out anyway. She needs to accept that you need some time to decompress."

"But—"

Ignoring her protests, he tapped the "accept" button and raised the phone to his ear. "Hi, Luz."

The de la Paz *prima* clearly didn't want to waste any time on pleasantries. Voice sharp, she asked, "Is Zoe with you?"

"Yes," he replied calmly as Zoe frantically shook her head in a vain attempt to shut him up. "We're at the hotel. She's fine."

"At the hotel?" Luz repeated, her tone sharpening further, if that was possible.

"Yes," he said. "She was a little upset. We're having a bite and a drink. She just needed to get away for a bit."

"Evan, I appreciate you wanting to help, but Zoe needs to learn that the future *prima* of this clan can't just run away when things get tough."

Oh, man. He ran a hand through his hair and attempted to think of a reply that didn't consist of telling Luz Trujillo to go screw herself. "I'm pretty sure Zoe knows that already, ma'am. But I don't think there's anything wrong with letting her catch her breath, so to speak. She's safe. Isn't that the important thing?"

A long pause. Then Luz said, sounding annoyed, "Yes, of course. But—"

"I think as long as it doesn't come back, you should give her some space. Maybe we'll go get some dinner, catch a movie or something. I'll look out for her."

Even though Luz didn't reply right away, Evan could practically feel her need to argue with him radiating through the air waves. However, when she spoke, she sounded resigned. "Fine. I understand that she just suffered a traumatic experience. But try to get her home at a decent hour. Agreed?"

He wanted to tell Luz that Zoe was an adult who could set her own hours. But he understood that Zoe wasn't exactly your normal twenty-one-year-old. As the prima-in-waiting, she had to be watched all the time. Clearly, Luz trusted him enough to keep an eye on her niece.

Evan just wasn't sure whether he'd really earned that trust.

Zoe watched as Evan ended the call and then set the phone down on the table next to his beer. "So she's not sending the troops after me?"

"Not yet." He drank some of his beer. Zoe found something oddly satisfying about watching the muscles of his throat move as he swallowed. "But she doesn't want you wandering around the city at all hours, either, wants to make sure you get home safely."

Of course not. Their little *prima*-in-waiting had to be kept under lock and key at all times. Okay, she knew that wasn't really true, that she had plenty of autonomy as long as she didn't test the limits too badly, but still. Annoyance flared once again. "Maybe I don't want to go home."

He raised an eyebrow at that remark. "Zoe, you have to go home sometime."

"Why? Because that's what I'm supposed to do?"

"They just want to make sure you're safe—"

"Why can't I be safe here?" she asked. "I could get a room, and we could run out and shop for a few things that I'd need, and then I wouldn't have to go home at all."

"I doubt that would go over very well."

God, was everyone against her? Deep down, she knew Evan was only trying to be the voice of reason, since he obviously thought she'd gone off the deep end, or at least was about to. But really, how would she be any safer at home than she was here? Neither of her parents was skilled at defensive magic, and Zander would be of no help, either. At least here in the hotel she'd be surrounded by people—not that that had stopped the creature from appearing in the middle of Scottsdale. Even so, she liked the idea of taking a room here, of asserting her independence. That way, it would be a lot harder for Luz to try to force any more horrible candidates for consort on her. Because although her aunt might let it go for now so Zoe could have a chance to recover, she knew that sooner or later—well, sooner, since she now had only a week before she turned twenty-two and lost her chance at receiving the full strength of her pow-ers—Luz would find someone else to try. She had to. It was her responsibility to make sure that the line of de la Paz *primas* remained unbroken.

"Maybe not," Zoe said defiantly. One thing she definitely wouldn't tell Evan was how much she'd love to share his room. But she knew he would never agree to such a thing, even on the pretext of feeling safer with him around. However, just staying in the hotel with him was better than being confined to her room back at home. "Right now, I don't really care. How much help have they really given me? I mean, the creature probably wouldn't have even shown up this afternoon if my aunt hadn't sent that horrible Carlos guy over to meet me."

Evan didn't say anything at first, probably because he couldn't argue with that comment. "Okay," he said. "I can tell your mind is made up. So let's finish our drinks, and then see if there are even any rooms available. The hotel might be full."

That particular possibility hadn't occurred to her. Yes, it was Saturday, but spring break was still a few weeks off. It couldn't be that busy, could it?

So she nodded and said, "Sounds like a plan," then swigged the rest of her chardonnay. Evan was a bit more measured about finishing off his beer, but only a few minutes later she laid down a twenty and a five to cover the drinks and the tip, and slid out of the booth so she could go to the front desk, her companion trailing reluctantly behind her.

It turned out that the hotel did have some empty rooms, including the one right next to Evan's, since she made sure to ask whether that particular room was available. He shot her a sideways look at that request but didn't argue. If he was going to be her bodyguard, so to speak, then he needed to be close by. Anyway, although the rooms were adjoining, the doors that connected them were kept locked at all times.

Not that witches and warlocks had too much of a problem with door locks.

Zoe scooped up her key card, beaming. This was all falling into place perfectly. Now she could go with Evan to the mall, do some shopping, and afterward they could have dinner, maybe go to that movie he'd mentioned on the phone to Luz. A nice, normal evening out together. That was what Zoe craved more than anything else after the tumult of the day. She had to stop and remind herself that the incident with the redneck out at the ATV staging area had only taken place that morning. It felt like a hundred years ago.

Should she go up to check on the room? No, what was the point? She didn't even have any luggage, no personal belongings at all except her purse. They should go out, get their errands done, and then…

…well, then she'd just see what happened. Because she knew for sure that one item she intended to pick up was something sexy to sleep in….

CHAPTER SIXTEEN

THIS WAS CRAZY. HE SHOULD HAVE TAKEN ZOE HOME, or at least convinced her to drive there under her own power. Instead, he was following her around Scottsdale Fashion Square as she bought what seemed like enough clothes and toiletries to last her a month at the CopperWynd resort, instead of just a few days.

He didn't protest, however. He knew better than that. Zoe was set on this course of action, and about all he could do was stay out of the way and promise himself that if something did go sideways, he'd be there to make sure the damage wasn't permanent.

At least there were restaurants and a movie theater here, so they shouldn't have to venture out to complete their evening's entertainment. Evan hoped that would be enough to satisfy Zoe; she had a rebellious glint in her eyes that seemed to indicate she wouldn't like being told it probably wasn't the greatest idea for them to be wandering all over Scottsdale just because she was pissed off at her aunt.

It probably wasn't so brilliant for the two of them to be here at all—what if the creature decided to drop in unexpectedly?—but Evan knew there was only so much he could do. While Zoe was in the lingerie department at Macy's, he made sure to stay safely away over in the accessories section, and then pulled out his phone and sent a text, not to Luz, who he guessed might go nuclear if she learned of Zoe's plans, but to Jack Sandoval. Zoe had said Jack was her favorite uncle, and maybe he'd be a little more understanding when it came to her current state of mind. But at least that way Jack could pass on the word, and Evan could stay safely out of the brouhaha that was sure to ensue. Maybe that was a coward's strategy. Right then, he didn't much care. The day's events had combined to make him feel vaguely shell-shocked, and if he could avoid any more de la Paz drama, all the better.

After Zoe had declared she was done shopping and they'd stowed all her loot in the Barracuda's trunk, they went to the theater to check on movies and times. In these doldrums before spring break, there wasn't much to choose from, but Evan was relieved to see that she was far more interested in the spy thriller on tap rather than a silly-looking romantic comedy. He would have sat through that if she insisted, true, simply because at this point he was ready to do just about anything that would keep her happy. Luckily, though, she didn't seem inclined to put him through that particular ordeal.

The movie didn't start until seven forty-five, so they decided to go ahead and have an early dinner. By that point, the tapas he'd consumed at Sofrita had long worn off, and he was hungry. Zoe, too, by the way she suggested appetizers first before they moved on to the main course.

To his surprise, she didn't order anything to drink except water. "I think it's all starting to catch up with me," she said after the waiter took their order and departed. "If I have another glass of wine now, I'll probably pass out asleep in the movie. So just water for me."

He was glad of that evidence of her level-headedness. Before they'd sat down, he'd already decided he wouldn't have a drink, either, but it was nice that they were reinforcing one another's choices. Even though he knew she probably wouldn't like the news, he thought he'd better tell her he'd been in contact with her family. Keeping secrets just wasn't his thing.

"I let your uncle know what we were doing," Evan said as he reached for his water.

Zoe's eyes flashed with surprise for just a second, and then she gave a resigned shrug. "Well, I suppose you had to," she replied. "And actually, good call on reaching out to him. He can usually talk Aunt Luz down off a ledge."

That was the opinion Evan had begun to form as well, but it was good to hear that Zoe agreed with his decision. "So we probably won't see your *prima* showing up to stalk us?"

"Hopefully not." Zoe lifted her own water glass, but she didn't drink. Instead, because they were sitting at a sort of conversation area with low couches and a cocktail table rather than in a booth, she set the glass on her knee and cradled it in her hands. "Really, I probably shouldn't be so down on my aunt. She's doing her best. This is the first time that a *prima*-in-waiting in my clan has had such a hard time finding a consort. So that has her stressed out. And then this latest thing...." She didn't mention the monster; she didn't have to. "Anyway, I guess I need to remind myself that she hasn't been *prima* all that long, either. That's got to be a tough gig."

Evan had no doubt of that. Was Zoe thinking of the day when all this responsibility would fall into her lap? Probably. But that day would be decades off, unless some other calamity befell the de la Paz clan. "It can be hard. My cousin Angela handles it pretty well, but then, her situation is kind of unique, since she and Connor do everything together. Usually a *prima* has to go it more on her own, even though she has a consort to bounce ideas off. Or at least, that's how it seemed with my Great-Aunt Ruby. Her husband died when I was really young, but she always seemed to be fully in charge even when he was around."

Her expression thoughtful and a little sad, Zoe added, "That's got to be the worst, though—being bonded that closely with someone, and then having them gone. I mean, in my *abuela's* case, she was probably more relieved than anything else, but hers wasn't exactly a typical situation."

"Great-Aunt Ruby's situation wasn't typical, either, I guess." The conversation had taken a melancholy turn, but Evan wasn't about to deflect. These things needed to be discussed, along with more cheerful matters. "I think she hung on a lot longer than she would have because she didn't want to leave us without a *prima* who was of age. Angela didn't have a consort yet when Ruby died, but at least she was twenty-one and starting to come into her powers anyway. At that point, I suppose Ruby hoped the universe would take care of it."

"And it did, just not in a way she could have imagined." To his surprise, Zoe shot him an impish little grin. "I mean, Connor Wilcox is *hot*."

That comment annoyed Evan, although he had a feeling Zoe had said it partly to see how he would react. Anyway, it wasn't as if he could argue the relative merits of Connor's hotness, not when he'd seen plenty of girls in his own clan get a little dreamy-eyed when Angela's consort walked down the street. Yes, Connor was more than taken, but, as a former girlfriend had once remarked when Evan was irritated by the way she'd eyeballed a couple of good-looking guys on the street, just because you look in the bakery window doesn't mean you're going to go in and buy a cake.

"So I've heard," he said dryly, and drank some more of his water. At the same time, he hoped the waiter wouldn't take too long with their appetizer.

Zoe seemed to realize she'd scored a point, because she settled back against the sofa cushions and said, "Anyway, I think Jack will be able to smooth things over. It's not like I've taken off for the Bahamas or something. I'm five minutes away in a hotel with plenty of people staying in it. If anything happens...." She stopped there, clearly uncertain as to how she should finish that particular sentence. If the creature did show up, there would be a hell of a lot of witnesses to its appearance.

Assuming, of course, that its appearance remained distorted. It seemed to be changing quickly now. For all Evan knew, the thing could show up looking exactly like Zoe's *telenovela* star, and instead of scaring the crap out of a bunch of people, the creature might have the women in the hotel lining up to get its autograph.

If they even recognized him. That crowd at the CopperWynd looked pretty white bread. Evan was fairly sure none of them had ever watched a *telenovela*.

"I doubt anything will happen," Evan said, more to reassure her than because he was actually certain of that fact. "We're just going to have a quiet night here, and then we'll go back and go to sleep. There's nothing going on that should arouse its protective instincts."

"Maybe," Zoe allowed. "But that wouldn't stop it from showing up someplace else. After all, it's appeared in places miles away from where I was."

"True. But if that happens, we'll sense it, or maybe your uncle will call to sound the alarm. Either way, I think the odds of a disturbance at our hotel are pretty low."

Right then the waiter showed up with their bacon-wrapped dates, so conversation on all sensitive subjects had to wait until he took off again, but not before he promised that their entrees would be out in another fifteen minutes or so. They both reached for the plate on the low table and snagged a date.

The savory little appetizer practically melted in his mouth. Evan had never had bacon-wrapped dates before, although he'd heard Angela mention them… with some sadness, because the little tapas place in

Flagstaff where she and Connor used to get them had since closed down.

Evan reached for another, and Zoe grinned at him.

"I told you they were good."

"No kidding. I'm going to have to start lobbying for one of the restaurants in Cottonwood or Jerome to start carrying these."

For some reason, her smile seemed a little muted after that remark. Disappointed that he was thinking about going home?

Don't flatter yourself, he thought.

But....

"They really should," she said, her tone too casual. "They go great with wine. Wine's a big thing up by you, isn't it?"

"Yes," he replied. "Lots of wineries in the area. Maybe some of the wine-tasting rooms could have them as appetizers."

"They're time-consuming to make. My mom makes them sometimes for family parties—immediate family," she added quickly. "If she was trying to make them for a clan get-together, she'd be stuffing dates for a week."

Her comment conjured an amusing mental image, and he chuckled slightly. "I suppose so. I hadn't thought about that particular angle."

"Well, you'd think about it a lot more if you ever got drafted for kitchen duty." She tilted her head to the side slightly as she gazed across the table at him. "You don't talk about your family that much."

"I guess it never came up," he replied with a shrug. "You already know about the McAllisters, anyway. My parents are still up in Jerome, in a two-bedroom cottage that's small but has some of the best views in town. I'm an only child. Not much else to tell."

"Really? No brothers or sisters?"

"It's not that strange. Down here in the Phoenix area, you guys have a lot of room to spread out. But Jerome is tiny. Yeah, we're down in Cottonwood and the rest of the Verde Valley, and as far as east as Payson, but we're still careful about family size. Usually people have one or two kids. Every once in a while you'll get more, but it's not common."

"I guess that makes sense." She picked up another date and bit it in half. How she managed to do that without having the feta cheese inside squeeze out all over the place, or mess up the soft coral-colored lip gloss she wore, Evan had no idea. A different kind of magic, he supposed.

But since staring at her mouth could create all sorts of problems, he went ahead and got another date for himself, and popped it in his mouth. Now there was only one left, but he wouldn't take it. Zoe should have it.

"Go ahead," she said. "They're rich. Two's enough for me."

"Are you sure?"

"Yes, I'm sure," she said, dark eyes dancing. "If I really wanted it, I would have taken it."

He couldn't argue with that. One thing he'd been able to determine about Zoe…when she wanted something, she went for it.

So where did that leave him?

Dinner was good. Friendly, casual, but Zoe was okay with that. The day had been tense enough. It was nice to see Evan slowly relaxing through the meal. Afterward, they had plenty of time to take a leisurely walk to the theater and still get decent seats. Since they were full from their meal, they didn't bother to get anything to eat, although Evan did buy them a couple bottles of water.

Sitting next to him was…well, she could have wished that an armrest didn't separate them, but it still felt wonderful to be this close, especially since before this they'd always sat across from each other at restaurants, and he'd always done what he could to keep her at arm's length. It was probably her imagination, but she almost fancied she could feel the warmth of his body next to her in the cool, air-conditioned space.

Even for a Saturday night, the theater wasn't that crowded. Other moviegoers filtered in until about half the seats had been occupied, which meant she wouldn't have to worry about being stuffed in like a sardine and having people in their row tripping over her and Evan as they went out to go to the bathroom or get more popcorn.

What would he do if she brushed her leg against his? No, that would be way too obvious. She'd have to sit here without moving around too much, but it wasn't the end of the world.

At least he'd agreed to being here at all, and that was something.

The theater darkened, and she felt Evan shift in the seat next to hers, settling himself in. His long legs stretched out in front of him, and she had to keep herself from staring at the muscles of his thighs as they strained against his Levi's.

Like you don't have a million other things to be thinking about, she scolded herself, but that wasn't enough to keep her from catching one last glimpse before the trailers started and she had to at least pretend to be paying attention.

The movie was, as she'd expected, kind of lackluster. However, it served its purpose of using up a few hours, and she relaxed as time went on and she didn't get a twinge from the monster, or a sudden flare of heat from the black tourmaline she'd put back in her jeans pocket. Neither had the creature appeared in the theater, bursting through the screen before it went on to terrorize the audience.

No, the whole experience had been entirely uneventful. They stayed through the credits; Zoe didn't know if that was because Evan wanted to kill time any way he knew how, or because he was just the kind of person to stay until the bitter end. She generally liked to stay, since so many movies had little "Easter egg" scenes at the end, although they didn't get that payoff here. The screen went dark, and it was time to get up and head out to the parking lot.

By then, full dark had fallen, with not even a faint glow to the west to show where the sun had gone down. She followed Evan out to his car and got in, and he drove them away from the city lights and back to Fountain Hills. Not that the suburb she called home didn't have its own light pollution, but it wasn't the same thing as the hundreds of square miles of artificial illumination that poured forth from the Phoenix basin at night.

While they were driving, she got out her phone and switched it on, fearing that she'd be confronted by dozens of missed calls and text messages from her aunt, her parents, maybe even Uncle Jack. But there was nothing. Well, a series of plaintive texts from her friend Amber.

Hey I'm home. Going to Max's party 2nite?

Oh, hell. The party had completely slipped Zoe's mind. Her parents weren't big on her going to parties, but they trusted Amber because she understood the situation and would always keep an eye on Zoe. Besides, the de la Paz clan was numerous enough that someone from her family always managed to get into these things as a friend of a friend or whatever. The chances of anything untoward happening were basically nil. However, Zoe still tried to go out as much as she could, just because at least that way she could pretend to be normal, even if she knew she really wasn't.

The next text was short, but not all that accusatory. Party's starting. *Where are U?*

It was followed by,

Thought we were driving 2gether?

And finally,

Fine. I'm going. See U later.

Well, that was going to be fun to smooth out. Amber had kind of a thing for Max, the guy throwing the party, who had recently broken up with his long-time girlfriend. No way was Amber going to miss an opportunity to swoop in now that he was single, even though Zoe had warned her about being a rebound girlfriend.

Like she would even know. She'd never had a single boyfriend, on the rebound or not.

She glanced over at Evan, admiring his sharp, clean profile, the strong lines of his throat, the way his heavy hair fell forward, partly obscuring his brow. He didn't look like anyone she'd ever met before, which, if forced, she would have admitted was part of the attraction. Exotic in a way she really hadn't expected.

But he'd also shown himself to be dependable and strong, and not someone to easily lose his cool. Since Zoe knew she had a tendency to fly off the handle at times, she thought his temperament was a good complement to hers. They seemed to be suited to one another in a way no one else she'd met had ever been.

Which meant basically nothing, because he just wasn't consort material. Or so Luz and her parents, and probably even Uncle Jack would say. Too old. Married before…and to a woman who clearly had no problem with extorting money to keep her mouth shut about her ex-husband's magical nature. From another clan. Her family might be willing to overlook one of those faults if necessary, and maybe even two of them, but all three taken together?

No way.

Evan pulled into the parking lot at the CopperWynd. The spots closest to Zoe's car were full, but there was one available only a few spaces down and across the row. He turned off the engine and said, "Well, I guess we'd better take all your loot inside."

"It's not *all* my loot," she retorted. "Four bags of stuff. You'd think I'd loaded up like what's-her-face from *Titanic,* you know, with all those steamer trunks. I saw it on Netflix once."

"Good thing you didn't buy that much, because then we'd need to get one of the bellboys to help."

He got out of the car, and she followed him back to the trunk, where they pulled out the results of her shopping trip. It wasn't all that much, not really. The mall wasn't the kind of place to get some necessities such as toothpaste, but she always carried a fold-up travel toothbrush in her purse, and she figured she could get those personal items at the resort's gift shop if they didn't come supplied with the room.

They rode up in an otherwise empty elevator. When they got to Zoe's room, she dug the plastic key card out of her wallet and opened the door. It did feel weird to have Evan follow her inside, but she didn't have much of a choice, since he was carrying half her shopping bags.

He went ahead and deposited them on the bed. "Well, I guess that's it."

"I guess so."

The tension in the air was so thick, Zoe thought he could have rested the bags on it instead of the bed. She didn't dare make a move, though. He'd be sure to avoid any advances she might attempt, or worse, laugh them off. He knew she was off limits.

"If you need anything, I'm just next door," he added.

"I know."

"Okay." He moved past her, coming fairly close as he did so, but not close enough for her to reach out to him. Not that she would have had the guts to do that, anyway. Right then, after everything she'd gone through that day, she knew she couldn't deal with the possibility that he might reject her. He paused at the door, then said, "Good night," and let himself out.

The moment was gone. Zoe wanted to swear, but she knew she had only herself to blame for not even trying to stop him. She glanced at the clock on the nightstand. Ten minutes until nine. If she wanted to get anything from the gift shop downstairs, she'd better do it now.

So she went down and bought toothpaste and deodorant and a little pack of floss. She'd already gotten stuff for her hair and face at the mall, so she figured she'd be covered for a stay of some duration, should it come to that.

It still felt early to be going to sleep, though, and she didn't feel like watching TV. She added a paper-back romance novel to the pile and tried to ignore the curious look the woman behind the counter gave her as she added up Zoe's purchases.

"Airline lost my carry-on," she said blithely, which only increased the woman's mystified expression.

Then it was back up to the room. Zoe tried very hard not to think about Evan on the other side of the wall separating them, but it seemed the harder she made the attempt, the more she ended up obsessing over him. Was he watching TV? Playing a game on his phone? Maybe calling the McAllister elders to tell them what was going on? No, probably not. It wasn't that late, but a little late to be making a call that wasn't an emergency.

Maybe he'd wandered out on the balcony to look at the stars. If she went out onto her own balcony, would she see him?

No, she told herself. *You are not going to do that. You are going to get ready for bed and try to act like a rational human being, not some lovesick seventh-grader.*

She went through the bags and got out the face-care products she'd bought, along with the stuff from the gift store downstairs, and took them all into the bathroom. The ritual of getting ready for bed helped calm her down a little. Changing out of her clothes brought on a pang, though, because she had to resolutely ignore the purple satin chemise with black lace trim she'd bought, and instead put on the much more sensible thigh-length sleep tank top she'd also purchased. That chemise had been too gorgeous to pass up, but she wasn't going to wear it unless Evan could see her in it.

Stupid, she knew. That wasn't going to happen. She'd probably end up returning the thing, or shoving it into a far corner of her dresser back home so it couldn't remind her of what an idiot she'd been.

Evening toilette complete, she went back to the main part of the room and climbed into bed, taking the paperback with her. If she couldn't have the man of her dreams, then at least she could read about someone else getting theirs.

It was hard to concentrate, though. The room felt too quiet, so she reached over and turned on the clock radio, tuning it to her favorite local station, although turned down low enough that it was only soft background noise, none of the songs recognizable unless she really stopped and concentrated on what was playing.

Eventually, although she tended to stay up later than this, her eyes began to slide shut with weariness. Long, crazy day. She should just go to sleep. Who cared if it was only ten o'clock?

She slipped the receipt from the gift shop into the book to hold her place, then set it on the nightstand. A flick of the switch, and the bedside lamp had been extinguished. Dark fell, but not utter dark, since she hadn't pulled the heavy blackout curtains all the way closed. A faint orangey light from the parking lot still penetrated the room, and that was just fine by her. Right then she really didn't want to be in utter blackness.

But that was what she experienced when she shut her eyes. Sleep came quickly, stealing over her tired limbs, despite her unfamiliar surroundings, despite the fact that she'd never slept away from the security of her family home before.

Something bumped into her bed. Although she'd been deep asleep, Zoe's eyes shot open in panic, even as she pushed herself up against the pillows. She strained to see into the darkness, heart pounding.

At first she couldn't detect anything at all out of the ordinary, and she wanted to tell herself that the slight shaking of the bed had only been herself as she adjusted positions, trying to get comfortable. Didn't that sort of thing happen all the time? She was just jumpy because she was in a place she didn't know.

But then she saw the dim light from the parking lot touch something pale. A glint of fair hair.

Her blood went cold. The creature's hair was blond because William Levy, the *telenovela* star she'd modeled it on, was blond.

Somehow, her shaking fingers found the little knob at the base of the lamp next to her bed. She turned it, and bit her lip to keep from screaming.

That was the creature, standing at the foot of the bed. It stared at her, head slightly tilted to one side, but did not speak.

Oh, God.

And it had changed again. If Zoe had passed it—*him*—on the street, she probably wouldn't have given him a second glance...except maybe to think that he was pretty damn gorgeous.

The transformation appeared to be complete. She couldn't see any traces of the deformities that had previously distorted his features. No, he was perfect. If anything, he was almost *too* perfect, with none of the small asymmetries and quirks you usually saw in even the most beautiful of faces.

She cleared her throat. "You can't be here."

He watched her and didn't answer for a moment. Then he said, his voice now as normal as his appearance, "Why not?"

"Because—" She floundered for an appropriate response. "Because I didn't summon you."

"But you did. You summoned me yesterday. I was not complete then. I frightened you. But now I am ready."

Oh, dear God. Zoe really didn't know if it was better to stay safely concealed by the covers, or to get out of bed. Doing so would reveal how short the tank top she wore actually was, but on the other hand, she felt curiously helpless being in bed like that, with the creature seeming to loom over her.

She decided to get up. She pushed back the sheet and blanket and duvet, and slowly climbed out of the bed. The whole time, the creature continued to watch her. It was impossible to avoid noticing the way his gaze flicked down to her legs and back up to her face, and a chill went down her spine.

I should scream, she thought then. *If I scream, Evan will come running. But then, probably so will everyone else on this floor.*

That wouldn't be good. She had to handle this herself.

"I know you don't—don't understand how everything works here. But our rooms are private. Where we sleep is private. You can't just show up in someone's room like this."

"But you are not just 'someone.' You are Zoe. You are the reason I am here."

Confronted with logic like that, she wasn't sure what to say. Because when you got right down to it, the creature was right. He wouldn't be here, in this world, if it weren't for her.

"Okay," she replied, after an extended pause, during which he continued to stare at her as if she was the most fascinating thing in the world. "I know I summoned you. And I know we—well, things got off to a sort of rocky start. But even so, it's not right for you to appear like this. I was trying to sleep. You—you really scared me."

His eyes narrowed. The lighting in the room was too dim for her to see clearly, but she knew those eyes were probably clear, bright blue. "I do not wish to scare you. I wish to be with you."

Zoe gulped in a breath. Should she scream now? Probably not. He hadn't made a move, was still standing there at the foot of the bed. She supposed she should be glad of that. And really, if she was going to be completely honest with herself, she had to admit that if he'd looked like this when he appeared yesterday morning, she would have happily fallen into his arms, thinking that the spell had worked perfectly.

Now, though....

Her heart and mind had undergone a transformation during the last thirty-six hours. Why conjure a man when the perfect one was there for you already?

Somehow she doubted the creature would respond well if she told him sorry, she'd fallen for someone else during the time he was growing into his human face.

Thinking quickly, she said, "Um...why don't you sit down over there, and we can talk?" She pointed toward the table by the window and its two accompanying chairs.

A faint frown marred the smooth skin of his forehead. "I do not wish to talk. I want to go there." His gaze slid past her to the bed, his meaning clear.

Great. So not only had she conjured a being from some other dimension, but apparently he was a horny bastard.

"I'm not the kind of girl to jump into bed with someone I just met," she said primly. Never mind that she would have happily fallen into bed with Evan within hours of meeting him, even if such a thing had been possible.

The creature straightened slightly, as if he had taken offense at her words. "No, of course not. You are Zoe Sandoval, future *prima* of the de la Paz clan. But you brought me here to be your consort, and so the situation is different."

Wow, he'd certainly made leaps and bounds in his vocabulary and in his grasp of the situation, she'd give him that. Had his mind and speech developed along with his face and form? That sounded plausible enough, although she couldn't think of a way to ask without sounding rude.

"Maybe," she allowed. "But I'd still like to sit down and have some water. Do you want some water?"

His head tilted again. "If you are having some."

On shaky legs, she made her way over the mini-fridge and extracted two bottles of water, then took them over to the table and set them down. After that, she sat, praying he would follow her lead.

Which he did, after a moment's hesitation. He took the seat opposite hers and then recommenced what seemed to be a ceaseless inspection of her face and person.

This was the closest they'd been so far, except for the time when he'd grabbed her arm back in the ATV staging area. As if in recollection of the injury, her wrist gave off a quick, sharp ache, one that Zoe tried to ignore.

She unscrewed the cap on her bottle of water and drank, trying to pretend this was all very normal. How in the world was she going to convince the creature to go back where he'd come from? He seemed so very determined to be with her. And though she knew she could mount a physical attack if she had to, she didn't like that idea very much. It was one thing to shoot fireballs at someone when they constituted an immediate threat. It was something else entirely to launch that kind of an offense at a person who sat calmly across a table from you.

Well, maybe not a physical offense, but a verbal one?

"Those other girls," she said abruptly. "Why go after them?"

The creature blinked at her, clearly confused. "Which girls?"

"The one down in Superstition Springs, in that condo complex with the pond. The girl this afternoon in Scottsdale by the museum. What was up with that?"

He wrapped his hands around the water bottle but made no move to open it. "I—" Breaking off there, he frowned, as if digging around in his memory banks for the right words to use. "When I was new, it was...difficult to always find you. Those girls had an energy similar to yours. It drew me. But then I saw they were not you, and I wasn't sure what to do."

Better to be confused than to take action. At least he hadn't hurt them. "So...you can sense me?"

"Just as you can sense me."

"Not always," she protested. "Here and there. A twinge. That's all."

"It is because I was becoming. Now I am this." He let go of the water bottle and touched a hand to his chest. "I am what you wanted me to be. So there is no need for us to be apart again."

Back to that. Zoe realized he'd always keep circling back to the issue of them being together, because in his mind, nothing else existed. She truly was the center of his universe.

And that scared her more than anything else.

"Where did you come from?" she asked then, desperately trying to come up with any way she could think of to keep him talking about something that didn't involve the two of them being together.

He made a vague gesture with one hand, pointing upward. "Somewhere out there."

"Out...you mean like in space?"

"No." A pause as he seemed to grapple with the question. "Someplace not here. Within, without. Both at the same time."

Another dimension? That seemed to be what he was saying, but she was having a hard time trying to comprehend his words. Quantum physics wasn't exactly her strong suit.

Definitely not here, though.

"Are there others like you?"

"No. I did not have being until you called me. Your words—the magic words—they made me happen."

Being from nothingness. A shiver crept down Zoe's spine, and she wished she'd turned down the A/C before she went to bed. But she supposed what he had said made sense. Spells were just thought made tangible, or at least something that had tangible effects in the physical world. She didn't see why conjuring a man would be any different.

Did that make the situation better, or worse? When he was finally sent away from this plane, would he dissolve back into the nothing he'd come from? Something about that notion made a wave of sadness go through her. She didn't know if she had the guts to do that to him.

But neither did she want to be his consort. She'd brought him here in a moment of foolishness and stubbornness, but that wasn't his fault. None of this was his fault.

On the other hand, she knew she didn't have the courage to admit to him that somehow she'd managed to fall in love, not with the creature she'd brought here, but with the man who was supposed to help send him back to the netherworld where he'd been created.

"I—" She stopped there, not sure what she'd meant to say. "Do you have a name?"

"No. It is for you to name me."

Great. If she named him, that would mean just one more connection between the two of them. "I think you should choose your own name."

"I do not know your names."

Well, this could go on all night. In desperation, she got up from her chair and went to the nightstand. Sure enough, there in the top drawer was a Gideon bible. "Here," she said, and placed it on the table in front of him. "There are all sorts of names in here. Pick one."

He lifted a curious eyebrow, then opened the bible. His brows drew together.

Oh, shit...maybe he can't even read.

But that worry disappeared soon enough, since she saw the way his lips shaped the words as he ruffled through the pages. Well, he could speak English, so she supposed he must be able to read it as well. Magic could do funny things.

"Leviticus," he announced after a long pause, and she had to fight back an incongruous giggle.

"That's a little unwieldy," Zoe said. "Could we shorten it to Levi?" And that was a little too close for comfort to the name of the man who had inspired her creation's face, but she knew it would be far too difficult to explain to the strange being who sat across from her. Levi he would be, it seemed.

"If that is what you wish."

What she wished was for none of this to have ever happened, but it was a little late for that now. "I think it would be easier," she said gently. "Anyway, Levi, it's late, and I don't think now is the time for us to be making any big decisions. Why don't you come back in the morning, and we can have breakfast and talk some more?"

And maybe by then I'll have figured out what the hell I'm supposed to do next, she thought. *Or at least I'll have had a chance to talk to Evan.*

"And then we will be consorts?"

"Um...not exactly. But it'll give you a chance to see a little more of how the world works."

He seemed to consider that statement. "Very well. I will be here in the morning."

"Not too early," she warned him. "Do you know how time works?"

"It is always around us, if that is what you mean."

"Not exactly." She pointed at the clock. "You see how it says '2:33'?"

"Yes."

"Well, that means it's very early in the morning, just a few hours past midnight. I want to meet for breakfast at ten. That's eight hours from now."

Frowning, he glanced over at the clock, and then back at her. "An hour is an increment of time."

"Yes. It has sixty minutes in it."

"I do not know what a minute is."

"Well—" She floundered for a second, then said, "Let's watch the clock together. It just turned over to 2:34. In sixty seconds, it'll be 2:35. Watch the clock, and you'll see how long a minute is."

"If you wish."

They were both quiet then, staring at the clock until the display showed the time as 2:35. Zoe looked over at Levi. "You get it now?"

"Yes. Sixty of those is an hour, and ten in the morning is seven and a half hours from now. I will be here then."

She summoned a ragged smile. "Ten it is. And Levi—"

"Yes?"

"You might want to find some shoes while you're at it."

A glance at his bare feet, and then he sent her beatific smile, one that would have made shivers go all down her back only a day and a half ago. "Shoes. I will do that for you, Zoe."

And then he was gone, vanishing into the darkness as if he'd never been there at all. Zoe drew in a breath and glanced around the room, but yes, she was alone.

What the hell she was supposed to do next, she had no idea.

CHAPTER SEVENTEEN

HE'D DEFINITELY HEARD VOICES NEXT DOOR. EVAN TOLD himself he should go back to sleep, that what he'd heard was just Zoe watching TV—for all he knew, she was a night owl, or an insomniac—but dammit, one of those voices had sounded like hers. The other was definitely male.

Silence fell once again, however, and he glanced at the clock. Two forty-two. Not exactly the best time of night to go knock on someone's door and ask if they'd had company recently.

He was here to watch out for her, though. What if the creature had appeared and had stolen her away, right under Evan's nose?

No, he doubted something like that could have happened. Zoe would have kicked up a ruckus, would have screamed and started fighting back. The whole hotel probably would have heard that kind of commotion.

Just do it, he thought. *If she's fallen asleep with the TV on or whatever, apologize and go back to bed. Better to embarrass yourself and know she's safe. You know you'll never forgive yourself if something really has happened to her.*

So he got out of bed and pulled on his jeans and the T-shirt he'd left draped over the back of a chair. He wouldn't bother with shoes, but at least he was covered enough to venture out into the hallway.

After sliding the key card for his room into his pocket, he went out into the corridor and then lingered for the longest time in front of the door to Zoe's room. He was going to feel like a real idiot if he woke her up.

She'd forgive him, once she knew the reason for his disquiet. Or at least he hoped she would.

He raised his hand and knocked softly on the door, saying, "Zoe? Are you okay?"

To his relief, she opened the door just a few seconds later. If she'd been asleep, he doubted she would have been that fast. Dark hair tumbled over her shoulders, and he tried very hard not to look any further than that, because he could see she wore a thin-strapped tank top that only came down to mid-thigh, baring her long, tanned legs. Also, that tank top wasn't doing much to conceal her chest.

Before she could speak, he said hurriedly, "I thought I heard voices."

She peered past him into the hallway, but since it was the dead of night, no one else was out and about. "Come in," she told him, her voice barely above a whisper.

Evan really wasn't sure how good an idea that was—not with her looking like that—but he also knew he didn't have much of a choice. He moved past her into the room. The bed was definitely rumpled, as if someone had slept there, but the lamp on the nightstand had been switched on. The TV, however, was off.

Well, of course she turned on the light, he thought. *You made her get up to answer the damn door.*

Since he didn't know where he should sit, he went to the window and stood there, pretending to look through the sheer drapes out to the parking lot below. Zoe came over and paused a few feet away from him, arms crossed.

"He was here."

Evan didn't ask who "he" was, even though in his own mind, he always thought of the creature as an "it." "Here?" he demanded. "In your room?"

"Yes, here," she said, sounding tired. "I was asleep, and something bumped into the bed...and there he was."

"Why didn't you yell for me?"

"And wake up everyone on the floor? That's a great way to keep this whole thing quiet." She pushed her hair back from her face. For the first time, Evan realized she didn't have on a speck of makeup, but he liked her this way. Something about it seemed more honest. Besides, those big dark eyes with their long, long lashes hardly needed any embellishment. "He didn't—he didn't hurt me or anything. We talked."

"You talked," Evan echoed, voice flat. "About what?"

"Well, he's still pretty insistent on being my consort. And...." She paused then, her gaze not meeting his. "He's changed again. He looks—well, he looks like the way I'd meant him to look when I first conjured him. You'd never think...anyway, he's not going to make any crowds of people scream and run away now, that's for sure."

Evan sure as hell didn't like the sound of that, just because it seemed to confirm the nagging fear he'd had for a while, that eventually the creature would come into its—his—own, and then maybe Zoe wouldn't be nearly as repulsed by him. She'd have the man of her dreams, and Evan would have to go back to Jerome, alone again.

Stop the "woe is me" shit, he thought, right before he said, "If he was so insistent about being your consort, how'd you get him to leave?"

"I promised him we'd have breakfast and could talk more in the morning, but it was way too late tonight for that sort of thing."

"And he agreed to that?"

"Yes," Zoe said, then burst out as he frowned at her reply, "Stop looking at me like that! What else was I supposed to do? I needed to buy us some time so we could figure out what to do next."

Any protests Evan had been about to make died then. She was right—they did have to come up with some kind of plan, even if he had no idea what that might be. "What time?"

"What time what?"

"What time did you tell him to come back?" he gritted.

Her eyes flashed with dark fire; he could tell she wasn't thrilled by his tone. But her voice was even enough as she said, "Ten o'clock. I didn't know if I could push it much later than that."

"We'll just have to work with it." He ran a hand through his hair, no doubt making it stick out every which way, but he couldn't worry about that right now. "At least now we know when he's going to show up, so we can be waiting for him. I've been working through your spell in my mind, and I think I have an idea on how to reverse its effects so we can send him back for good this time."

"No," Zoe said, and Evan's scowl deepened. He wondered if he somehow hadn't heard her correctly.

"What?"

"No," she repeated, her voice firm. "I know this is going to sound crazy, but—but I *talked* to him, Evan. I don't care if I somehow managed to conjure him out of nothing. Now he's a real person, with thoughts and wishes and needs of his own. Sending him back, making him nothing again...it would be like murder."

He couldn't be hearing this. Had Zoe just gone right off the deep end? Wasn't the whole point of this exercise to get rid of the creature she'd summoned?

"You're right," he said, and watched her expression relax slightly, right before he added, "It does sound crazy. So, what—you're going to make him your consort after all?"

"No." She glanced away, small white teeth working at her lower lip. "I don't want him to be my consort. I want—" The words broke off as she appeared to wrestle with herself. "I want *you* to be my consort, Evan."

She might as well have punched him in the gut. Such a blow would have produced pretty much the same effect—the sensation that he couldn't quite breathe, that there wasn't enough air in the room to fill up his lungs. Never mind that he'd been doing his best to ignore his attraction to her, the growing need that he'd never be able to satisfy. He couldn't be her consort. He was absolutely the worst person in the world for that particular job.

Somehow he managed to get out, "I can't."

He'd expected her face to fall in disappointment. Instead, she raised her chin and said, "I don't think that's your decision. I think that's for the universe to decide."

Which was true enough. The individual wishes of the *prima*-in-waiting and her consort didn't factor into the matter. Either they were compatible, or they weren't. Still, Evan wished he could come up with some sort of logical argument as to why her suggestion was all kinds of crazy. But with those big dark eyes staring up into his, her full mouth parted slightly, the logic centers in his brain seemed to have taken the night off.

Apparently taking his silence as tacit agreement, Zoe went on, "I've spent the past year kissing guys I really didn't want to kiss. Now I have someone standing in front of me that I've wanted to kiss almost since the moment I saw him. Just let me have that, Evan. Maybe you're right. Maybe you aren't the one, and it'll just be a kiss. At least it'll be a kiss I actually wanted. Anyway, the universe will tell us one way or another, won't it?"

"I—" He shook his head. Right then, in the depths of the night and with his brain fogged with weariness, maybe it didn't seem like such a bad idea. No, he really didn't think he was her consort. But to be able to kiss her just once, to feel those soft, full lips against his, to take her in his arms and hold her...well, he'd be crazy to pass up that opportunity, wouldn't he?

Or maybe he'd be even crazier to take it. For the longest moment he stood there, gazing down into her lovely face as he warred with himself. This had the potential to go so horribly, horribly wrong.

On the other hand...maybe it would go completely right. Right then, he just didn't have the strength to fight the attraction any more.

"Yes," he said, "let the universe tell us."

She smiled and came to him, wrapping her arms around his waist. Ah, she was a goddess, the sweet scent of her hair, the sensation of her full breasts pressed against him, unencumbered by a bra. Hot, cramping need went through his body, making him grow stiff already, and they hadn't even kissed yet.

Well, he'd just have to remedy that situation.

He bent his head, and claimed her mouth with his.

Pure, sweet golden light. That was what it felt like, arcing along every nerve ending, rushing through every limb. None of the other candidates' kisses had felt anything close to this, even the ones who seemed to know what they were doing. No, their kisses had left her cold, because they weren't the one.

But Evan was. Heat flooded all through her, the need for his mouth, his touch. At the same time, she could feel her powers waking even further, energy humming in all the cells of her body. Her aunt had told her this was what it would be like, and yet Zoe had still found it difficult to believe her words, to think that one man in all the world would be the match to her soul, the single person to ensure that she would be a *prima* in possession of all her powers.

The kiss lasted forever, an eternity in which their mouths touched and their spirits mingled. At last, though, she knew she'd have to come up for air, and so she pulled away ever so slightly so she could gaze up into his face…his dear, perfect face.

His breath was ragged and hoarse, a glow of perspiration on his forehead. "Was that—?"

"Yes," she said. "Yes, Evan. That was the soul-mate bond waking up. You're my consort."

He still looked completely dazed. "But…how can I be? I'm too old, and—"

"I suppose the universe doesn't care about that as much as you think it did," Zoe replied with a smile. Her whole body was thrumming, and she had to make herself stand there and talk rationally with him when all she really wanted was to push him onto the bed and let him finish sealing the bond between them. "Luz tried to explain it to me. She said that there were probably several people at any one time who could be a *prima*'s consort, but they wouldn't necessarily cross paths. Maybe there was someone else in New Mexico, or Colorado or Wyoming. That doesn't matter, because the person here and now who is best suited for me is you, Evan McAllister. And anyway, that whole thing about candidates being under twenty-five is really just tradition." She didn't mention him being divorced, even though she knew that no de la Paz *prima* had ever bonded with a divorced man.

Until now.

Pulling in a breath, she added, "It's not like someone came down from the mountain with it written in stone. Understand?"

"I think so." His gaze traveled to her mouth. "Can I kiss you again?"

"I'd be pissed if you didn't."

In the next second, their lips were touching again, all sweet fire, and her body throbbed with need once again. She wasn't even sure who made the first move toward the bed, only that suddenly they had both fallen onto the mattress, mouths devouring one another as she grabbed his T-shirt and pulled it over his head, and he pushed up the tank she wore so his hands could close on her breasts. His touch made her gasp. She'd never realized her breasts could be this sensitive, that the whisper of his fingertips across her taut nipples would be enough to make her ache with desire.

Then he let go so he could grasp the hem of her tank and pull it all the way up, drawing it over her head just as she had with his shirt a few seconds earlier. The cool air of her hotel room washed over her bare skin, and she sucked in a breath.

"You're perfect, Zoe," Evan whispered. His hands moved over her, tracing a path from her waist back up to her breasts. "Every inch of you."

"So are you," she said, which was only the truth. He still wore his jeans; however, the light from the bedside lamp sent the defined muscles of his stomach and chest and arms into sharp relief. She'd hoped he would be built like that, but somehow seeing his body revealed made her want to just stare, to drink in all of him, every perfectly sculpted detail.

His fingers hooked into the waistband of her panties, but then he paused. "Is this—is this what you want?"

Was he kidding? Right then she couldn't think of anything she wanted more. "Of course it is. It's what we're meant to do—to seal our bond." As he still seemed to hesitate, she added, "And if you stop now, I will *never* forgive you."

She'd said the words in a halfway teasing tone, but they seemed to be enough to convince him. He pulled down her underwear, while at the same time she reached over so she could undo the buttons of his Levi's and yank them down along with the black boxers he wore, although she was careful not to get them hung up on his obvious erection. He was big. She'd sort of expected that, because he was tall, but being confronted by the reality of him was a little overwhelming.

He must have noticed where she was looking, because he said, "Are you okay, Zoe?"

"Yes," she replied. The last thing she wanted him to think was that she might be hesitant. To prove she was the exact opposite, she took him in her hand, stroking gently. At once he let out a low, sighing moan, eyes shutting halfway so all she could see was his thick dark lashes.

"Goddess, Zoe," he managed, then slumped back against the pillows.

She knew he was only swearing by the goddess the McAllister clan followed, but still, the juxtaposition of her name and the word "goddess" made Zoe smile slightly. Anyway, even though she didn't have any real-world experience, she knew well enough what she should try next. Bending down, she took him into her mouth, tasting the heat of his flesh, feeling the softness of his skin against her lips. She loved the feel of him, and loved the way he groaned, his back arching with pleasure.

Good, then she must be doing this right. She kept going, sliding him in and out of her mouth, sometimes speeding up, sometimes slowing to a drawn-out, tantalizing motion that teased him to end of his cock before moving languorously back down his shaft.

"Zoe," he whispered. "You need to stop."

"Why?" she asked, although she could guess at the answer.

"Because you're going to make me come, and I want to do that in you."

Well, who could argue with that? She raised her head from him, and in the next instant he'd pulled her to him, was kissing her roughly as his hand moved between her legs. Then it was her turn to moan as he caressed her, fingers skillfully moving over her, eliciting waves of pleasure so intense that she had to keep herself from crying out. If this had happened in the privacy of a house, she might not have worried, but she really didn't want the hotel guests on the other side of the wall to hear everything she and Evan were doing.

So she had to settle for little sighs and moans as he bent his head to take her nipple into his mouth, his tongue and his fingers working together to bring her closer, ever closer....

The orgasm burst through her with roughly the same heat level as a supernova. This time she had to cram her fist into her mouth to keep from screaming, the shockwaves flowing through her body in ripples of almost cramping pleasure. When they'd finally subsided somewhat, she fell back against the pillows, gasping.

Evan nuzzled against her neck, kissing her throat and making more exquisite little shivers go through her. She moaned again, even as he shifted so he was on top of her, those misty hazel eyes meeting hers, seeming to penetrate to her very soul.

She could feel his erection touching her, but he didn't move again, waiting there at her entrance. "It's okay, Evan," she said. "I want to. Please—be with me."

A breath escaped his lips, and he nodded. And then he was pushing into her, the heavy shaft of his cock filling her. Yes, it hurt a little, but not too badly. She concentrated on how good he had made her feel just a minute ago, how ready she was for him, and the pain subsided as he began to move slowly in and out, with each stroke going a little deeper, each passing moment bring them closer and closer together.

This was the soul bond. Every inch of her body responding to every inch of his, the empty places in her spirit filled and soothed. She'd understood this was how it was supposed to be, but until she'd experienced it for herself, she'd had no idea how complete this kind of contact would be, consort and *prima* coming together.

She'd heard that the McAllister witches had some sort of charm to prevent pregnancy, and there were spells the witches in her own clan had devised for that same purpose, but Zoe wouldn't use any of them now. This was only natural, Evan and her. The prima was supposed to have a family, and start young, so the clan would have more strong witches and warlocks, and very possibly the next *prima*-in-waiting. If God decided to bless them from the very beginning, she wouldn't deny her destiny.

At last Evan's breaths began to grow ragged, and his movements speeded up. Zoe could feel her own body responding, knew that the climax was approaching for her as well. She wrapped her legs around him and pulled him even deeper into her, tangled her fingers in his thick hair the way she'd wanted to ever since she first saw him.

When he came, it was hard, rocking into her with an intensity that made her suck in a surprised breath, even as the second orgasm of the night swept through her. She hung on to him until he slowed, then stilled. Without speaking, his mouth found hers, kissing her again with an intensity that took her breath away.

At last, though, he lifted himself from her, and leaned back against the pillows, his breathing still heavy, strained. Only a second later, though, he reached over to pull her next to him so her head was pillowed on his chest. She could hear the beating of his heart, hear how it gradually began to slow.

Neither one of them said anything for a long while. Zoe was still trying to gather herself, to realize that she truly was bonded to Evan McAllister, that the universe had decided to bless her with her perfect consort. His hand ran over her tumbled hair, the caress unexpectedly gentle after the intensity of their love-making.

When he spoke, though, he sounded almost amused. "You want to tell me where you learned how to do that?"

"'That'?" she repeated, then chuckled as she realized he was referring to the oral sex. She gazed up at him guilelessly. "Come on, Evan—you know the internet is for porn."

His eyebrows lifted. "Zoe Sandoval, you're telling me your parents let you watch internet porn?"

"Like they knew." She gave him a sly grin. "Private browsing history, you know? Anyway, I told myself that I wasn't going to be a complete innocent when the time came. I couldn't date or have a boyfriend, but that didn't mean I couldn't learn what I needed to ahead of time."

"You're amazing, you know that?"

"So are you."

He didn't reply, but just a second or two after she'd spoken, he was pulling her to him again, kissing her as she felt him begin to harden once more. It appeared he was ready to seal their bond all over again.

And she was just fine with that.

CHAPTER EIGHTEEN

EVAN'S EYES OPENED SLOWLY. IN HIS IMMEDIATE FIELD of view was a pile of pillows, covered by a scatter of long dark hair. For just a minute, he couldn't figure out where the hell he was. Then the events of the night before came back to him in a rush—going to Zoe's room. A kiss that wiped out the memory of every other kiss he'd ever had.

The two of them making love over and over, until at last they'd passed out around four-thirty in the morning.

He directed his bleary gaze toward the clock. Eight fifty-two. Could be worse, although normally he didn't sleep that late. Then he froze. The promise she'd made to her creature. Breakfast at ten o'clock. That didn't give them a whole hell of a lot of time.

"Zoe."

A muffled groan was her only response. Apparently she wasn't much of a morning person.

Evan sat up, then reached out and touched her shoulder. "Zoe, it's almost nine. Didn't you say that breakfast with your—with *him*—was at ten?"

That question made her push herself up to a sitting position. "Shit." Her eyes met his, wide and dark. Her full mouth looked swollen from their kisses, and he could make out a few marks on her neck as well.

Hope she bought some concealer yesterday, Evan thought. *Because I doubt her creature is going to be too thrilled to see those…if he even knows what they mean, that is.*

"What are we going to tell him?" she asked.

"The truth. What else can we do? For all I know, he'll be able to sense what we did without you telling him anything."

She nodded, although she still looked worried. "I don't—I don't know how he's going to take it."

Neither did Evan. Not well, he assumed. Maybe they could convince him to take a walk on the grounds before breakfast. At least that way if the worst happened and the creature exploded in some kind of supernatural rage, it wouldn't be in the middle of the restaurant at the CopperWynd resort.

"Only one way to find out." He pushed himself out of bed and began to pull on his discarded clothes, which were strewn all over the floor. "I'll go back to my room and take a shower. You do the same. Can you be ready in an hour?"

"Of course," Zoe replied, looking somewhat indignant. Underneath the indignation, though, appeared to be a trace of worry.

Well, not much Evan could do about that. He'd gotten the impression Zoe was a little high-maintenance, but he found he didn't mind too much. However long it took her to get ready, she'd be worth the wait.

So he came around to the side of the bed where she sat, and bent down and kissed her. The sensation of her warm mouth touching his was enough to make him want to push her down onto the bed and go for round four—or would it be five?—but they really didn't have time for that.

"I'll come back over when I'm done," he said, and she nodded.

"Love you, Evan," she said swiftly.

Of course he had to kiss her again after that. "I love you, Zoe. But we have got to get moving."

She smiled, then nodded, and he went ahead and let himself out. Luckily, no one seemed to be around, although he noticed a few empty room service trays on the floor outside several of the rooms.

He went to his room and climbed out of his clothes, then headed into the bathroom and turned on the shower. It seemed a shame to wash Zoe's warm scent from his skin, but he reassured himself that there was always tonight.

Or this afternoon, he thought with a grin.

First things first, though. They had to get through this meeting with the creature. Although Evan was doing his best to understand her opposition to just banishing the thing to whatever plane it had come from, he still couldn't quite agree with her reasoning. Did she think the creature would just calmly accept that she'd chosen a real human man as her consort, rather than the being she'd summoned to take that role in the first place?

Hard to say. After all, she'd spoken with it—with *him*—more than he had, so quite possibly she'd had more opportunity to take his measure. But even if her creation didn't completely flip out about being passed over, what in the world did she think his eventual fate would be? To simply stay here and make some kind of life for himself?

Well, he supposed they'd all find out soon enough.

He went back out to the main part of the room and got some underwear from his duffel bag, along with a fresh shirt and a pair of jeans. Unfortunately, he hadn't brought anything remotely resembling "dress-up" clothes with him, but at least everything was clean and not too wrinkled.

Getting dressed didn't take very long. He didn't need to shave because he tended to go around stubbly half the time anyway, letting his beard grow out for a week or so until it started to drive him crazy, then shaving it back down so he could start the process all over again. Some goop in his hair to keep it from falling in his face, and he was about done.

He went to the nightstand and got his watch, then strapped it on his wrist. Nine thirty-five. Probably a little too early to head back over to Zoe's room. Instead, he pulled out his phone and checked it for messages. Nothing, which didn't surprise him too much. The elders wouldn't want to interrupt him while he was in the middle of helping the de la Paz clan with their little "problem," and his parents would have gotten the word from the elders to leave him alone, too.

Everything had changed last night, though. Now he was Zoe's consort. Which meant he'd have to say goodbye to his life in Jerome and Cottonwood. He'd be expected to live down here in Phoenix—or, more likely, in Fountain Hills or Scottsdale. A small sacrifice, when in exchange it meant he'd be spending his life with Zoe, but even so, there were a lot of adjustments that would have to be made. And plans. They'd need to get married, and probably quickly. He doubted the de la Pazes, who seemed pretty old-fashioned, would be okay with him and Zoe shacking up for any extended length of time.

Evan shook his head. If anyone had asked him even two days ago whether he planned to ever marry again, he would have looked at them like they were high on crack. After Kelly, he certainly hadn't been eager to jump back onto the matrimony train. But now he was calmly contemplating the notion as if it were a foregone conclusion.

Because of Zoe. He wouldn't have done this for anyone but her.

So he looked at his phone, and thought for a long moment, then slowly put it in his jeans pocket. The first people who needed to know that she'd found her consort were Zoe's parents, and then Luz. After that, the news would spread like wildfire among their clan. Only then would Evan feel comfortable contacting his own family.

And sometime before all that, they'd have to meet the monster she'd created.

A little Sunday brunch with a creature, Evan thought, mouth twisting. *Only in a witch clan.*

By then it was almost a quarter to ten, so he figured enough time had passed that he could head over to Zoe's room. She did take a while to answer when he knocked, and when she answered the door, he could see why. Her hair was dry but not styled, and she held a tube of mascara in one hand and the wand in the other. As far as he could tell, the rest of her makeup was done.

"Come in," she said. "I've been rushing as fast as I can, but—"

"It's okay," he reassured her. "We've still got about fifteen minutes."

"Fifteen minutes," she repeated. "I can do that." And she disappeared back into the bathroom.

Since he figured he might as well make himself useful, Evan headed farther into the room and began to make up the bed, fluffing the pillows and smoothing out the sheets and the duvet. Sure, the maids would probably be along to do over his work, but at least it wouldn't be such a mess when they did arrive.

He was just finishing up when Zoe came out of the bathroom. It looked like she'd completed her makeup application, but her hair still hung straight down, rather than falling in the long, loose curls she'd worn the day before.

"No time for my hair," she said. "That usually takes me at last half an hour. Does it look like complete ass?"

"No," he replied. "I like it." And he did. Something about it lying so sleek and straight seemed to accent the exotic beauty of her features, her high cheekbones and almond-shaped eyes, as if maybe the de la Pazes had some Native American blood a few generations back, just like the Wilcoxes did.

"Good." She went to the dresser and pulled out a little fabric bag with flowers woven into the material, then started digging around in it. Jewelry, he supposed, since she pulled out one dangly earring, then another, and put them on. Bangles, and a turquoise ring on her right hand, although he noticed she didn't bother with a necklace or a watch. She turned back toward him. "Do I look okay?"

Evan almost wanted to ask her why she cared what she looked like for this meeting, but he decided that would be rude. She probably wanted to appear as if she cared, to do what she could to ensure that the being she'd summoned understood she wanted to treat him with respect.

"You look great," he said. "I like that color on you."

Her top was almost the same deep sky-blue as the ring, a sort of peasant style that was quietly sexy when paired with those snug-fitting skinny jeans and a pair of silvery thong-style sandals. The color of her blouse brought out the warm tones in her skin, and her hair looked shimmering black against it.

"Thanks, Evan," she said, as she pushed her hair back over her shoulders. Then she shot a worried glance up at him. "I guess we need to do this."

"We do," he agreed calmly, although inside he felt just about as nervous as she looked. This whole thing had so much potential to go wrong. But he knew they couldn't blow off the meeting; Zoe's creature had amply demonstrated that he was just fine with seeking her out and appearing out of nowhere. Evan went to her and took her hand in his, pressed it to his lips. She shot him a grateful smile, even as he said, "Let's do this."

The hotel seemed so normal. How could it look so unchanged, so happy-Sunday-busy, when her whole world had tilted on its axis the night before?

Evan had held her hand in the elevator during the ride down. The middle-aged couple who shared the car with them had greeted them pleasantly and wished them a good morning, and Zoe was glad of that. Some people could get downright bent about seeing a white guy with a Mexican girl, and she didn't feel like dealing with that sort of ugliness on such a bright, friendly-looking morning.

But nothing like that had happened, although Evan had let go of her hand as soon as they emerged into the lobby. He probably didn't want to tip off Levi that things had changed with her and Evan, and she couldn't blame him for that.

As they approached the restaurant, she spotted Levi waiting outside. Evan went tense, and she could practically feel the shock radiating through him. Not surprising; she'd seen Levi's final transformation, but Evan was probably still picturing him as the distorted monster they'd banished back in Scottsdale, rather than the model-handsome man standing in the lobby. Zoe couldn't help but notice the admiring glances Levi had just attracted from a group of girls around her age who were passing by on the way to the pool. He, on the other hand, appeared completely oblivious to their stares.

Also, he seemed to have taken her advice about his attire to heart, because he was wearing clean, new-looking clothes, jeans and a polo shirt and loafers. In fact, he appeared far more at home with the preppy, well-dressed people around them than Evan did in his faded jeans and henley shirt with the sleeves pushed up.

Levi spotted them, and Zoe watched as a frown marred his perfect forehead when he realized she wasn't alone. Putting on a smile, she went up to him and said, "Hi, Levi. Evan and I thought we should talk to you before we eat. Why don't we go outside for a little walk first?"

She'd rehearsed this speech in the shower, because she knew that when the moment came, she'd be all too likely to lose her nerve and blurt out something completely inappropriate. Now she sounded almost natural, casual, as if this was a completely normal request.

Like there was anything normal about this whole situation.

Still frowning, Levi looked over at Evan, who didn't move. "Why is he here?"

"Because we all need to talk together, Levi. Please—can we go outside?" Zoe stepped away from Evan and laid a hand on Levi's arm. A tremor went through him at her touch, and then he gave a very faint nod.

"If you wish it."

She couldn't allow herself to be too relieved. Getting him out of the hotel was just the first step. She still had a lot of talking to do.

The three of them moved away from the restaurant as the hostess gave them a curious glance. She was probably wondering why they hadn't come up to request a table, but Zoe couldn't worry about that now. The important thing was to get outside, where it would be easier to perform damage control if Levi freaked out after learning how Evan was now her consort.

A warm wind blew around them, but it wasn't too hot yet. Off to one side, Zoe spotted a clump of trees that provided some shade—and privacy. It seemed like as good a place as any for them to have their talk.

So she moved a little ahead, walking quickly so Evan and Levi would have no choice but to follow her. Once they reached the stand of trees, she turned back toward both of them. Levi's expression was impassive, but she didn't know if that was because he'd decided to withhold judgment until he heard her out, or because he hadn't completely mastered human expressions yet.

Either way, she knew she couldn't avoid what she had to say. "Levi," she began, and then noticed how Evan's eyes widened slightly. Right—she'd completely forgotten to tell him that Levi had given himself a name the night before. Well, she and Evan had been a little preoccupied ever since then. Blood rushed to her cheeks, but she gathered a breath and went on, "I'm not sure how to say this, but—"

Levi's clear blue gaze flicked from her to Evan and then back again. When he spoke, his tone was flat. "He is your consort."

Shock pulsed through her, sharp and as unexpected as if Levi had just punched her in the gut. "I—how did you know that?"

"I sensed it. Your aura is different now. Brighter, more powerful."

"You can see people's auras?" she asked as Evan crossed his arms and stared at Levi as though he'd never seen him before. Well, in a way, he hadn't. At least not Levi as he appeared to them now.

"Yes. Can't everyone?"

"Not really," she said. "That is, I guess there are some witches who can, but we don't have any in my clan. In yours?" she added, with a quick glance at

Evan. He shook his head. "Anyway…yes, that's what we needed to tell you, Levi. I know it must seem strange, when I brought you here to be my consort, but I should have trusted the universe to know what it was doing."

He didn't respond at first. His gaze kept moving from her to Evan and then back, although Zoe wasn't sure what Levi might be looking for. Some evidence that their bond wasn't quite as close as it should be?

"If that is the case," he said slowly, appearing to choose his words with care, "then it won't matter if I kiss you, will it?"

Her throat went dry. She hadn't been expecting that sort of request. Confused, she looked up at Evan, whose mouth had compressed to a flat line. It was pretty obvious that he didn't like the idea at all. But he didn't say anything. It seemed clear enough to her that he was going to allow her to make this decision on her own.

She wanted to refuse. What point would there be in sharing a kiss when she'd already sealed her bond with Evan? But as she glanced back over at Levi, saw the painful hope in his clear blue eyes, the hurt he was trying to conceal, she knew it would be cruel to say no. She'd brought him here, and she would do whatever it took to make sure he would want for nothing now that he was a person as real as she was, or Evan. Anything else just wouldn't be fair.

"Yes," she said. "Yes, you can kiss me, Levi."

Even though she'd given him permission, he hesitated, his eyes meeting Evan's. Almost imperceptibly, Evan nodded, even though his jaw was tight, and Zoe could see how much he hated the idea of having to stand there and watch another man kiss the woman he'd just soul-bonded with.

Then Levi stepped forward and twined his fingers with hers. His skin was warm, his hands strong and very human-feeling. They didn't send any particular spark through her, not how Evan's merest touch could seem to make her very blood turn to fire, but at the same time, she wasn't repulsed by his touch. If he'd reached out to her like this, looking like this, only a few days ago, she wouldn't have recoiled. And that was shallow, because she didn't know how much of his mind and spirit had changed over those two short days, except maybe his ability to articulate his thoughts. But she needed to be truthful with herself.

Anyway, it wouldn't have mattered. Even if she had gone to him willingly, she wouldn't have felt the consort bond forge itself between them, because he wasn't the one.

Then he bent and placed his mouth very gently against hers, an almost tentative brush of lip against lip, as though he knew what the mechanics of the act were supposed to be but was concerned about how to carry them out in practice.

No heat, no spark, nothing except the realization that she'd done a terrible thing to this man. Tears started to her eyes, and she blinked them back. She'd have to make this right, no matter what.

He seemed to understand as well, because he gave a sad nod, then stepped away from her. "It's true, then," he said softly. "This man is your consort. I had hoped—"

"I'm sorry," Zoe told him, throat tight. She hadn't meant for this to happen. She hadn't meant for any of this to happen, and yet here they were.

His shoulders lifted, and he turned away, as if he intended to walk off into the parking lot...and go where? She had no idea where he went when he disappeared from one place and didn't reappear for hours later. Would he just blink himself out of existence, disappointment taking him far, far away from her?

"Wait," Evan said, and Levi paused, expression puzzled. "Were you just going to walk off into the sunset?"

The bewildered look Levi wore only deepened. "It is only ten o'clock in the morning," he pointed out.

"Right. It's just an expression. What I meant was, where will you go?"

"Around," Levi said, making a vague gesture toward the hills behind the hotel. "Out. Now that I have been brought here, I can move from place to place easily enough, although I cannot return to the place I was when Zoe first summoned me."

She let out a relieved little breath. "So you're stuck here."

"In a manner of speaking."

Evan glanced at her, hazel eyes questioning. She nodded. She'd already vowed to make this right, but she was relieved beyond measure to see that he agreed, that he wouldn't leave her to clean up this mess, even if it had been of her own making.

"Well," she said, going to Levi and slipping an arm through his, "that doesn't necessarily have to be a bad thing. Let Evan and me introduce you to something called Sunday champagne brunch."

As she led Levi back toward the hotel, Evan came up next to her on her other side. He didn't make a move to take her hand, but she caught his gaze for just a second, saw the approval and love in his cloudy hazel eyes. In fact, the warmth of his affection was almost a tangible thing, reaching out to wrap around her like a warm desert breeze.

In that moment, she was pretty sure everything was going to be okay.

CHAPTER NINETEEN

SO MANY EXPLANATIONS. SO MANY PHONE CALLS, SO MANY arrangements.

Evan had thought he was prepared for the hubbub that would result from Zoe's announcement that he had turned out to be her consort, but he was so very mistaken. Her mother had looked shocked for a split-second, right before she threw her arms around him and told him she was thrilled he would be a part of the family. Zoe's father Luis was somewhat more restrained, but his smile was laden with relief as he said, "It will be a good thing—another connection between our clans."

He was speaking of Caitlin McAllister's marriage to Alex Trujillo, Luz's son, but Evan knew this was a far bigger deal. This was the joining of their clan's *prima*

to a man from another witch family, something that
didn't exactly happen every day.

More than that, though, was their reaction
to Levi. Luz came over to the house to meet him,
and inspected him carefully from head to toe, as if
she was doing her very best to find something off
about the guy, something that would keep him from
mingling with regular people. She didn't succeed,
though, because he looked perfectly normal—normal for a TV star, that is.

"Well," she said briskly after giving Zoe's creation the sort of scrutiny usually reserved for live-
stock at the county fair, "he'll definitely pass. So I
suppose the next thing to do is figure out what we
should do with him."

Zoe winced at her aunt's comment. "Maybe we
should ask him what he wants to do. I mean, he's
standing right here."

Those words made Levi smile slightly. "It is all
right, Zoe," he said. "I know this is an unusual situation. Your *prima* is just being careful."

"Thank you, Levi," Luz said, a smile of her own
touching her lips. "All I'm saying is that he can't stay
at the CopperWynd indefinitely."

Because that was what Evan and Zoe had decided
to do, in the interim before they could figure out anything more permanent. After their brunch, they'd
gone to the front desk and asked about available

rooms. Since it was Sunday and people had begun to check out, there were a few empty ones, and they had Levi set up in one not long afterward.

They'd gone on their own to the house to make the announcement to her parents, but once that was done, they'd returned to the hotel to fetch Levi. Now Luz still appeared abstracted, her mind clearly racing to come up with a solution for this unexpected stranger her niece had dropped into the middle of their clan.

Levi was also somewhat bemused, although it seemed to Evan that he was willing to let those around him decide on his fate. Actually, for someone brought to this world for an express purpose that didn't exactly pan out, he was acting pretty damn mellow. Maybe any kind of existence here was better than where he'd come from, in which case Zoe had actually done him a favor, even if Evan could tell she was still wracked with guilt over the whole thing.

Also, a kernel of an idea was beginning to hatch in his mind. Levi had managed fairly well at brunch, but it was pretty obvious that the hustle and bustle of the hotel had begun to overwhelm him. At the same time, Evan didn't know how beneficial it would be for him to be someplace where he could see Zoe and Evan all the time, or even merely hear about what they were doing. Although he wasn't acting horribly disappointed about not being her consort, Evan had to think that Levi might do better someplace where he wouldn't have that particular reality shoved in his face all the time.

"How about Jerome?" he asked, and everyone looked at him as if he'd sprouted wings. Well, Luz and Zoe's parents, anyway. Levi frowned—Evan wondered if he even knew what Jerome was—and Zoe's eyes lit up with sudden interest.

"Why Jerome?" she asked, speaking quickly so as to get the words in ahead of any protests from her aunt or Luis and Andrea.

"Well, think about it," Evan replied. "It's kind of a funky place to begin with, so Levi wouldn't stand out so much. Also, there's my flat. Obviously, I'm not going to need it anymore, but it would be perfect for him—it's right in the middle of town, so people can keep an eye on him and help him out."

Luz and Andrea exchanged a dubious glance, but Luis nodded, his expression thoughtful. "It does sound like it might be a good setup. And your elders would agree to this?"

"I'd have to ask them, of course," Evan said. "But I think they'd be okay with it. More to the point, I'm pretty sure Angela will want to help out, and that's the really important thing, isn't it?"

"True," Luz said. "Your *prima*'s wishes would, of course, supersede those of your elders. If you really think she'd agree to it—"

"I do. But obviously I'll need to call her first before I promise anything else."

As if noting the rather strained look on Levi's face, Zoe got up from where she'd been seated in one of the living room's side chairs and went to sit down next to him. "Would you be all right with it, Levi?"

"I—I'm not sure." He glanced over at Evan. "What is this Jerome?"

"It's the town where I grew up, a little more than a hundred miles from here. The weather is cooler, and it's much smaller. Here." Evan pulled his phone from his pocket, then unlocked it so he could go to his photos. Last summer, he'd been up in the mountain town and taken some fairly spectacular pictures during monsoon season, especially one where the clouds had broken and shone golden light over Sedona's red rocks while a rainbow formed overhead. He walked over to where Levi sat and held the phone out to him. "See? That's taken from Main Street in Jerome. It's basically the view out the bedroom window of my flat."

Levi peered down at the image on the screen, and his eyes widened slightly. "I would be able to see that all the time?"

"Well, not exactly like that, because the weather is always changing. But the red rocks, and the mountains beyond—yeah, you'd always be able to see that except on really cloudy days."

"I like this Jerome," Levi announced, and a palpable wave of relief swept over the room.

"Then that's where we'll take you," Zoe said. She glanced up at Evan, her dark eyes shining with gratitude. "Just as soon as you want to go."

She'd never been any farther north than the outlet mall at Anthem, on the far northern outskirts of Phoenix. Zoe didn't know whether it was Levi or she herself who was more fascinated by the landscape passing by outside the car windows. The highway climbed, gaining altitude, and the saguaro cactus disappeared. Evan explained it was because they got snow up here, and the cactus weren't hardy enough to survive at this altitude.

It had all been easier to arrange than she'd thought. Evan had spent some time on the phone with Angela—Zoe supposed it was a story that needed a good deal of explaining—and then gave Zoe the thumbs-up sign, indicating that his clan's *prima* was just fine with taking on a man who hadn't even been a man up until a few days earlier. After that, Evan was on the phone even longer with his cousin Kirby, whom she gathered was his caretaker for the apartment over the kaleidoscope store in Jerome.

"I've been renting it out as an Airbnb flat," he explained once he got off the phone. "But luckily, it's been a kind of dead time of year, and so we didn't have any bookings until the end of the month. Kirby is going to cancel them for me and then help the people who had reservations find something else."

"That sounds like a lot of work," she said. "Is he okay with handling all that?"

"I'll make sure he gets a nice bonus," Evan replied. "He's kind of bummed that he won't have the caretaker gig anymore, but I assured him it was all in a good cause."

"Ack, now I feel bad about it."

They'd been sitting in Zoe's room at the CopperWynd, since they'd decided that was the best place to live until they got more permanent digs. It would have been too weird for both of them to stay in her room at her parents' house, and they certainly weren't going to be separated, even though she'd informed him that it was sort of the custom in the de la Paz clan for the *prima*-in-waiting and her consort to stay in separate homes until they were married. But she could tell Evan wasn't too thrilled by that idea, so the CopperWynd seemed like the best interim solution.

At any rate, Evan got up and pulled her into his arms, holding her close so she could hear the comforting beat of his heart, the strength of his embrace.

Her body thrilled, and it was so hard not to take him over to the bed so they could make love once more—but she managed to keep it together. They had the rest of their lives to be with one another, and right then they had a whole lot of logistics to work out.

"Don't feel bad," he told her. "Kirby gets his stipend like everyone else in the clan. It's not like he's going to be out on the street or something. And, since it's Kirby, I'm sure he'll have another side gig going within the week. That's kind of how he operates."

"I think I like Kirby," she said with a grin.

"Everyone likes Kirby. And they're all going to love you." Evan bent and kissed her then, and all her good intentions about staying focused went out the window. But that was all right. Making love with him was damn important, too.

So now she watched as they cut off the highway and headed through open country for a while until they came to the outskirts of Cottonwood. She couldn't say she was that impressed by most of it, since it felt small and shabby to her, although the downtown area was cute and looked like someplace she might want to explore.

First things first, though. After passing through Cottonwood, Evan guided the Barracuda up a winding mountain road, steep hills on every side, the landscape just beginning to be flushed with the first green of spring. And then they were in Jerome itself, old buildings of clapboard and brick on either side, so close to the street that they seemed to loom over it.

Evan pulled off into a sort of alley behind a row of tall buildings and parked in one of the spaces there, right in front of a sign that said "Residents only. Violators will be towed."

Zoe raised an eyebrow at him.

"I am a resident. Well, sort of. I mean, I've been living down in Cottonwood. But the flat's still mine, so I get parking privileges if it hasn't been rented out." He glanced over his shoulder into the back seat. "Ready to check out your new home?"

Levi nodded. "I want to see the view."

"And you will. Come on."

They all got out of the car, and Evan opened the trunk so Levi could get out the bags of belongings Zoe and her mother had put together for him—toiletries, and changes of clothes, and a few more necessities. Then they headed into the building through the back entrance. Immediately inside the door was a staircase, and Evan took them up two flights until they emerged at a landing on the top floor. From his pocket, he produced a tooled leather fob with one key attached.

"Here," he said, handing it to Levi. "You should do the honors."

Levi took it and turned it over in his hand.

"You put the key in the lock," Zoe began, pointing, but he cut her off gently.

"I know how to use a key. I've been learning a great many things during my time here."

So he had. She was still startled by how much he'd been able to assimilate of how modern American society worked, although of course there were still many gaps in his knowledge. Even so, she thought he'd be able to manage well enough.

He unlocked the door and went inside, Zoe and Evan following a few paces behind. This had all sounded like a great plan, but inwardly she couldn't help worrying. What if the flat really wasn't that great, was too small or smelled weird or something like that?

When she looked around, though, she saw her fears had been for nothing. Yes, it wasn't all that big, but the living room area was large enough for a smallish couch and a coffee table, and a bookshelf filled with books stood against one wall. Off to one side was the kitchen area, with new-looking stainless appliances and a little table for two placed up against the window. In the other direction was a short hallway, with a bedroom on either side and the bathroom at the end of the hall. The whole apartment was decorated in simple dark oak furniture, with an antique rug under the couch and coffee table combo, and plain, sheer white drapes at the windows.

Overall, the flat had a feeling of peace and serenity she really hadn't been expecting, and she looked over at Evan and gave him a grateful smile.

Levi went at once to the window and opened it, letting in a fresh, wild breeze that sent the draperies fluttering. He stood there for a long moment, taking in the view of Sedona's red rocks off in the distance, the slanting afternoon light that painted the landscape in shades of gold. Did it match his expectations?

Apparently so, because he breathed in deeply, then nodded. "Yes. I like this. It's clean here, not like the city."

Zoe opened her mouth to argue that particular point, then shut it just as quickly. Wasn't it better for everyone involved if he did think that Jerome was better than Phoenix? He needed to be happy here. She wanted desperately for him to be happy.

There was a soft knock at the open door, and Zoe turned around to see a pretty woman with graying auburn hair, probably in her early fifties, standing there. "Hi, Evan," she said. "Just wanted to check in."

"Hi, Rachel," he responded. "Levi, Zoe, this is my cousin, Rachel McAllister. Or wait—I guess it's Rachel Miller now, isn't it?"

She shook her head. "I didn't bother with all that nonsense. Tobias doesn't care, and it's not like we're going to be starting a family." Smiling, she stepped forward and extended a hand to Levi. "Hello, Levi. I'm in the apartment just a few doors down, above the old mercantile, so if you need anything, you just come find me."

"Of course," he said, looking both confused and relieved.

"And Zoe," Rachel went on, surprising Zoe by taking her in her arms and giving her a quick hug. "I suppose I should be angry with you for taking Evan away from us, but frankly, I think a change of scenery will do him good."

"Rachel," he said in pained tones, while Zoe smothered a smile.

"Well, I promise to let him come up and visit," she said. "Actually, we'll both come up and visit. Jerome is adorable—I wish we had more time to stay, but we've got a million things to do back in Phoenix."

"I can imagine. Wedding and house shopping, in that order?"

"Something like that." The de la Paz clan had several real estate agents among its members, and they were already hot on the hunt, looking for the best house for the family's *prima*-in-waiting and her new consort. And her mother had started getting the wedding organized, but Zoe knew she needed to get back and pitch in.

"Then you do what you need to do, and we'll take care of Levi." Something about the appreciative glance Rachel gave him made Zoe think that Levi was going to do just fine here in Jerome. The girls here were probably starving for some new blood, and open-minded McAllister witches most likely wouldn't have too much trouble with Levi's unorthodox origins. "In fact," Rachel added, "Angela and Connor are driving down tonight so we can all have dinner together. Does that sound okay to you, Levi?"

He nodded. "Thank you. I feel very welcome."

She beamed. "Well, then, I'll let you get back to it. And I'll be back to fetch you in a few hours for dinner, Levi."

After that, she disappeared into the hallway, and a moment later Zoe could hear her footsteps on the stairs.

An awkward silence fell. She knew she and Evan should get going, because it was a long drive back to Phoenix, but something in her quailed at the thought of leaving Levi alone here, even though it seemed clear enough that he wasn't going to want for company.

Apparently sensing her unease, he came forward and laid a hand on her arm. "Zoe. It is going to be fine. I like this place very much."

"You're going to like it even better after you've had dinner at Rachel's," Evan put in. "She's got to be the best cook in Yavapai County."

"You see?" Levi offered Zoe a reassuring smile. "Go back to Phoenix. You gave me this life—now it is up to me to do something with it."

Tears started to her eyes, but she resolutely blinked them away. "You're a much better person than I made you, Levi."

He put his arms around her and gave her a quick, fierce hug, then let go just as swiftly. "And you're a better person than you believe yourself to be, Zoe Sandoval."

After that, she really couldn't manage to say anything, because her throat was too tight, and she knew she was going to start bawling like a baby if she didn't get out of there right away. She hurried to the stairwell, heard Evan murmur a few words to Levi, and then he was there next to her, his arm around her waist as he helped guide her down the stairs.

They were quiet as he pulled out of the alley, then made a treacherous left turn onto Main Street so they could head down the hill. It wasn't until they were almost at the bottom that Evan spoke.

"You okay?"

She nodded. Her tears had begun to subside almost as soon as they left Jerome's town limits, and now she thought she could speak without bursting into sobs. "I—I think so. It was just…leaving him there like that…."

"I know. But he needs the opportunity to make his own way in the world, and he has a much better chance here in Jerome. Everyone will look out for him. We're like that."

It was on her lips to say that all witch clans were like that, but she had to admit that the McAllisters were closer-knit than most, probably because they were so few of them. The de la Paz clan did what it could to keep in touch with one another, but there were so many members of the family scattered over such a large area that the task felt downright impossible sometimes.

So she only said, "Good," and fell silent again as he cut off the highway into a neighborhood of smaller but well-kept homes, all with a gorgeous backdrop of high mountains looming in the near distance.

They'd already planned to stop in at Evan's house in Cottonwood so he could gather up more of his belongings. Eventually he'd have to come up here and empty out the house for good—or pass it on to one of his cousins, he hadn't decided which yet—but for now this was just a brief stop.

Zoe looked around in curiosity as they stepped inside. Pale tile covered the entryway, but other than that the house had wall-to-wall cream-colored carpet. She wondered how he kept it so clean-looking when he was working on his car all the time.

And it didn't feel much like him, with the modern, square-looking red couches in the living room and the other pieces of steel and glass. Vertical blinds covered the windows.

It wasn't that the decor wasn't masculine; it just didn't feel like Evan's brand of masculine. The clean, simple pieces of age-warmed wood in the flat up in Jerome seemed much more his style.

"I didn't choose any of this stuff," he said, and Zoe started.

"What?"

"Kelly picked it all out. She wanted it to look like something out of a magazine. Which I guess would have been okay if she was decorating a condo in New York or something, but it really doesn't work with a ranch-style house in Cottonwood, you know?"

"I guess you're right," Zoe admitted. "I promise—no red leather couches."

He grinned, then bent down to kiss her on the cheek. "Like I was worried. Let me just go get my stuff. Could you do me a favor, though? I didn't have much in the fridge, but what's in there probably needs to be tossed. It's not like I'm coming back. But it would speed things up if you could take care of it while I'm packing."

"Sure," she said. Not that she really looked forward to the task, but its very nature proved that he didn't have any plans to change his mind, to say that he knew he was her consort, but he just couldn't leave his home here in the Verde Valley. She didn't even know why she should be worried about such a thing, although she supposed her grandmother's sad example had proved that not all consort-*prima* pairings ended in bliss.

But she was not going to think about that now. Evan was nothing like her grandfather. Jaw set, Zoe went into the kitchen, saw that it was very neat and clean, no dishes on the counter or anything like that, even though she knew Evan had to have departed for Scottsdale in something of a hurry.

He'd been right about one thing—there really wasn't much in the refrigerator except a container of leftover Chinese and a pizza box with a couple of forlorn pieces of pepperoni lingering inside. Well, and a six-pack of Kilt Lifter ale with four bottles remaining. That should be safe enough to leave behind, maybe a little present for the next person to live in the house.

She found the trash bags under the sink and disposed of the leftovers, then took them outside to the garbage cans. As she came back into the kitchen, she saw Evan waiting for her, a beat-up-looking duffle bag that was a match to the one he'd left in the hotel lying on the floor next to him.

"There was beer in the fridge," she said. "Do you want to bring it?"

He shook his head. "No, don't worry about it." Then he paused and looked around, as if trying to commit one last image of the house to memory.

"Sad?"

"No," he replied with some vehemence. "No, just...sort of saying goodbye, I guess. I actually kind of always hated this house. It was what Kelly wanted, not me. But still...Jerome...Cottonwood... it's all I've ever known."

She went to him then and put her arms around his waist, hugged him tight. His lips brushed the top of her head, and just that light touch was enough to awaken the bond between them, strong and shining and sure as the sun gleaming outside the windows, fresh as spring, and just as brimming with promise.

"And we'll make a new home of our own in Fountain Hills," she said. Then she looked up at him, and couldn't help smiling, just a little bit. "I promise I'll let you help pick out the furniture."

"Promise?"

She nodded, still smiling, and he bent down and kissed her, mouth warm and wonderful, and promising her far more to come when they got back to Phoenix. And then they would make their home together, but the important thing—the really important one—was that no matter where they ended up, *he* was home, the match to her soul, the missing piece of her heart.

The *prima* energy glowed within her, and was content.

The End